THE ICY TOUCH

GRIMM

COMING SOON FROM TITAN BOOKS

Grimm: The Chopping Block by John Passarella
(February 2014)

THE ICY TOUCH

GRIMM

JOHN SHIRLEY

BASED ON THE NBC TV SERIES

TITAN BOOKS

Grimm: The Icy Touch
Print edition ISBN: 9781781166543
E-book edition ISBN: 9781781166550

Published by Titan Books
A division of Titan Publishing Group Ltd
144 Southwark St, London SE1 0UP

First edition: November 2013
10 9 8 7 6 5 4 3 2 1

A CIP catalogue record for this title is available from the British Library.

Printed and bound in the United States.

TITANBOOKS.COM

For all the fans of *Grimm*

"Could you tell me whether my bridegroom lives here?" asked the bride.

"Oh you poor child," the old woman answered. "Do you realize where you are? This is a murderer's den! You think you're a bride soon to be celebrating your wedding, but the only marriage you'll celebrate will be with Death!"

"The Robber Bridegroom", as per the Brothers Grimm

PROLOGUE
FRANCE, 1815

Once upon a time, a Grimm embarked on a voyage with an Emperor…

On a cold dawn, on March 1, 1815, six ships arrived together on the Mediterranean coast of France. The flagship of this small fleet was the brig *Inconstant,* carrying the exiled Emperor Napoleon Bonaparte and his retinue. The vessels dropped anchor in the Golfe-Juan, near the Cape of Antibes, just a 147 miles north of Corsica, where, not much more than forty years earlier, the Emperor's destiny had begun to unfold.

Johann Kessler waited in the launch for the return of the Emperor of France. Kessler's tanned, dark-eyed face was impassive, but his heart was troubled because amongst the other seven men waiting in the gently rocking boat with him was one Alberle Denswoz—and Kessler was sitting beside him. The irony fairly tingled in the air: Denswoz was *Hundjager Wesen*, after all. Kessler had only recently discovered the man's Wesen nature when Denswoz let down his guard, briefly revealing his true bestial form.

Not so long before, the old folk tales collected by the Brothers Grimm—tales of witches, wolf-men, dragons, and many others—had become enormously popular. Few readers knew that the creatures described by the Grimms actually *existed*. The brothers themselves had assumed they were only mythology.

But in the dark heart of each fairy tale was something true; something fantastic yet real: the *Wesen*. Some were essentially beast-men, and women, disguised as human; some were more monstrous.

Another ancient line of beings, both human and more than human, sought out the more dangerous Wesen and destroyed them. Lately, in sardonic homage to the compilers of the fairy tales, these secretive hunters were called... Grimms.

As far as Kessler knew, Denswoz was unaware that one of these almost superhuman beings was seated next to him.

Now, the Emperor climbed lithely down to the boat that would take him ashore. Colonel Mallet helped the great man into the stern sheets.

The Emperor was a compact, pale, slightly plump, long-nosed man with deep-set eyes and black hair. He was wearing a long black overcoat, and a white weskit over which slanted his sash; his famous bicorn hat adorned his head. He peered through the streamers of mist rising from a sea the color of his gray-blue eyes; he strove to see if anyone awaited them on the shore. Napoleon would have preferred to take a place in the bow, but Colonel Mallet had begged him to sit in the stern, for fear of hostile sharpshooters awaiting them on the beach. They had escaped easily from Elba, with almost 1,100 grenadiers, while the British and Bourbon ships were away; but the journey to the French coast had been tediously dragged out by contrary winds, so that the Emperor joked that *Inconstant* had lived up to its name. In that time, word may have reached France of the Emperor's impending return. Enemies could be waiting.

Kessler was half expecting to see Bourbon soldiers on the shore, perhaps a detachment from one of the hostile garrisons in Provence, training cannon on the launch. He had no wish to die in a cannon fusillade, nor did he wish Napoleon's death. But the Emperor's own scouts stepped into view on the beach to wave the all clear. Kessler's spirits rose—and though it was a chill daybreak on a cold sea, everyone in the boat was smiling, their eyes bright. They were back in France after ten months of exile on the island of Elba. *La France!*

Johann Kessler was German, but had become a French citizen under Napoleon; Denswoz was Austrian but when Austria had been annexed by Napoleon, he had eagerly sought to advise the Emperor—only recently had he been accepted, on sailing to Elba. In fact, Kessler suspected that Denswoz was in part the cause of the Emperor's decision to return to France. Denswoz—and the coins. Kessler had only caught a glimpse of the large, curious Greek coins that the Emperor kept in his coat pocket; that he took out from time to time; that seemed to transfer their ancient shine to those gray-blue eyes...

If Kessler's theory was confirmed, these were no ordinary coins. They were strange and powerful artifacts, created on an island of Greece centuries ago—they'd passed through many hands: Caligula had clasped them lovingly; Nero had caressed them. They had vanished into China, last seen in the Han Dynasty. If they'd reappeared, and if the dark Wesen had given them to the Emperor, it might be that Kessler's true, secret cause was hopeless.

The coxswain directed the sailors to begin rowing, and

the launch set off, as the Emperor Napoleon Bonaparte turned to speak to Colonel Mallet.

"Yonder is an olive orchard, Colonel," he said. "Let us bivouac there until everyone is ashore and organized for the march."

"Very good, my Emperor."

The orchard was barren of olives at this time of year but Napoleon was pleased by it.

"Happy omen!" he said, striding up to his retinue, a sprig from an olive tree in his hand. "The olive is the emblem of peace."

Kessler stood beside the command tent nibbling a biscuit as Bonaparte arrived. He swallowed a bite of the hardtack with difficulty.

"God willing the omen is a true one, my Emperor," he said. "Peace is always a blessing."

"I will fire no shot," Napoleon said. "Except in dire necessity." He turned to survey his soldiers. Mallet had deployed the grenadiers about the outskirts of the orchard. Over a thousand men milled restlessly there, or leaned against trees, talking in low tones, wondering if they would be shot by royalist troops—or elevated within Napoleon's army if he succeeded in restoring himself to the throne.

Since he'd first spoken of his return, Napoleon repeatedly vowed that no shot would be fired during his journey to Paris. The Bourbons, who had been installed in his place, would have to order their armies to fire first. And many a French soldier would in fact refuse to fire upon Napoleon. Perhaps the Emperor guessed that the skittish Louis XVIII would fear that the French army would turn upon him if he issued an order to attack their former leader.

The Emperor sat in a camp chair and opened a map of the

coast, frowning as his finger traced the roads to Grenoble.

"Do you propose, my Emperor, to take an indirect route to Paris?" Kessler asked, surprised at his own boldness.

Napoleon nodded briskly. "I do. If we're to avoid unnecessary conflict, we must take the mountain roads that avoid the garrisons. It will be slow. But it will give us time to gather our strength."

Kessler had been present when Napoleon had told Marshal Pons that he was planning a return from exile, and he'd gathered that the Emperor was counting on a degree of surprise and more than a degree of confusion to make it possible for him to establish himself in France again. "They will be astonished," Napoleon had said, "and astonishment paralyzes." During the hoped-for paralysis of the Bourbons, the French people would stand behind him; so Napoleon believed. It was true that all France had been frustrated with Napoleon's fevered overreaching into Russia; had been appalled at the loss of 700,000 men who'd died in his wars of conquest. But the feeble efforts of the Bourbons to restore France's economy were not working. The triumph of revolution was fresh in the public memory and the return of an unpopular monarchy was a bitter pill to swallow.

When Josephine died at Malmaison, Napoleon was crushed. Though they were divorced, he still loved her. He had refused to come out of his suite for two days. When at last he emerged his emotional ferment had been apparent—and that's when the Hundjager, Denswoz, had begun to spend more and more time around the Emperor. Denswoz always seemed to be prodding Napoleon with whispers. And at some point he'd pressed those mysterious coins upon him.

Were they in fact The Coins of Zakynthos—the playthings of Caligula and Nero? Kessler was not yet certain.

Johann Kessler was an envoy to Germany from

Napoleon's "court" at Elba, tasked to find financial support for the Emperor's return from amongst those German noblemen who were at odds with the Archduke Charles of Austria. It was a task that would never be completed, since Kessler was in fact an undercover agent for Charles. The Archduke hated Napoleon Bonaparte.

Kessler himself had come to admire Napoleon. The genius and vision of "the little general" were beyond dispute—and Kessler preferred he remain safely in Elba. But he'd found out about the escape from Elba too late to stop it. And his genuine friendship with Napoleon had restrained him from taking more ruthless steps.

Napoleon glanced up from the map as Denswoz arrived on horseback accompanied by a balding, baby-faced man whom Kessler had only seen once before: Jean-Baptiste Drouet, the comte d'Erlon and one of Napoleon's Marshals. Drouet wore a resplendent coat, much decorated with braid and lace.

"General Drouet!" Napoleon said, standing. "You have come! And with horses!"

"More horses are on the way, my Emperor," Drouet said, dismounting. "And your carriage! But we have not horses for one thousand men, not yet."

"It is very well, we shall march, slowly and peacefully, back to Paris." The Emperor bent to pluck a violet, and held the flower up to admire it in the morning sun. "How early they are blooming, even for Antibes. Another good omen."

"You are still determined to walk through France defended only by posies and a merry smile, my Emperor?" Denswoz asked, as he dismounted and gave his bow. He spoke in a silky, gently facetious way that removed the sting from his acerbity.

"We will be armed, Monsieur Denswoz," Napoleon replied, shrugging. "But we will not seek to use the weapons."

"The Bourbons may suffer your return, my Emperor. But the allies will not."

"We shall sue for peace, and if it is refused us, we will fight," Napoleon replied. "Now, let us examine our route, General Drouet…"

It seemed to Kessler that Napoleon Bonaparte's confidence waxed and waned by the hour. An unusual penchant for superstition had settled on the Emperor—the normally rational Bonaparte was giving credence to omens, and Kessler had noticed him repeatedly fingering those curious coins. And yes, he had confirmed—they were the Coins of Zakynthos.

Johann Kessler had seen the coins up close, for a few moments, on the wood and brass folding table in the Emperor's tent, at the second camp after a long day's march. The Emperor had stepped over to a chest, to obtain another map, and Kessler had seized the chance to examine the gold coins. They were identical, and without a doubt the same ones depicted in the grimoire. The old book on ancient mysteries asserted that they'd been minted in the eighth century on the Greek island of Zakynthos. On one side of each coin was a swastika—in ancient times, a symbol of good luck in the Far East—on the other was the Nemean Lion. Kessler felt a mild stinging sensation when he touched the coins, as if sensing the legend that reverberated around them: they were said to convey to the bearer a mystical power over men, imparting inspiration, charisma, and an almost divine glow. But the gold of the coins was also said to be somehow poisoned. And the bearer's powers corroded, over long use, charisma decaying to become madness and despair.

Still, if the legend were true, then Napoleon might use the coins to retake power; they might give him an infallible command that could break the back of the allies. And as Kessler was the agent of the Archduke Charles, he was obliged to head Napoleon Bonaparte off. If the coins were genuine, he must take them. They should not be in the hands of men like Denswoz—or Napoleon.

But he had to put them down when Bonaparte turned back to him.

"Curious coins," Kessler remarked, to see how Napoleon would react. "Greek, I believe?"

"Yes," said the Emperor snappishly, quickly scooping the coins up. "Greek."

Just outside Lyons, in a rainy dusk, they were confronted by an army of 6,000 men. This opposing force was tasked to disperse the Emperor's army—or destroy it.

A royalist officer stood before Napoleon, towering over the smaller man yet trembling in fear, as he awaited Napoleon's answer. Everyone watched the Emperor; everyone waited.

Standing a few paces to Napoleon's right, Kessler expected that the Emperor would first order his men to withdraw, then redeploy them for attack. But Napoleon hesitated, scanning the opposing troops, reading the eyes of the men who looked back at him. He seemed to waver…

He glanced back at the force he had with him. They were badly outnumbered. But his brave men had their weapons pointed toward the royalist forces. He murmured an order to Colonel Mallet.

"Tell the men to lower their weapons."

Then Denswoz stepped up and whispered something in Napoleon's ear.

The Emperor nodded, reached into his right-hand overcoat pocket, and drew out the Coins of Zakynthos. He did it almost absentmindedly, as if wanting something to clink in his hand as he thought the matter over. But the instant he clasped the coins he began to change. The change was subtle, but clear to Kessler, who was sensitive to the influence of the miraculous.

Napoleon seemed to swell, just a trifle, when he grasped the coins. He stood straighter, and his sunken eyes suddenly seemed brighter. He lifted his head, and when he spoke to the assemblage—to every man there—his voice boomed out with the echoing power of a cannon discharge. And it seemed to Kessler that waves of energy pulsed out from Napoleon—energies invisible to ordinary men...

"I see many faces I know, of men who fought beside me, before!" Napoleon called out. "I see the faces of brave men who drove the English back from our borders!" He paused dramatically, then, with a flourish, opened his coat, baring his weskit. "If any man here would shoot his Emperor— *shoot him now*!"

The opposing troops stared.

Then one of the soldiers reached up and tore the white plume of the House of Bourbon from his hat and threw it down. He reached into his coat, and drew out the old, soiled tricolor of Napoleon, and inserted it into his hat.

A cheer went up, and other men flung down the plume of the Bourbons. First a few—and then hundreds, thousands.

The men roared *"Vive l'Emperor!"* And the 6,000 soldiers who had opposed him became part of Napoleon's army.

Kessler looked at Alberle Denswoz—and saw something that he alone could see, of the thousands of men here: Denswoz's face transforming, becoming the furred, savage, snouted visage of a Hundjager; the muzzle of a vicious feral dog. It seemed to snarl in brutal triumph...

Kessler looked quickly away, and was careful to add his cheers to the huzzahs of the soldiers, as Napoleon waved his hat to them, glorying in their loyalty.

* * *

June 18, 1815. Waterloo—the *morne plaine*—in the United Kingdom of the Netherlands.

The ground was softened by rain, but it had cleared up that morning, and near midday Napoleon Bonaparte judged that the battlefield was firm enough. He ordered the *grande batterie* of cannons be fired at the ranks of British soldiers, led by the Duke of Wellington, and followed up with a frontal assault in a tight, relentless column. Kessler watched in horror as the army of the Republic charged down onto the plains from the ridge to the south, attacking Wellington's position head-on.

Wellington's dense ranks of musketry played havoc with the Napoleonic forces. Men fell by the score, dead or dying, torn to pieces by chain shot and musket balls, cavalry horses screaming as shrapnel tore into them. Smoke billowed over the battlefield, carrying the reek of gunpowder, followed by the distinct smell of blood—a great deal of blood.

Kessler looked at the fallen French soldiers through his small brass telescope; saw them lying across one another, a few twitching and groaning, blue coats staining red. Strange to think each fallen man had been born, had lived a life of hopes and plans, only to end here, breathing his last in this muddy battlefield...

Standing near Napoleon now, Kessler lowered the telescope and turned to see the Emperor once again clasping the Coins of Zakynthos, clicking them together like a gambler flipping chips between his fingers as he gazed broodingly out over the field of battle. He'd had the coins constantly within reach since the day Denswoz had urged them upon him outside Lyons. But in Kessler's view, their effect on Napoleon was increasingly dismaying.

The great man seemed to be gradually wilting, becoming sickly, complaining of kidney afflictions and malaise. He rarely sat on his horse, and appeared to have difficulty seeing the battlefield clearly.

As Kessler watched, Napoleon seemed to become aware of his scrutiny. The Emperor put the coins back in his coat. But they were never far away from him.

The coins have turned against him, just as the legend warned, Kessler thought. Still, their effectiveness in ensuring the loyalty of his soldiers was undiminished. If Napoleon continued to hold the coins, he might well win this battle. And if Napoleon won the battle, it would only bring more war and chaos on Europe.

Napoleon. Kessler felt some anguish, thinking about Napoleon's undoubted civilizing influence on the world. The great man's dreams of a rational, enlightened empire sometimes seemed the best course for Western civilization. But Kessler's loyalty was to Germany, and the Archduke Charles. And Napoleon had subjugated much of Germany.

And yet—Kessler regarded Napoleon as his friend.

In many ways he felt it would be doing his friend a service, in the long run, if he could get the coins away from him. Once he'd lost the Coins of Zakynthos, Napoleon might lose heart. He had become dependent on them. Without them, he would likely lose the battle—a defeat that Kessler's employer desired—and perhaps Napoleon would be saved from the madness and physical deterioration contact with the coins would inevitably bring.

Napoleon took off his overcoat as the afternoon grew warmer. Kessler waited his chance… and when Denswoz had gone to get them some water, Kessler stepped up beside Napoleon as if joining the Emperor in examining the maps. With his left hand Kessler reached into the coat folded over the back of the camp chair—and quickly filched the coins.

He straightened up in time to see Denswoz striding toward them, carrying a canteen of water and frowning. In his position bent over the maps, Napoleon blocked Denswoz's view of Kessler as he entered the field headquarters, so he could not have seen the theft. Not directly. But something had aroused his suspicion.

Kessler looked quickly away, and said something about "seeing that my horse is watered as well." He headed to the edge of the camp, then glanced back at Napoleon—his last sight of him ever—and went quickly out to where the horses were picketed.

He had another duty, he reflected, as he strode to his chestnut mare—when the time came, he must kill Denswoz. Alberle Denswoz was a predatory Hundjager and Kessler suspected him of feeding on dying soldiers and killing peasants purely for the sake of amusement along their route. But there would be time to execute Denswoz later. First Kessler wanted to uncover his agenda and killing him might sever traceable ties. And Denswoz would not be hard to find when the time came.

The sentries were used to seeing Johann Kessler come and go and no one said a word as he rode past them into the damp Sonian Forest. Ghosts of misty evaporation ascended from the ferns like the souls of fallen soldiers. The sounds of battle echoed between the boles of the beech trees, growing muted as he continued along the sunken, winding lane. His horse's hooves gave out a lonely clopping as his mount trotted along.

He would skirt the battle in the forest, then head east to Germany...

But the urgent hoof-beats of galloping horses came drumming behind him. Kessler turned in his saddle, half expecting to see a troupe of cavalrymen coming after him. But it was Alberle Denswoz who pursued him—accompanied by a young man Kessler hadn't seen before. The brutal, fixated look on their faces made their intentions clear.

They came on rapidly, galloping up to either side of him, the young man on a roan, Denswoz on his burly cloudy-white horse. Kessler reined in so that their momentum would carry them past. He prepared to turn, thinking to dodge into the depths of the forest. But Denswoz turned in his saddle and fired a pistol—striking Kessler's mare in the head. The horse collapsed beneath him and he was only just able to jump clear.

Kessler regained his footing and drew his dragoon saber with his right hand; the saber had a falcon worked into its pommel, a part of his family crest. He had a loaded pistol in his sash, ready to draw if he had a clear target.

The two horsemen had already turned their mounts, and were riding hard at him—but then Denswoz reined in his horse so abruptly it skidded on its hooves, neighing, eyes wild.

"Did you think I couldn't track you down?" Denswoz snarled.

"I should have known you would," Kessler admitted. "Tracking is a Hundjager gift, after all."

"I'll kill you face to face, up close, you thieving scum," Denswoz growled. His face was transforming, as he dismounted, devolving into the Hundjager's doglike features; the Wesen's eyes, the color of the juice of blood oranges, glinted with bloodlust.

Denswoz came at him, uplifted dragoon saber shining in a shaft of light angling down through the trees. Kessler moved whiplash quick, and sidestepped out of the saber's whistling arc, at the same instant stabbing his own blade deeply into Denswoz's left armpit. The agonized Hundjager howled, the sound distinctly wolflike, and twisted loose from the blade. He stared, blinking, seeming startled by Kessler's speed.

But a powerful Wesen was not so easy to kill, and the Hundjager squared off with him again, teeth clenched, growling, upper lip peeling back in a snarl. The boy, no more than fifteen, climbed off his horse with less skill than Denswoz had shown, and came at Kessler from the left.

"Lukas, stay back!" Denswoz growled.

"Father—let me help! You're wounded!"

So this was Denswoz's son, Lukas. He'd heard it mentioned that the boy was meeting Denswoz at Waterloo.

"Listen to your father," Kessler urged. "I don't want to have to kill you too."

Blood was leaking from Denswoz's Hundjager muzzle. But he charged Kessler, leaping and swinging the saber at once. Kessler's Grimm reflexes did not fail him: he ducked easily under the assault, and let Denswoz's momentum carry him past, so that the Wesen fell heavily on the path close beside Kessler's fallen horse.

Kessler spun toward the boy, who was aiming a pistol from four paces away. Lukas Denswoz fired, and the ball hissed past Kessler's left ear. Lukas cursed, and threw the pistol aside, raising his saber. The teenager's face was transforming—the Hundjager in him forcing its way into view.

Kessler drew his own pistol—a Lepage that was a gift from Napoleon himself—and aimed carefully at the boy's right shoulder. He fired, and the boy yelped, stumbled, and fell groaning. The pistol ball had shattered the bone of his shoulder.

Kessler turned just in time to see that the older Denswoz was up, his bestial mouth bubbling with red foam.

"Kessler—throw the coins down and walk away! I will let you live a while longer!" he demanded.

"Why did you use the damned things to prod Napoleon into all this?" Kessler asked.

"That you will never know!"

Denswoz rushed him, but the deep wound under his arm was draining his strength, and his sword stroke at Kessler's head was clumsy.

Kessler parried, slipped aside with Grimm rapidity, and struck down hard, cutting through the back of Denswoz's neck—and severing the Wesen's head from his body.

The body staggered, spurting from the stump—and then fell twitching to the clay.

"No!" Lukas howled, swaying as he struggled to his feet.

"You cannot hope to kill me, boy," Kessler told him.

The young Wesen took an uncertain step toward Kessler, staring at his father's severed head. Then the saber fell from his nerveless fingers to ring dully on a stone.

Kessler walked to within a pace of the boy and pressed the tip of his blade to Lukas's jugular.

"Just a short thrust and a twist, and you will join your father," Kessler told him. "You'll be with him in Hell— damned like all Wesen as you are unchristian." He had heard that this was not entirely so, that some Wesen were indeed Christian. But Kessler wanted to make the boy's flesh creep.

The boy gaped at him, and licked his lips. His right arm hung limp, and useless.

"I...have to try to kill you."

"No, no you don't. I should, in fact, kill *you*. But...my people only kill Wesen when they have to. You are young, and you could learn to live off cattle, and lambs—you could swear to never prey on a man or woman born."

"I...I swear it."

"But you must do one other thing, if you want to live. You must tell me why your father gave Napoleon the coins.

Why did he want him to attack the allies again?"

The boy shook his head. "I don't know." He averted his eyes.

"Indeed. Then—greet your father for me." He pushed minutely on the sabertip.

"Wait! Father said...the war would not last. Napoleon would win for a time—and then fail. And there would be chaos afterward. And the chaos would suit those he'd sworn to uphold."

"And to whom had he sworn himself?"

"He said I was not to know until I was a man. He said it was 'those who feed on war and human dissolution.'"

"Indeed. You have no names to give me?"

"No!" Lukas put a shaking hand up to cover his tearful eyes. "Oh my father, I have betrayed your trust."

Kessler snorted. "You have told me little enough. But— you may go. I give you your life. Remember that there is greatness in being merciful. It has given you another chance to see the deeper truths of the world. Take your saber, and depart."

He lowered his saber, and nodded toward the young Wesen's horse.

Lukas caught up his saber and backed away from Kessler, then turned quickly to the horse. The injured boy had difficulty mounting but at last he was galloping back the way he'd come.

As Kessler watched, after about thirty yards, the young Wesen reined in the horse and turned toward him, face drawn in pain and frustrated rage.

"You sir!" the young man shouted. "You and all your family will pay the price for this deed! I swear it now!" Then he turned and galloped away.

Kessler walked over to his saddlebags, retrieved a few things, including the leather bag containing the Coins of

Zakynthos. Then he mounted Denswoz's horse and rode off toward Germany.

He told himself that there was no need to be troubled by Lukas Denswoz's oath. The boy was injured, emotional, and not the ruthless operative his father had been.

But intuition told Kessler that he had made a dire mistake in letting the young Hundjager live.

And that intuition was correct. Johann Kessler's mistake would crystallize like roof water in a wintry blast of wind. In time its poison would trickle like drips from melting ice; like frosty fingers it would stretch out, seeking with an icy touch...

Captain Sean Renard stared at the badly burned body on
the morgue table. It smelled of smoke and burnt flesh—
and methane.

"How'd they find this guy?" he asked. Though he had
his suspicions, he had encountered the odor before.

"Fire Department got a call about smoke coming out
of the ground in a vacant lot," Sergeant Wu said, blinking
in the glare of the bright light over the stainless steel
table. He tugged nervously at the jacket of his new police
department uniform. "Damn thing doesn't fit right," he
muttered. The new dark blue uniforms had been hastily
made up, and didn't seem to hang as well as the old two-
tone ones.

"Cause of fire determined?" Renard continued.

"Just guesswork, Captain. Some guy walking by the lot
saw smoke, thought it might be some kind of underground
natural gas fire so they called the gas company and the
fire department. Gas line was ruled out. Firemen looked
down in the hole, saw this guy's legs down there. Like he'd
crawled down and died there. I've felt like crawling in a
hole and pulling the dirt over me in my time but..."

Renard noticed that Wu was glancing around the room, looking at anything but the body. It was indeed a repulsive corpse. The skin had been scorched off most of the upper half, exposing charred muscles and membranes. The eyes had melted out. The hands too were badly burned…

Wu glanced down at the body, winced, looked away.

"Weird about that donut box…" he said.

Renard nodded. The corpse's clawlike right hand gripped a piece of torn, charred cardboard. All that was legible on the cardboard was the name, "WICKED DONUTS" and a shop address on Halsey.

"And look at that hand," Wu went on. He was clearly trying to find something he could deal with to make an observation about. "Like a sloth's claws. Kinda weird."

"*Enforcer des portes ouvertes,*" Renard muttered.

"What's that mean?"

"Hm? Oh it's a French expression about 'breaking down open doors.' Stating the obvious. Okay…" He drew the sheet over the body, to Wu's visible relief. "Let's get the coroner on this."

As they went to the door, Wu said, "I figure he was a bum getting sloppy with Sterno, or something. Tries to crawl down a hole to put the fire out, maybe."

"The boys in rubber boots find anything else down in that hole?"

"Naw, just hooked the guy out with a grabber. Firemen's job isn't to climb down holes. Well, except now and then. I knew a case where this Chihuahua was stuck in a—"

"Never mind the Chihuahua, Wu. Have the report on my desk."

"You got it, Captain. You want that hole excavated?"

Renard shook his head. "Not yet. Let's see what the coroner says about this guy."

"What's up with the sloth claw?"

"Deformity. Or damage to bone from fire." Renard didn't want Wu thinking about it too much. "Who knows?"

That telltale claw might be left over from a *woge* event, Renard figured. Maybe it hadn't disappeared on death, the way they usually do, because of the fire trauma. But he was pretty sure he knew what kind of claw that was.

Chances were, it was the claw of a *Drang-zorn*.

"You know," Wu said, frowning, as they walked up the hall to the elevator. "I saw something about Wicked Donuts on an incident report... Yeah. Guy over on Halsey said his store was robbed. But they only took donuts." After a moment he added, "Perp mighta been a cop."

Renard winced.

"Sorry, Captain. It had to be said."

"Just—send me that donut shop report, Wu."

"Nick—you're joking, right? You don't really want me to climb inside that weird little *thing* do you?"

"Hey, it wasn't my decision, Hank."

Hank Griffin snorted. "Suppose the Sheriff's department sees us? We'll be a laughing stock. We're supposed to be homicide detectives, not circus clowns."

Nick Burkhardt nodded slowly, looking at the little car.

"It *does* look like a clown car."

It was a wet October morning and they were standing in the Portland Police Department parking lot staring at the tiny vehicle, each of them with take-out coffee cups in hand.

"Is that a whatsit—a 'Smart Car?'" Hank asked.

"Um... no. This is a new thing. It's called a 'Pocket Car.' Kind of a Mini Cooper, kind of a Smart Car. Even a little smaller. More... sustainable? The City is trying to be environmentally conscious."

"Nick—screw this. Why don't we just drive my car?"

"Department policy. They want someone to show off

how-concerned they are. They mean well."

"I'm all for clean air, Nick, but this thing, forget it. Hey...I don't see any others in the lot."

"Department only has one other so far. Renard wants us to have this one." Nick chuckled, and opened the passenger side door. "I mean—can you see a couple of street cops driving in something like this? I heard they're gonna get Chevy Volts for patrol cruisers."

"Patrolmen gonna get Chevy Volts?" Hank went around to the driver's side, and angrily yanked the door open. "A Chevy Volt'd be a damn Humvee compared to this thing. And it's got that PPD rose painted on the side, too." He climbed in, grimacing as he folded his long legs into the car. Hank was a tall black man, and had a hard time fitting into the seat. "I've heard patrolmen grumble about that rose symbol on the cruiser. 'Other cops get a bad-ass badge symbol.' But I never minded it till today. Now I feel like I should put on a clown nose and find the Rose Parade."

Nick wasn't much shorter than Hank. He squeezed in, putting the seat back as far as it would go. But he still felt like a hunchback.

"Yeah. It sucks," he said. "It's just for now, Hank. Let's see how it drives."

As they pulled out of the lot, he turned to look out of the side window. The glass was glazed to reflect heat, which inside made it almost mirror-like. A dark-haired man in his early thirties looked back at him; the man had rather large, dark eyes. Not bad looking. A little too baby-faced, perhaps. It was his own reflection. He could almost see the Grimm in that shadowed face...

They were out on the street, heading up NE Sandy Boulevard, wheels sluicing the wet streets of the gray Portland morning, before Hank delivered his verdict.

"You want to know how it drives? Like a bumper car at a carnival. This thing is a *diss*, man." He swore colorfully for awhile.

"You interested in our first call?" Nick asked.

"Another diss, from what I heard. Now they got us investigating donut shop robberies!"

"You are in a *bad* mood, Hank. You went to that new club last night... You hungover?"

"Hungover? Me? No!" He put on a pair of sunglasses with one hand, driving with the other. "Not much."

"Renard asked us to take the donut shop. There's a connection with that possible homicide in Precinct Three. The guy found burned to a crisp. Renard seemed to think we might have something to bring to this one..." He looked at Hank. "You and me particularly."

"Wesen connection?"

"Must be. Take a left here..."

Ten minutes later they pulled up in front of Wicked Donuts at NE Halsey and 57th. A teen skateboarder drifted by, his wheels clacking. He stared at their car.

"Yeah, kid, that's my ride," Hank muttered, grunting as he eased himself out of the enclosed space.

They went into the donut shop. There was no one behind the counter, and the only customer was a big-bellied middle-aged hippie guy finishing a jelly donut. He was wearing a fading T-shirt that said "Set Cannabis Free." Passing the hefty, bearded guy, Nick could smell marijuana.

"Serious munchies?" Nick asked, looking at the remains of the donut.

The bearded guy stared at him and then got up, and walked hastily out the door.

"Skittish, isn't he?" Nick said, looking around the shop. There were old-timey pictures of flappers and Roaring Twenties showgirls, some of them dressed in dancing donut costumes; above a juice cooler was a framed slogan, "Wicked Donuts, Wicked Good!"

"The donuts do taste damned good," Hank said. "But how come they got to *look* like that?"

Some of the pastries under the display's glass were shaped like coiled vipers; some were like flotation devices with *SS Titanic* written on them, others resembled opened mouths, or sharks. There was a bearclaw shaped like a bear trap. Others were baked in peculiar, abstract shapes and wild colors. Flavors included Licorice Goat Milk and Acai Berry Cactus.

"That's just Portland," Nick said. "You know: 'Keep Portland Weird.'"

"Long as you and your shape-changing pals live in this town, Nick," Hank said, his voice low, "not much chance it'll be anything else."

"Anybody working?" Nick called. "Or are the donuts free?"

Almost instantly a man in a smudged white apron sped from a back room, dusting powdered sugar off his hands. Nick could see the clerk was anxious, and his emotional state immediately exposed his Wesen nature. For a moment Nick saw the Wesen's true form shimmer into visibility: a gray-furred rat-like face, protruding front teeth, no real chin, red eyes. A *Reinigen*.

Then the Wesen visage disappeared, and he seemed an ordinary man with a weak chin, small brown eyes set closely together, an overbite, and a receding hairline.

But he'd somehow sensed that his true Wesen nature had been seen. He turned to Nick, eyes narrowing.

"You! You're that Grimm with the cops!" he snapped.

Hank snorted. "There any of these guys who don't know about you, Nick?"

"Fewer and fewer," Nick said. It bothered him how

many Wesen knew about him. It was dangerous. "I'm Detective Burkhardt, this is Detective Griffin." Nick glanced at the name on a sheet of paper Sergeant Wu had given him. "Are you Mr. Popatlus?"

"Yeah, yeah, I'm Fritz Popatlus. Wait—they sent detectives out here over some stolen donuts?" He sniggered. "Figures. Cops. Donuts. *Priorities*, right guys?"

Hank sighed. "There's a connection to another case, here. Maybe. Tell us about the big donut heist."

"Hey, it was just about every pastry in the shop. Whoever it was broke in the back door, took a lot of catering boxes, filled 'em up, and about cleaned the place outta pastry. Several hundred dollars worth, retail price. Bastard snagged five bottles of Healthjuicer too, from the cooler over there."

Nick glanced at the door to make sure no customers were coming in. He didn't want his next question overheard.

"You know any Drang-zorn?" he asked.

"Drang-zorn?" He glanced at Hank. "Can I talk in front of this guy? He a Grimm too?"

"Hell no, I'm not a Grimm," Hank said.

"'Hell no', he's not a Grimm," Nick said, amused. "But you can talk freely in front of him."

Popatlus shrugged. "Sure, I know a Drang-zorn. Regular in here. Sorta pal of mine. Haven't seen him for a while. Used to bowl with him, but you know how they are—those badger guys. Ill-tempered bunch. Can't stand losing. So we stuck to watching football games together."

"What's his name?"

"Clement. Buddy Clement."

"Big fan of your donuts, was he?"

"Yeah, practically *lived* on 'em. Well, you couldn't live on 'em but you know what I mean."

"And you had a falling out over bowling?"

"Nah—'cause I wouldn't loan him money. He wanted to get out of town. Said he had to do it in a hurry. Said they'd done something to his bank account—couldn't get any cash."

"He wanted to get out of town? Why?"

"Don't know. Seemed kinda scared. Tell you the truth, I felt guilty saying no, went to his place later, to try to see if I could help him and his wife out. But they'd moved out already. Landlady said he just split overnight, owing two weeks' rent."

"You know his wife too?"

"Yeah. Ruby."

"A Drang-zorn?"

"Who else would marry a Drang-zorn but a badger babe?"

"What was his address, before he moved?" Nick asked.

Popatlus wrote it down on the back of a receipt and handed it to Nick.

"So you think Buddy stole my goods?" he asked.

"Seems like it."

"You guys gonna get my pastries back?"

"You wouldn't sell stale pastries pawed over by some badger guy, now would you?" Hank asked, looking at him innocently.

"Well…"

"Never mind. You got anything more here, Nick?"

Nick shook his head. "Someplace else I want to have a look at."

"You officers like a dozen donuts on the house?"

"Yeah!" Hank said.

"No," Nick said.

"Oh, come on, Nick, Jeez, sure it's *technically* illegal for us to take 'em but…"

"I'll *buy* you a dozen of your choice, Hank."

"I'm totally taking you up on that. I'll have six of those jelly fire hydrants and half a dozen coiled vipers, the ones with sprinkles."

CHAPTER TWO

"You going to tell me why I'm standing in a vacant lot staring down into a hole?" Hank asked.

Nick nodded. "This morning Renard left the report on my desk about the guy they found burned up down in this hole. Body was likely a Drang-zorn, holding part of a Wicked Donuts box. Drang-zorn like to hide in burrows if they get stressed out."

"The *report* said Drang-zorn? No way."

"No, of course not, but Renard had circled the place they found the body—and something on the coroner's report. Unusual features on the stiff's hand. Couple of fingernails like a sloth's claws. Only I figure it wasn't a sloth. They were more like badger's claws. Sometimes a Wesen will woge under traumatic circumstances—and some part of the woge stays after they're dead. Just a little telltale."

"Renard and his sneaky little ways of talking about stuff we're not supposed to talk about..."

"Yeah. And this lot is just two blocks from the last address for Buddy Clement."

Hank glanced up at the sky and Nick followed the look.

"Starting to rain," Nick said.

"Never worth mentioning in this town."

"It didn't rain for several weeks in August."

Nick hunkered down, peering into the hole. It was about a yard wide, at the top, narrowing as it slanted down into darkness. A rich smell of mud, minerals, and animal rose from the shaft.

"You got a flashlight?" he asked Hank.

"Little one."

As a thin rain fell, Hank reached into his suit pocket, pulled out the small flashlight he always carried, handed it to Nick.

Aiming the light into the hole, Nick could make out the packed mud and clay walls of the circular shaft. There were regular marks down the walls where it had been dug out—claw marks.

"That little hidey-hole," Nick remarked, "is probably snugger than it looks, you go down far enough. Drangzorn pack the walls tight, work out some drainage, make a nice little apartment down there."

"That hole is *snug*? You been watching that kids movie, what is it—*The Wind in the Willows*?"

"Not my brand of fairy tale." Nick glanced around, saw that no one was watching. The lot was enclosed on three sides by a wooden fence. He leaned closer to the hole, and called down it, "Mrs. Clement! Ruby Clement! We want to help you! It's Nick Burkhardt, from Portland Police! Could you come up and talk to us? I promise no one's going to hurt you!"

There was no response—except, very faintly, Nick heard a scrabbling sound. And he had a Grimm intuition: he could often sense Wesen around. She was down there.

"Mrs. Clement! They will excavate this hole! You may as well come out!"

He aimed the flashlight as deeply as the beam would reach…

After a few moments, two red eyes reflected back at him. He glimpsed a wedge-shaped head, the fur striped white on black. Then the Wesen appearance melted away—and it was a human woman's face. She looked frightened.

Nick waved his badge. "Detective Burkhardt, ma'am! We want to help—we'll protect you. I know about Drangzorn—it's all right!"

"I… can't get up there, like this!"

"Go ahead and woge," he called. "We'll move back. You come on up and shift back and we'll talk."

It took her a couple of minutes to make up her mind, and work her way up the shaft and out of the hole. Back in her human form she was a stocky little woman with a wide face, just faintly badger shaped; there was a white streak in her black hair. She wore a dirty raincoat, jeans, sneakers. Her hands were mucky from clawing at the dirt walls, fingernails caked in mud. A brown leather purse dangled from a strap over one shoulder. She was almost hyperventilating with fear as, wide-eyed, she looked back and forth between Nick and Hank.

Her voice quavered as she asked, "You're both really police?"

"Yes, ma'am," Hank said gently, showing her his badge.

"How do I know you're not… not *bad* cops. Bought out by those people?"

"Which people, Mrs. Clement?" Nick asked.

She hesitated, and gnawed on a soiled knuckle.

"Those men from the organization," she said eventually.

"You know what the organization was called, ma'am?"

"I don't know—Buddy said something about ice."

"Ice?"

She nodded, and her lips quivered. "Buddy…"

"You know how he died?" Nick asked. "What caused the burns?"

She pursed her lips, as if she was afraid to say it.

At last she whispered, "*Daemonfeuer.*"

"What's that?" Hank asked.

"You remember that fire-dancing case?"

"Yeah. I knew there was something hinky in that one. It was a Wesen?"

Nick nodded. "Fire breather." He looked at Mrs. Clement. "How'd your husband run afoul of a Daemonfeuer?"

"It wasn't exactly like that. The Daemonfeuer was working for someone else. The organization."

"Some kind of… enforcer?"

Ruby Clement glanced past him at the place where the wooden enclosure became a hurricane-fence gate. Maybe worried someone might be out there on the street, watching and listening.

"Yes. Buddy and me, we always stayed on the right side of the law. Always! One of these people asked Buddy to do some special underground engineering, at a construction site. Well, that's what Buddy *does*, so he thought it was just another job. But when he got there they wanted him to tunnel up under a warehouse of some kind. They want to put a hidden underground entrance, like a trapdoor, too, so they could go into this warehouse without anyone knowing. And—they wanted him to join their organization and… They said he had no choice."

She began wordlessly crying, shaking her head, covering her eyes as if that would blot out the memory of her husband's face melting in dragon fire.

"And he said no," Nick said, softly. "And they sent the Daemonfeuer—to make an example of him."

"Please. I can't stay here. They'll come for me next."

"Did he mention any names?" Hank asked, putting a

reassuring hand on her arm. "Anything that can help us?"

She shook her head. "He didn't tell me anything else. He said we had to hide and… he dug this place out till we could think of something else…"

"Where was this warehouse?" Hank asked.

"Gresham Industrial Park, he said. A drug warehouse. You know—pharmaceutical drugs." She looked toward the gate again, lips compressed thin with fear. "I don't like to be out in the open like this. They could be looking for me. Oh God, I don't want to die like that. It was so awful. It breathed fire on him and burned him and he screamed and his eyes…"

"I don't think they're looking for you," Nick said, "or they'd have been back by now. You have any relatives you can stay with?"

"Yes. I have a sister in Woodburn."

"I'll have a policewoman come and give you a ride down there. You'll be all right, Mrs. Clement. I'm sorry about your husband. We'll do what we can to… bring them to justice."

"How can you? Without telling people? I mean— without telling them about… Wesen?"

"We have ways, Mrs. Clement…"

As Nick and Hank walked into Portland Police headquarters, Hank asked, "You and Juliette wanna do a double date thing, this weekend? I can get free tickets to Princess."

"What's Princess?"

"Prince cover band, man. Girl singers. Maya Rudolph. It's awesome."

"*Prince*? You're old school! I'm up for it if Juliette is."

I'm up for it if Juliette is. Nick smiled. That covered a lot of territory. Nick would be up for marriage, if Juliette was. Only, since she found out about the Grimm thing— and how he'd kept it from her—there was still some distance between them. Be awhile before she'd trust him enough to consider it.

Maybe stupid to get married anyway, being a Grimm. Tough enough to marry a homicide detective. Always a high risk that the next time she sees him after that last kiss goodbye, he'll be in a body bag. But a *Grimm*? The risk was even higher. And it was risking Juliette's life, too. She'd already almost gotten killed because of her association with Nick.

As they rode the elevator up, Hank asked, "What's this damon thing Mrs. Clement was talking about?"

"Daemonfeuer—a Wesen that's kind of a dragon man. They can incinerate their own fat, inside, breath flames out. Tough and nasty. You wouldn't like 'em."

Hank did a short leg squat, grimacing, as the elevator door opened.

"My legs are cramped from that damned car. They want to discipline me, they can talk to the police union. But I'm not getting inside that thing again."

Nick chuckled, leading the way down the hall.

"I hear you. You know, Renard could've picked a lot of guys to drive that thing. But he picked us. Like he was trying to kind of… send us a message."

"Yeah? That we're clowns?"

"That we shouldn't get too big for our boots, maybe. That he's still got his thumb on us. He's always had a Napoleon complex. Even looks like Napoleon some."

"You're right, he does! Remember that press conference, the way he was talking as if he was going to *conquer* the town to bring order? He had a whole megalomaniacal thing going on, man."

"Yeah. About that…" But they'd just reached the door of Renard's corner office. Through the office windows Nick could see Renard at his desk. "Tell you later." Nick hadn't briefed Hank on the Coins of Zakynthos—and Renard's period of being under their influence.

Nick knocked on the captain's door.

"Come in," came Renard's voice. They entered but Renard didn't even glance up from the report he was scanning on his computer. "Shut the door and sit down."

"Yes *sir*," Hank said, a hint of rancor in his voice, as they sat.

"About that car you wedged us into, Captain," Nick began. "Message received, but we—"

"Not going to argue about your vehicle assignments," Renard interrupted snappishly. "I want to know what you found out this morning."

"You mean at the *donut shop*?" Hank asked. "Found out the price has gone up on the jellied fire hydrants."

Captain Renard looked coldly up at him. His face looked distinctly Napoleonic in that moment.

"You have any Bonaparte blood, Captain?" Nick asked, to head off more friction between the two men.

Renard looked at him in mild surprise.

"Some. How'd you know that?"

"Just wondered. What we found out this morning—if you were hinting at Drang-zorn in that report, you were right. Burned body in the morgue is probably a Drang-zorn named Buddy Clement—same guy who broke into the donut shop. He was hiding in that hole from some organized crime outfit. His wife says they tried to strong-arm him into tunneling up under a pharm warehouse in Gresham. She says he was killed by a Daemonfeuer."

"A Daemonfeuer!" Renard leaned back in his chair, and tented his hands. "Thought it might be. They're rare. Didn't think we had any more in town. But then..." He glanced at the computer screen. "Looks like there's a big influx of Wesen, lately."

"How do you know?"

"Doesn't matter. I've got my sources…" Renard picked up a coffee cup, looked in it, apparently found it empty and put it back on his desk. "What organization was it?"

"She didn't know. Her husband said something about ice. That's it."

"Ice." Renard nodded to himself. "Here." He pushed a folder on his desk toward them. "This is for your eyes only. It's all I've got on The Icy Touch. Ever hear about them?"

"Nope." Nick looked at Hank, who shook his head.

"Not likely you'd have heard much," Renard said. "They were out of business, for a long time. And when they were active they were smalltime, compared to the mafia. Kind of an offshoot of the *Hasslich*, going way back."

"The Hasslich…" The name struck a chill through Nick. It was an organization that existed only to kill Grimms. "Great."

"Grimms aren't an Icy Touch priority, especially now," Renard said. "They've got some other agenda. I keep reading between the lines on FBI reports, and Interpol—I suspect it's gone Wesen."

Hank snorted. "The feds know about Wesen?"

Renard shook his head. "They don't have a clue what they're dealing with. They just know Icy Touch is a growing organized crime outfit making a big move. Extortion, drugs, sex slavery, major stolen goods. But Icy Touch is Wesen—and they could have a much bigger agenda than just cashing in on crime."

"How many of them are there?" Nick asked.

"Don't know. More than I'd thought, judging by these reports. Looks like they're making a move on Portland. I'm putting you two on it, so start digging. But report only to me. Keep your mouths shut—and your heads down…"

CHAPTER THREE

A misty dusk. Monroe stood on his front porch and sniffed the October air.

Across the street was Forest Park, 5,100 acres of wildness on the west edge of Portland, where shadows were gathering like flocks of dark birds. The sun was going down beyond the park; the line of firs and deciduous trees broke up the reddening sunlight into a trembling coinage of scarlet-gold. Forest Park, his second home.

Monroe inhaled deeply, taking in the woodland's damp exhalation, parsing the scents with a clarity an ordinary human could only dream of.

Exquisite.

Overtop were the distinct fragrances of evergreens, western red cedar, Douglas fir, western yew, grand fir, all mingled with the decay-rich scents of fallen leaves from black cottonwood, bigleaf maple, red alder; piquant notes of wild blackberries and salmonberries struck through like thorns on a vine. He scented dozens of varieties of mushrooms and tree fungus; he caught the smells of Oregon Grape, trillium, Morning Glory and... Hooker's Fairy Bells. That one made him smile.

Fairy bells. Grimm's fairy bells? In the back of his mind Monroe wondered what Nick was doing today.

Then the lower notes of living fauna rolled over him and he inhaled again to savor them: the Northern flying squirrel; the acrid smells of birds; the sharp tang of frogs and salamanders in Audubon Pond. He caught the rank odor of a fat old raccoon; the distinct rodent aroma of a creeping vole. There—the scent of black-tailed deer. That one made his mouth water. Imagine tasting it freshly killed…

No. You're a vegetarian. For a reason.

But he sniffed again. He could smell scat—guano from bats, droppings from possum and bobcat… and there, the smell of marijuana. Probably someone harvesting it. There were a number of hidden marijuana patches in Forest Park. He chuckled. Smelled like strong stuff.

He could see birds in the foliage, from where he stood: flitting, foraging. There, a woodpecker, getting its evening meal as it paused in climbing bark, drum-rolled its beak into an oak; there, an orange-crowned warbler, heading for its nest; there, a great horned owl, swooping between trees, hunting for a delicious mouse to start off its evening.

Unconsciously, Monroe licked his lips.

Vegetarian, Monroe. It's part of your recovery program. "Hi, I'm Monroe, I'm a predator…"

He had to stay with his program. He was a *Wieder Blutbad* now. But still—he ached to just dive into the forest at random, get deep inside it and then let loose; just woge and explore… and hunt. It'd be sublime to take Rosalee there. She was a *Fuchsbau* Wesen. A fox-woman. She could relate to his urge to plunge into the woods; to take off his shoes and run through the trees in full-on woge. Foxes loved to stalk as much as wolves did.

Rosalee. Was it crazy for him, a Blutbad, to be involved

with a Fuchsbau? Like he cared. But if they had kids would the children be hybrid chimera? He wasn't entirely sure. At some point he'd have to talk it over with her. Right now he couldn't imagine breeding with any other woman, Wesen or human. If not for his long, happy history of living alone, making his house exactly the den he wanted it to be, he'd have asked her to move in with him by now. Eventually, when he was ready for the Big Commitment, he'd have to face up to her natural female desire to redesign the den the way she'd want—fewer clocks, maybe. She might say no to moving in with him, of course. But he doubted it. She was crazy about him. Which made perfect sense. At last. He'd always been puzzled that so many other women had failed to be crazy about him, after Angelina... Dating had been rough until Rosalee...

The shadows deepened in the vast park across the street. They called to him. Another cool exhalation rolled across him, the woods giving out moisture, and fresh oxygen, cooling as the sun set.

Come, Monroe, the forest murmured. *Come, Blutbad. Run. Howl. Feed. Full moon tonight, Monroe. Vegetarian? Don't be silly. That's not what you need! I've got what you need. What you hunger for...*

Monroe sighed, shook his head, and turned away, going quickly into the house.

Not going out there, not tonight. I'm not feral, I'm domesticated, now, and that's a good *thing. Gotta hold onto it, for Rosalee's sake and for Nick and for the Perkins family and... just for me.*

He couldn't run free, not anymore, not like that. Not since that day he and Angelina stumbled on the ranger...

He shuddered, and his stomach lurched at the memory. The ticking of his clocks reassured him. He went quickly to his workbench. Working on restoring an old Swiss pocket watch—that was his refuge. It consumed his full attention to tinker with clockwork, to find the heart and soul of the mechanism and bring it to life. There was no room for restlessness, or temptation. Clockwork was soothing; so much simpler than organic life...

Ridiculous, he thought, to think of clockwork mechanisms as alive at all. But secretly, that was how he felt.

He picked up the jeweler's loupe, held it over the mechanism, peered through it. *Mainspring needs adjusting.* He reached for a tool...

And then his cell phone rang.

Nick had made him get rid of the howling beast ringtone—he'd gotten Howling Wolf instead. *"That's evil, evil is goin' on wrong..."* sang Wolf's gravelly voice.

Monroe cursed under his breath. Wanted to be left alone right now.

But then again, it might be Nick—or better yet, Rosalee. He suddenly felt like answering. Didn't even look at the number.

"Yo, it's Monroe."

"Monroe?" The man's voice was husky, familiar—and hesitant. "It's Smitty."

"Smitty! My man! How are you, bro?"

"Um—been better."

"Uh-oh. You have a little relapse? Listen, relapse is part of recovery."

Smitty was Blutbad, like Monroe, and one of the first Monroe had met as an adult. And like Monroe, Smitty was in recovery from "over indulgence", as Monroe liked to put it. Which was his polite term for going crazy bloodthirsty feral.

"Listen, uh—I know you're busy, Monroe, but..."

"You want to talk, bro, I want to listen."

"Could I see you in person? Rather not talk on the... I'd

just rather talk in person. Right away."

"Huh. Yeah, okay. You were there for me, going back, man. Where you want to meet?"

"How about… Marine Terminal 2—on Northwest Front. Right outside the main gate to the docks."

"Out in all that industrial stuff? Sure, okay. Will I be able to find you, out there?"

"I know your truck, man. I'll see you."

"When?"

"Soon as possible. I'm in trouble, Monroe. So… soon as possible. Thanks, man. I owe you."

And he hung up.

Hank walked up to the desk with the take-out.

"They didn't have the sweet and sour chicken," he said, sitting in the chair across from Nick. "I got you that prawn thing you like instead."

"It's all good," Nick said distractedly, turning the page on the report. He glanced at his watch as Hank pushed the cartons of Chinese food over to him.

"Almost seven p.m," Hank said. "Another dinner at the precinct. Hell, you shouldn't be here, you got someone prettier to have dinner with."

"Prettier than you? Come to think of it, she is." Nick hadn't heard from Juliette that evening. But they hadn't had a date for dinner. He'd just been kind of hoping she'd invite him over. She worked late at the veterinary clinic, sometimes. Maybe that was it. Or maybe she was just brooding about whether or not she could trust him. They were back together—and then again, they weren't.

"So, to review…" Hank prompted, as he spooned broccoli beef from his carton.

"To review," Nick said, "the cartel's based in France, Marseilles."

"Ah. Good old Marseilles. Happy home to many a criminal concern."

"Yeah. Maybe they figure that's protective coloration. The Wesen organization is camouflaged by the human ones. Around there they call it *La Caresse Glacée*. Meaning touch of ice, or the icy touch. Rumor has a guy named Denswoz running it. Another rumor here says he's just the American boss. Just rumors."

Denswoz.

Something about the name made the hair stand up on the back of Nick's neck. Had he heard his mother mention the name, once?

"What other places they known to get down and dirty?" Hank asked, reaching for his coffee.

"Uh… Germany, Argentina, Russia, Mexico… America. More rumors say they've chosen Portland as their West Coast headquarters."

"Why Portland?"

"No one knows. Shipping, maybe?"

"Any local names?"

"One guy arrested. Died in jail. Found slashed up."

"Slashed up. Like, with a knife?"

"Coroner says more like…" Nick read the report aloud. "'Possible weapon: multi-pronged gardening implement.'"

"Garden implement. In prison?"

Nick shrugged. "Or maybe… claws."

Hank stopped eating, and looked at him.

"Claws. Wesen again."

"Could be. Fits with other reports of Icy Touch victims—people who didn't want to be extorted, didn't want to pay up—didn't want to work for them. Bodies slashed, multiple wounds. Some found burned same way as Buddy Clement. One with his guts melted out of him…"

"Like that thing, what was it…" Hank glanced around

to see if anyone else in the office were listening. No one was nearby.

"*Spinnetod*. Spider people."

Hank grimaced. "I hate that one."

"Lot of people with bite marks attributed to attack dogs. But…"

"Could be Blutbad."

Nick nodded. "Or *Schakal*. Jackal people."

"Sounds like they're using Wesen to terrorize people. Scarier than a thug with a gun."

"Using Wesen… maybe. But there's so much of it— could be they are Wesen."

"Yeah. You want to check out that warehouse Buddy was supposed to be digging up?"

"Oh—sorry, should've shown you this." He handed Hank a two-page report. "Renard sent a team over there. Some indication that a tunnel was begun, and abandoned. Like they found out the department was interested. What's interesting is the place doesn't warehouse finished pills. It's only ingredients—chemicals, hormones, enzymes, everything that goes into big pharma medicine. Like they wanted a steady, quiet supply of something… Could be a lot of stuff."

"Morphine, something like that?"

"Maybe. Or maybe something else. Something a *Hexenbiest* might combine with traditional herbs, maybe…"

"You just guessing?"

"Just… a hunch."

Hank let out a long breath.

"I've learned to trust your hunches. And I don't like the sound of that one. You want some broccoli beef?"

The road to the Marine Terminal was a lonely one after dark. Monroe drove just under the speed limit, not wanting to accidentally drive past Smitty. There was no traffic, no one to honk at him to hurry up. A few lights shone coldly from a big container ship at the river dock, beyond the hurricane fence. Enormous industrial cranes for lifting multi-ton shipping containers stood poised like dinosaur skeletons over the dock; a freight train clunked and chugged slowly down a confluence of tracks, between the road and the river, carrying a load of intermodal containers and tanktainers.

Up ahead was the turn-in for the dock. The silhouette of a man was just visible against the closed gate. Monroe turned carefully into the drive, and pulled up. Smitty hurried to his passenger side, opened the door and climbed in.

"There's a river park, not far away," Smitty said, pointing farther down the road. "Let's go there, sit in the parking lot."

"Sure."

Monroe put the truck in reverse and glanced over at Smitty. His friend was a broad-shouldered, heavyset guy with a ragged beard, he wore a plaid coat. But there were circles under his worried eyes and he looked more haggard than Monroe had ever seen him.

Monroe pulled onto the road, heading toward the park.

"You look kinda like crap, bro."

"Not getting much sleep."

"Sleep's important. I can't sleep, I get outta bed, go to the fireplace, chuck a log on there, curl up on the rug with a pillow. Pretend I'm camping. Usually slip into dreamland. But I get cramps in my neck the next day."

Smitty didn't answer, so Monroe kept quiet till they got to the park, and he'd pulled up in the empty parking lot. He switched off the engine, and the lights. They looked out toward the river. The park was flat, green, with little stubs of recently planted trees. Not much of interest.

"Nobody ever goes to this park," Smitty remarked. "There's your tax dollars at work."

"What happened, Smitty? We talking about a relapse?"

"Naw. Could've been one. They'd like that. They want me to relapse."

"They who, man?"

"They came around when I was working in crane maintenance." Smitty nodded toward the big cranes, over by the river. "I was replacing the lights on 'em, and greasing. Guy walks up to me and says, 'Hey, Blutbad. I hear you gave it up.'"

"Just some random guy you don't know?"

"Yeah. But he made sure I got to know him. He was a *Siegbarste*."

"Ugh. An ogre. I hate to be prejudiced but... those guys even smell bad. Under bridges or not."

"Said they needed me to start moving some stuff off a ship for them, into some kind of old tunnel—I guess it was one of those Shanghai tunnels. You know, from back in the day."

"Those things? They wouldn't reach all the way out here."

"They dug part of it out, with a crew of Drang-zorn. You got a cigarette?"

"Nah, I gave up smoking."

"Smoking, hunting... red meat. We gotta give everything up?"

"I can eat store-bought meat, if I want to. I just gave it up because it helps my recovery, man. And there's a lot I haven't given up. I like a good aged single-malt Scotch. I like... well, I'm not a monk, know what I mean?"

"The Drang-zorn—you hear about that one they found cooked, other side of town? Legs sticking up outta some hole in a vacant lot."

"A badger boy? No. I'm surprised..." He started to say

51

he was surprised Nick hadn't told him about it. But his friendship with Nick, his consultancy, was something he didn't want getting around. "No, never heard. *Cooked* you said?"

"Burned—word is, it was a Daemonfeuer."

"Daemonfeuer! A dragon?"

"They got a few enforcers in town. Stuff that'll make you sit up and pay attention. Hasslich. Daemonfeuers Couple of rogue Blutbaden, too."

"Yeah? Who're the Blutbaden?"

"I don't know their names. From out of Chicago, I guess." Smitty cracked his knuckles nervously and looked in the side-view mirror.

"You think they're out here looking for you?" Monroe asked.

"Looking for me anywhere they can find me." He sighed. "I need a smoke. And a drink."

"You wanna come back to my place? We can stop on the way, get you a pack of smokes. I'll provide the drinks."

"No, I appreciate it, but... I couldn't do that to you. You were always a good guy."

"Whatya mean, 'do that to me?'"

"They're after me, man. Because I wouldn't play ball. They wanted me to smuggle shit for them. And act as guard for the stuff too. Meaning if anyone walks in on it, I'm supposed to go full woge and kill 'em."

"Really. Who *are* these guys?"

"They call it... I can't pronounce the French name. In English it's Icy Touch."

"Icy Touch. You give that a ring like *La Cosa Nostra*."

"That's the idea. But they're Wesen. Most of 'em. Some humans. But the humans work for the Wesen."

Now it was Monroe's turn to look nervously in the truck's side mirror.

"Any chance that ogre knows where you are now?" he asked.

"Doubt it."

"Kinda surprises me that they kill the uncooperative types with Wesen weapons, teeth and claws and… fiery breath. I mean—you'd think they wouldn't want to draw that much attention."

"They're trying to scare their way into power with the cartels. I hear it's working. And maybe… they got something else planned. Who knows. Maybe some of them are tired of staying hid. I know I am."

"I'm just used to it." Monroe reflected for a moment on the double life he'd lived for so long. It had been a relief to "come out" to Nick and Hank. And, finally, Juliette. They were humans who accepted him as he was. "So—how can I help you, man? No way these guys are going to let me talk them out of trying to recruit you. And no way, to be honest, I'm going to try. I don't want them to know about me."

"They probably do know. They seem to know about pretty much every Wesen around. Made it their business to know. They got some Hexenbiest who's helping them out on that."

"Hey, that's just wonderful."

"So, uh… I was hoping you could get that cop friend of yours to help me. Maybe protect me or… get me outta town or something. I'm broke, haven't got a car, figure they've got people watching the bus. I don't know what else to do…"

"Dammit! Does *everyone* know I've got a friend in Portland PD?"

"Naw. But word gets around. Some *Eisbiber* guy…"

"Oh. Him. Crap. Let me think…" Monroe shook his head. "My friend in the PD's not a bodyguard. This ogre—you know his name? Where he is?"

"Don't know where he lives. His name's Bonfield. Charley Bonfield. People on the street call him Snarfer."

"Snarfer? Why? Never mind, I don't want to know. Let me talk to my guy, see what he can do. Can you stall these guys?"

"Naw. I already told them I wouldn't play ball. They gave me some time to think but… they'll know, when they see me. You know. Wesen instincts. They'll know. I've been sleeping out here…" He hooked a thumb toward the docks. "Sleeping in a shed, Monroe, on a big coil of cable."

"Ouch. Okay, bro. Go home, pack your stuff up, I'll pick you up and, I don't know, rent a car and loan it to you. You can drop it off for me down south somewhere."

Smitty gave him a long, grateful look.

"That's taking a big chance on me. Something happens to that car…"

"I'll take that chance. Call me when you're ready, I'll pick you up. And I'll see what my friend can do…"

CHAPTER FOUR

Night on the freeway, wending up through the Willamette Valley. Santiago was feeling nervous. What he had in the trunk of his Toyota Camry could get him twenty years in prison, maybe thirty. But the *Sombra Corazón* had told him this was his load, so he must carry it.

Santiago Mendoza had no love for the *Sombra Corazón*. He hadn't even wanted to get the tattoo under his right arm. They'd made him. But the "Shadow Heart" made it possible for him to stay in this country. It had made it possible for him to pay his mother's hospital bills. The gang had paid for this car. And after all, he didn't have to sell any drugs himself. All he had to do was pick the stuff up, and take the risk of driving it from the laboratories and warehouses in southern Oregon, up to a place south of Portland and another near Seattle. Sometimes it was bricks of marijuana, grown in Humboldt County, in Northern California, warehoused in Southern Oregon. He usually pinched out a gram or so of that for himself. This time it was about ten pounds of yellow-white powder. Probably raw, pure crystal meth. That, he wouldn't touch. He'd seen what it could do to people.

Another few minutes, and he could drop it off in Canby. There was a farm on the edge of town where the stuff would be cut and redistributed, in an old barn that had once contained numerous doomed pigs and still smelled of it.

His headlights cut through the night and caught the reflective sign he was looking for. There—the exit.

He took the exit, careful not to take it too fast, to always drive smoothly. Do nothing to make a Highway Patrolman stop you.

Santiago drove around the curve, onto the utility road. He continued carefully for another quarter mile south, then turned left onto Strawberry Farm Road. He drove along an old concrete highway through a series of strawberry fields, already harvested, then turned right at the big redwood mailbox. Another short drive down a gravel road, then he was pulling up in front of the big aluminum-sided barn.

He stopped the Camry, feeling relief. They'd have something for him to transport to Seattle but he was glad to have this leg of it over with. He walked toward the partly open barn door, a little yellow light spilled out from inside. It took him a moment to see Juan standing by the door, submachine gun on a strap over his shoulder. The slim but deadly sentry was almost hidden in the shadow, but his glowing cigarette had caught Santiago's eye.

Juan's pockmarked face lit up red when he drew on the smoke.

"Que pasa, Juan. Todo bueno?"

"Bueno," Juan replied hoarsely, exhaling.

They performed the distinct *Sombra Corazón* handshake and then Santiago stepped into the big room, where a row of men and two women worked at a long metal table in front of the row of old aluminum stalls, cutting the dope. All of them were wearing respirator masks. Another guard stood at the back, a mestizo Santiago didn't know.

Donny Diaz, the boss of the operation, had his feet up on an old dented, gray steel desk, a bottle of tequila propped in his lap, a glass in his hand. A big wide smile, big black eyes. A sleeveless T-shirt, baring tattooed arms, though it was cold. He waved the bottle at Santiago, offering him a drink.

Donny was not supposed to be drunk right about now. He was a pretty decent guy, and Santiago hoped Donny didn't get caught by some cartel captain.

Over by the table, Jimmy Hernandez waved and then pulled the goggled mask off his face. He came toward Santiago, smiling, shotgun cradled in his arms, and showed a mouthful of big white teeth under a small black mustache.

"Hey, bro. *Cómo te va*?" Santiago called out.

"*Nada, aquí*, man. You deliver?"

"Shit's in the car, man. *Diez libra*."

Then Santiago realized Jimmy was staring past him, gaping in shock.

Santiago turned, and saw Juan staggering into the room, head hanging half off his neck, spouting blood like a fountain. His submachine gun was gone, his hands were shaking at his sides. Santiago was reminded of one of those zombies you saw in the movies, coming at him all bloody, empty-eyed and lurching. Then Juan fell facedown on the wooden floor at Santiago's feet, twitching. It looked like Juan's head had been torn half way off his neck.

"*Mierda!*" Santiago swore, backing away from the door.

The big door slid aside, revealing, as it went, one man, then another, and another, until there were five men standing side by side. Three of them were gringos. One Mexicano, one black.

They were clearly not friends of *Sombra Corazón*.

Remarkably, only one of them had a weapon—he held Juan's submachine gun in his hands.

Santiago heard metallic squealing, and a shout, turned to see the mestizo being pulled through the back wall. It had been ripped open from outside, as if the aluminum wall had been as frail as a piece of foil.

Massive clawed hands had thrust through the gap. They gripped the mestizo, wrenching him back through a jagged-edged hole too small for his body. The hole ripped asunder, spurting crimson as the man screamed... and vanished.

A shotgun boomed, and Santiago—taking all this in over a few seconds of paralytic horror—turned to see that it had fired uselessly into the air as someone... some*thing*... thrust Jimmy back to the floor. Was it a werewolf? Something close. Ripping out Jimmy's throat.

The women at the worktable screamed; the men swore in Spanish.

The other strangers at the door rushed into the room. One, who looked too big to be a human being, his face craggy, ears pointed and tufted, tossed Donny's desk aside with his left hand, as if it were an empty cardboard box; with his right he grabbed Donny by the throat, lifted him off his feet. Donny gave out a choked, gurgling cry. The tequila bottle fell from his hand, but Santiago didn't see it break on the floor because he was falling himself, struck in the left side of his head, knocked down by a furry fist. He caught a blurred glimpse of cat-like eyes, whiskers, snarling muzzle, bared tigerish fangs—and then he lost consciousness.

When Santiago came to himself, he was lying on his back, looking at the dusty peaked ceiling of the old pig barn. His head banged, his left ear throbbed and whistled. He heard the sound of women weeping somewhere. A man was speaking in a low voice.

"Donny Diaz, do you hear me clearly? You understand the Inglés, yeah?"

"We all understand…" came Donny's voice, thick with fright.

They continued to talk, as Santiago slowly sat up. A buzzing filled his ears, so that he couldn't hear most of what was being said. Blood trickled from a wound in his scalp; he could feel it running over his left ear. The whole room stank of blood. A lot of it was Jimmy's, in a reflective scarlet puddle around his body. He lay, staring in death, throat missing. Just an exposed vertebrae, white and pink, between his collarbone and his chin.

Standing over Jimmy's body was the…

Was that a werewolf? Almost, but not quite a werewolf. More like one of those men who grew hair all over their faces—Santiago had seen one on the *Ripley's Believe It or Not* television show. But this one had big fangs, too, and long black claws. He stood straight, and wore a blue suit. The suit looked strange on him. The front of it was heavily stained with blood.

Why wear a suit, Santiago wondered dazedly, *if you're going to get it covered in blood?*

The wolflike man in the suit was chewing something meditatively, as he watched Donny's interrogation. A piece of flesh and skin dangled from his mouth, on one side. Santiago could see a little bit of a tattoo on it. The tattoo that had been on Jimmy's neck.

The creature casually sucked the skin and flesh into its mouth, and swallowed.

Santiago's stomach rebelled; he doubled over and vomited. The other creatures in the room looked at him. The buzzing gradually simmered down in his ears, so he could hear a little better. The sound of his own retching. Donny saying something like, "We do what you say."

A man with a face like a cat turned toward Santiago, and gestured with its pawlike hand.

"You—come here."

Santiago could barely make out the words through the purring growl of the thing's voice.

"Yes," Santiago said. "*Si.* I have no guns. Don't hurt me."

He forced himself to stand. The room reeled, and then stabilized. He saw two other bodies, a woman lying under the table, her respirator mask down around her bloodied neck; a man lying nearby, goggles spattered inside with blood. Something was hunched over that one, seemed to be sucking at the body's innards…

The hulking one, standing over Donny, turned to look at him. It was almost as if his face was carved in stone. Like some church gargoyle.

"You…" he rumbled. "You can live—or we'll eat your flesh for a long time before we kill you. From now on, you serve Icy Touch. Or you die real nasty. You got me? The *Sombra Corazón*—that don't exist for you no more."

"Yes," Santiago said. "*Si. Te lo suplico. Si.* No more. I serve your *banda*. Before God I swear it."

He did not want to be eaten. Especially not eaten alive.

Maybe this is a dream, a nightmare, he thought. Then he looked down at his own vomit, and then over at the shining pool of syrup-thick scarlet around Jimmy. He knew it was no dream. This was real. The *espiritu bestia* of legend must be real. His uncle had told him stories of them and Santiago had not believed. But they had returned, and they were reclaiming the world…

"*Si,*" he said again, retching. "*Si. Si…*"

CHAPTER FIVE

"Nick? You awake? This is Monroe."

"I know it's Monroe, dammit. What time is it?" Nick sat up, saw that Juliette had already gotten up. She had an operation on a golden retriever scheduled early.

"Six-thirtyish in the morning. Okay, six-fifteen... Sorry about that, Nick. I *totally* knew something had happened when I woke up and realized I hadn't heard from Smitty—"

"Wait, who's Smitty?"

"You didn't get my message?"

Nick turned on a light by his bed. It was still mostly dark outside.

"No. I haven't checked voicemail since I went to bed, naturally."

"About a Wesen, in danger, a Blutbad, Smitty..."

Nick rubbed his eyes. "What can I do for you at six-fifteen in the morning on my only day off, Monroe?"

"It's this outfit, The Icy Touch, he—"

"Wait. You said Icy Touch?"

"That's what he—"

"Hold it. Just... wait." Nick thought about it. "Monroe? You at home?"

"Yeah."

"Wait there, I'm gonna come and pick you up."

"Not only on your day off, but this early, damn," Hank said, as Nick got into the car.

"Just drive," Nick said, putting his coffee in the cup holder. "Monroe's place."

Hank ran the windshield wipers for a few swipes, then turned them off. The rain was just stopping.

"Man, you're nearly as bossy as Renard." He drove the Crown Victoria onto the street. "Look at you, Mr. Up-at-Seven-Thirty-on-His-Day-Off."

"Not my idea. Monroe's. Looks like I'm working on my day off too. He's got an Icy Touch connection. Friend of his…"

"Yeah? Wesen?"

"Blutbaden. What's up with this ride? No clown car?"

"Hey, nothing to stop me from checking out an unmarked car, is there?"

"Good thought. Funny they use these Crown Victorias as unmarked cars. They look so damn much like cop cars even without the lights. Because they *are* police cars, almost everywhere. Stupid."

"Stupid? Police department planning? Is that possible?"

Nick laughed and sipped his coffee.

When they got there, Monroe was waiting out front in the drizzle. He had a watch cap on his head; rings under his eyes.

"Monroe looks more tired than you," Hank remarked.

Monroe got in the back, passing Hank a slip of paper with the address.

"Thanks for this, you guys," he said.

"You're helping us," Hank said. "I mean, if this really has an Icy Touch connection. But don't let anyone know we're checking them out, will you?"

"Me?" Monroe sounded offended. "When have I ever been big mouthed, y'know, talking out of school, all that?"

Nick turned and stared at him.

"Well, okay, a little, but…"

It was about half an hour to Smitty's place, with the early morning traffic. Nick's stomach was starting to react against coffee, more coffee, and nothing else, when Hank pulled up in front of the apartment building.

It was the grungy sort of place built on the cheap in the early seventies, big and blocky, with a vague modern look, covered in gawdy red and yellow paint. The landscaping around the front was overgrown with weeds. A grimy concrete donkey, once part of the landscaping, seemed trapped in the overgrowth.

"He's second floor," Monroe muttered, jumping out of the car before Hank had turned the engine off.

Hank and Nick climbed out and followed him through the open gate into a courtyard, up pebbled concrete steps to the row of apartments along the second-floor balcony.

Monroe knocked on Number 27. They waited. No answer.

Monroe got out his cell phone, tapped a redial.

"Come on, Smitty, answer…" he murmured.

They could hear a phone ringing inside.

"He got a landline?" Hank asked.

Monroe shook his head. "Don't think so. He wasn't even staying here—he was in a damn shed over by the Marine Terminal. But he came back here to get his stuff this morning… and he was supposed to call me…"

The phone rang, and rang. Monroe shook his head and hung up.

Nick peered at the door, examining the lock. It seemed bent out.

"Hank—that look like it was jimmied or… something?"

Hank leaned forward to take a closer look.

"Or something," he agreed.

Nick shoved the door—and it swung open. The lock, he saw now, had been snapped. That was probable cause for police entry. So was the trail of blood inside the front door.

"Looks like he tried to stop them coming in," Hank said, as he drew his side arm and entered.

Nick pulled out his own gun, gestured for Monroe to wait outside.

Nick followed Hank into the dank hallway and from there into the living room.

Seconds later Monroe rushed in behind him.

He stared in horror at the blood on the carpet, the blood splashed on the television screen, the blood on the wall. For a moment Nick got a psychic glimpse of the Blutbad's face, complete with fur, animal eyes and fangs, his Wesen form revealed by anxiety. At this stage Monroe's Blutbad appearance would be invisible to anyone but a Grimm or a Wesen. It vanished as Monroe pointed at the door which must be the bedroom.

"You guys—go! I can't…"

Nick gripped his 9 mm Glock, and followed Hank to the bedroom.

Hank pushed the door open. The remains of the body were spread all around the room. Parts of it were stuck to the walls. A man's head was set up on a pillow, on the bed, without the rest of the corpse. The victim's eyes stared at the ceiling, looking as if he'd just awakened without his body. It seemed someone had left it there as some kind of morbid joke.

A fly buzzed over the dead man's mouth. The room smelled heavily of blood, feces, sweat, and death.

The claw marks on the face were clear-cut. The man's

torso, lying on the floor chest down, was clawed up, his clothes shredded.

Nick squatted down—at his feet was a man's arm, and hand. The hand clutched a hank of fur—orange-golden fur, with a little black in it. Like a jaguar's.

Balam Wesen, *maybe*, Nick figured. Jaguar people. So many different types of Wesen seemed to be caught up in this thing...

Nick picked up a wallet from the floor, and opened it. He could see the cash and credit cards were still there. He stood up, silently handed the wallet to Hank.

"Here's the ID," Hank said. He looked at the driver's license photo and then at the head on the pillow.

"Monroe—don't come in here," Hank called. "But is the guy's name Lemuel Smith?"

"Yeah..." Monroe's voice sounded half strangled. "Smitty."

Nick sighed. "Okay, let's send for forensics, the body bag boys, and..." His voice seemed to trail off of its own accord. The vic was Monroe's old friend. This was gonna hit Monroe hard.

Hank nodded and they turned away, grateful to leave the charnel house bedroom, and went back into the living room.

Monroe was already out on the balcony, leaning on the iron railing.

Nick went out and stood beside him, looking down at the concrete courtyard. A child's plastic tricycle, missing a wheel, lay on its side next to a rusty charcoal barbecue grill. Monroe was frowning down at the barbecue as if he was hoping to find an answer there.

"Sorry about your friend," Nick said. "Wish we could've..."

"You couldn't," Monroe said, his voice husky. "Because

I didn't get on this fast enough."

"Not your fault, Monroe."

Monroe shook his head. "Theoretically—no, it isn't. But still…"

Nick nodded. "I know how you feel."

"You know—you're not a Wesen. That's something you don't know—what it's like for us."

It began to rain again, the first drops freckling the concrete below them. The smell of concrete in rainwater rose to meet them. A few steps down the balcony, Hank was calling the crime scene in.

Monroe cleared his throat, and went on, "See, Nick… an ordinary human being gets scared, they can go to the nearest police department, or the FBI, and they can get help. But not a Wesen—not if the danger is from other Wesen. Or…" He smiled sadly. "Or from a Grimm. Nothing personal, there, bro. No offense."

"None taken."

"But—you know what I mean… We got no place to turn, really. I mean, there are Wesen organizations but they can't do much. And when it's something like this…"

"Yeah. We'll find a way, Monroe. We can't save everyone. But we'll find a way to take these guys down."

Monroe shook his head. "Hard to see how. I mean—I smelled cat in there. A big cat…"

"Yeah, maybe. Balam, I think. Jaguar people."

"More than one. Maybe two of 'em. Least he didn't get cooked alive like that Drang-zorn. Daemonfeuer hunting people down "

"You heard about that?"

"Smitty told me. This Icy Touch, it's leaving messages, man. Messages for Wesen. Newspapers will say drug-crazed killer, or something, when they report on Smitty's murder. Chainsaws or whatever. But Wesen will know…"

"Looks that way. I figure the Drang-zorn death was another message. 'If we come for you, you play along or you die ugly.'"

Monroe rubbed his eyes. "Man! Daemonfeuer and now Balam. What's next, Spinnetod? How many kinds of Wesen are they bringing into this thing?"

"I was thinking about that too."

Sirens sounded in the distance. Ambulances. Patrol cars. The body bag guys.

"That many types of Wesen—kind of says that this thing is big. And they plan to make it bigger…"

"So this guy Smitty said there was a tunnel, here?" Hank asked. He sounded doubtful.

Nick and Hank were walking along the dock under the massive freighter. It was still drizzling but they were used to it, and hardly noticed. To their left was the sheer black steel cliff of the freighter's hull. The ship was called *La Conquete*. Above the ship towered the white painted cargo cranes.

"Not using those cranes today," Hank said. "But it's morning. There oughta be work getting done. And there's containers up there to offload."

"I thought that too. There could be reasons. But… yeah." Nick replied.

No sound came from the ship at all, except a faint creaking. They could hear their footsteps echoing on the dock.

They walked past the high prow of the ship. Hank paused and looked up and down the terminal's long metal and concrete dock.

"How could there be a tunnel here nobody would notice? Does it come out under water, or what?"

"I was thinking about that. There's one possibility. Might be a culvert there, see it?"

"Where?"

"Over here…"

Nick walked quickly up the dock, stopped another fifty paces on, Hank jogged after him.

Nick could see the outflow from the culvert, the wrinkling of the water's surface as run off flowed at right angles into the river. Nick lay down on his stomach, shuffled forward, and looked over the edge. The culvert was hard to see from the dock, but from here it was a barred opening about twenty feet in diameter, stretching into darkness. Water ran along the bottom, just a stream about three feet wide, to a concrete lip where it spilled into the river. A rusty barred gate closed the culvert off, just above the outflow.

Hank laid down beside him.

"You wear those cheap suits, doesn't bother you to lie on the damn ground. Nick, that thing's all locked up."

"It's closed. It's got hinges on it. There's a padlock. Padlocks can be opened."

"You think they load stuff in and out from a boat?"

"A big launch could lower off the far side of that boat at night, carry stuff over here. They could get it up there and into the tunnel."

Hank stood up, dusting himself off. "Wrinkling my clean pants," he muttered. He indicated. "That ship there, you think?"

"Hard to say. But they were kind of pushy about getting Smitty to help them with something. Like it was happening soon. And there's the ship."

"That's not probable cause. We need a warrant to get on that ship. We could call the Coast Guard, I guess…"

"Rather we searched the ship ourselves. I'll call Renard about the warrant."

"They don't give out warrants like French fries at a drive-thru. Going to take some time."

"Something else we can do in the meantime. You hear that?"

Hank shook his head. "What?"

Nick cupped his ear and pretended to hear something.

"There's someone yelling for help from that culvert."

"No, there isn't. If there were, protocol would be call the fire department."

"No time for that. Sounds urgent."

"We even need a warrant for a culvert?"

"I don't think so. But we should have a reason for going in there, just in case."

"Like imagining we hear someone down there?"

"I almost do hear them. Kind of."

"Okay, Nick. Well, you enjoy hunting around in there."

"Not going alone, Detective Griffin. Need you there, pal."

"No way, not in these shoes. Not going to do it."

"We can get some wading boots from somewhere. Hey, look—" Nick pointed at a blue and white boat moving slowly up the river. "—one of those little Coast Guard river boats! We can wave 'em over, get 'em to loan us some boots, take us in a boat right up to the culvert..."

"Hey, wait—what if that gate's locked?"

"I can accidentally break the lock. Accidents happen, Hank."

Monroe knew he shouldn't be following Nick and Hank like this. He shouldn't have followed them in his truck, and now on foot. He was using Blutbad skills to evade their notice, following back at the fence, moving along parallel to them as they walked up the dock. Keeping his distance—knowing if he got any closer Nick's Grimm abilities would alert him.

This is wrong.

They were his friends, Nick even more so than Smitty.

But his loyalty to Smitty was paramount just now. Smitty had been a fellow Blutbad in recovery who'd died—at least from Monroe's point of view—for ordinary humanity. He'd died for refusing to revert to Blutbad predation. Because when Blutbaden tried not to be predators, they did it partly to protect human beings. Of course—they also did it to protect themselves *from* human beings; from being hunted in retaliation… And they did it to escape the notice of Grimms, of course.

Why were Nick and Hank waving to that Coast Guard boat? He could see the gleam in Nick's badge in his hand. It was coming over to them…

Monroe waited, and watched.

Shouldn't be doing this…Nick's gonna be mad…

But Monroe *had* to know what was going down. Who, exactly, was behind Smitty's death. If he found out who they were, maybe he could get in touch with the Verrat, the Royals, *someone* who could rein these bastards in. Or maybe he could get the Wesen who'd torn Smitty to pieces himself. Get the scumbag alone. Take him down.

He'd sworn no more predation against animals or people.

But against a Wesen murderer… that was a death he could live with.

What would Rosalee say, if she knew what he was thinking? What would Nick say, for that matter. *This is nuts…*

But still Monroe waited, and watched.

CHAPTER SIX

Nick led the way, gun in one hand, Hank's flashlight in the other.

"You know," Hank whispered, as they waded quietly up the culvert, into ever deeper darkness, "I used to work in Vice, busting crack heads and tweakers. They'd be outta their damn minds every single time. Never knew what they were going to do. Some of 'em bit you when you arrested 'em."

"So I've heard," Nick replied. They'd gone about fifty yards into the culvert, after using a Coastie's crowbar to break the lock on the gate. Now and then something other than their boots splashed in the darkness. Rats, Nick guessed.

"Yeah. Twice I had to get antibiotics and tetanus shots, from crackhead bites. But you know what, that's starting to sound pretty good to me right now. I never had to wade up a stinking culvert, stepping on rats, looking for..."

"Shhh..." Nick stopped, aiming the light on the curved cement wall to their left. There was a dark place there, oblong, rough-edged. In a barely audible mutter, Nick added, "Might have our Drang-zorn tunnel..."

Nick moved toward the tunnel, trying not to slosh too loudly—it was difficult in hip waders on a curved, slime-slick surface, to keep from slipping and making a lot of noise.

Yes. A side tunnel.

It was cut into the wall—broken through, really—just above the water level. The tunnel beyond was formed of packed clay and rock, with characteristic Drang-zorn marks. They'd evidently found some other badger people to dig for them. Maybe the Daemonfeuer had scared them into it.

Nick moved up to the side of the tunnel, leaned out to look without showing too much of himself. He angled the light down and peered along the tunnel, hoping to see someone, or something, that might give him a clue what he and Hank were getting into.

"Let's just do this, at least then we'll be out of this rat waterpark," Hank said.

Nick holstered his gun, and climbed up into the tunnel, keeping the light angled down. Hank climbed after him. Nick created a pool of light so they could see what they were standing on then, hunched over a little beneath the dirt ceiling, they moved off down the tunnel. It smelled of clay and worms and wet rock.

Near as Nick could tell they were moving along at a sharp angle from the culvert, heading for Old Town Portland.

After an indeterminate distance, Hank whispered, "That flashlight goes out, I'm gonna light your hair on fire, so I can see my way. I don't like rats. Did I mention that?"

"I inferred it."

"That look like light up ahead to you?"

"Yeah…"

Another forty steps and they came to a wooden door, loosely fitted in a brick frame. A little light showed around the edges.

"Got a locked chain on it," Nick said, inspecting it with the flashlight. "You didn't bring the crowbar?"

"Wasn't our crowbar. But you know what, I didn't come all this way to stop here. Let me get out of these damned waders..."

They both discarded their waders. Then Hank looked at the door, searching for the right spot. He took a step back.

"You hear someone yelling for help, right?" he asked.

Nick put his hand to his ear, made a great show of pretending to hear something.

"Definitely."

"Okay then."

Hank gave the door his best kick-boxing slam, hitting it right by the chain. The frame shattered with a sharp *crack* and the door teetered inward.

"So much for surprising anyone," Nick said, putting the flashlight away and drawing his Glock.

But the door opened to reveal another empty tunnel. This one was made of brick, stone, and old timbers. The light came from electric lanterns which hung from the ceiling. Water dripped, hissing as it fell onto the lamps.

"Smells like river water," Nick said. "Must be right up close to it."

"Shanghai tunnels," Hank said.

"Yeah, they connected the culvert to their own tunnel and hooked that one up to one of the old underground tunnels," Nick murmured, looking around. Given the noise they had made breaking down the door, he was fully expecting any second some woged Wesen to come snarling around the curve up ahead, fangs bared and claws slashing. But he heard nothing apart from a faint hissing, and sizzling.

"I thought there were people going on tours down in these things..." Hank said.

Nick nodded. "I heard the tours were shut down

because of some structural problem. Which maybe they faked up so they could use them."

They started down the tunnel toward Old Town, Nick ahead, Hank close behind him.

"They really Shanghai sailors in these things? Smuggle heroin, all that?" Hank asked.

"I think the tunnels were supposed to be for moving freight from the docks to the old-timey shops, without having to get past all the wagons and traffic. But they found other uses for 'em. Knocking sailors out, dragging them through a tunnel to a ship they didn't want to ship out on..."

Another fifty paces, they came to a corner... and Nick stopped in his tracks.

Someone was behind them.

Nick spun round, signaling to Hank for silence, and listened. There was a squelching sound behind them, like wet, hesitant footsteps.

Nick eased back, waiting at the corner, his back against the dirt wall by the turn, gun raised. Hank was about three paces past, waiting silently, gun aimed at the bend in the tunnel.

Monroe stepped around the corner—and froze, seeing Hank.

"Oh. Hi, Hank. Um...you like to come down here too, huh?" Then he sniffed the air, turned and looked at Nick. "Well, well. Nick. There you are. Uh..."

"You just 'like to come down here'?" Nick said, lowering his gun. He pointed at Monroe's soaking pants legs and shoes. "And you like wading around in your best loafers, I see."

Monroe looked at his feet. "Oh, yeah. That's probably what you heard. Damned shoes were so loud with the water in them."

"Why are you following us, Monroe?" Hank asked softly, walking up to him, gun now at his side.

"Because—I feel responsible. I mean, not directly but… you know, Smitty was my friend and I just feel like I should be in on this. Not in on it like, I'm a cop, I know, but maybe an advisor, civilian advisor, or…"

"Or pain in the ass?" Hank suggested.

"Hey, I'm gonna be a help, I promise, I just need to know what's going on with this thing, you know, as much as you can tell me, which should be, I'd hope, a lot, because—"

"Monroe? Keep your voice down," Nick told him. "Since you're here, let's see if you can make yourself useful. Come on. Stay behind Hank and keep as quiet as you can."

Nick started off down the tunnel again, Hank and Monroe following…

Squelch, squelch, squelch.

Nick threw Monroe a look of irritation.

"Sorry!" he whispered. "They're wet… Hold on… screw it…" He rolled his pants legs up, and quickly pulled off his shoes and socks. "Always feels better to me anyway."

Nick nodded, and they continued on their way.

Another thirty paces… and voices reached their ears.

Nick could smell Wesen; could *feel* them nearby, a kind of subtle electric tension in his jaw and forehead. He could feel his Grimm side coming alert: colors and shapes suddenly seemed more vivid, and smells more potent.

Nick looked at Hank. Hank nodded and drew his 9 mm automatic.

They crept forward, quickly reaching another bend in the tunnel. Nick peeked around the corner.

Three Wesen stood in a small chamber, little more than a widening of the corridor, around a half-size fiberglass pallet stacked with pound-sized bricks of yellow-white powder. A "Lift'n Buddy" electric hand truck stood against the wall. Leaning beside that was a woged Blutbad, in black T-shirt and jeans, growling to itself, its furred arms folded on its chest. A submachine gun on a strap hung over one of its shoulders.

The other two figures were just finishing stacking powder bricks on the palette. They appeared human—but using his Grimm sight, Nick could see they weren't. One of them, short, thick, and blunt featured, was a Drang-zorn. The other was bigger, scowling… probably a Hasslich.

Nick drew back, and pulled out his cell phone. Perhaps if the Icy Touch thugs were surrounded by uniformed officers, they'd revert to human appearance and come along quietly. Maybe. But his cell phone had no signal. Figured, this far underground. Nick sighed, shook his head at the others, and put the phone away.

They'd have to come up with something else—maybe a decoy, someone to distract them while he and Hank got the drop… Since Monroe was here, he might as well be useful.

Nick turned to Monroe, signaled with a finger on his lips for silence, and tried to mime what he wanted Monroe to do—as if he were playing charades. He acted out a woge, miming turning visibly Wesen, making fangs with two fingers at Monroe. Aware, as he did this, that despite the danger, Hank was covering his mouth to keep from laughing. Monroe just gaped at him in puzzlement, and then started to speak. Nick quickly put a hand over Monroe's mouth and shook his head. Then he enacted the woge again, pointed toward the Wesen guards… and Monroe's eyes lit up.

Monroe nodded, closed his eyes for a moment, concentrating—and then became, visibly, a Blutbad, sprouting fur, fangs, his eyes becoming feral. And not a moment too soon.

A gruff voice spoke from around the corner.

"I smell someone—visitors. You guys getting that scent? Someone close…"

"Yeah, that'd be me, fellas," Monroe said, chattering as he stepped out into view. His voice was altered, made more guttural by the transformation. "Ha, shoulda taken a shower this morning. Got all kinda smells on me, from, uh, fighting humans, and… you know how it goes. I guess I shoulda called ahead. But, hey, no cell phone service down here."

"Who the hell are you?" asked the gruff voice.

"Boss sent me to tell you guys the stuff here's going to be picked up sooner'n planned. The other guys are coming pretty quick to get it…"

"We were told we'd be standing guard for a few hours. Only been an hour."

"Sure, that's why I'm here…"

"I don't remember you from the meetings," the gruff voice went on.

"You don't remember this?"

Nick looked around the corner in time to see Monroe grab the submachine gun hanging on the Blutbad's shoulder. He broke the snap, but, before he could turn it against the Icy Touch Wesen, the guard had lunged at him, knocking him back…

Nick and Hank darted around the corner, guns in hand.

"Police!" Nick shouted. "Get down on the ground!"

Only the Drang-zorn obeyed. Near the Drang-zorn, in mere seconds, the other man transformed, a full-on woge into Hasslich: his ears went pointier, tufted; his face became chiseled and gaunt; his eyes turned red, pupils slitting; his teeth became serrated as a saw blade; and fingers extended claws, muscles stretched, ripping his clothes.

The Wesen troll charged at Hank.

Nick ran to help Monroe who was rolling across the ground, fighting with the other Blutbad, both of them snarling and snapping. No way to shoot the guy without risking shooting Monroe, so Nick reversed his Glock and hammered at the Icy Touch Blutbad's head with the butt. The Blutbad howled and tried to twist away.

Nick reached between them with his free hand to try to get a grip on the Icy Touch Wesen—and a mostly feral Monroe bit his hand.

"Ow! Dammit, Monroe!" Nick said, snatching his hand back.

The submachine gun, compressed between them, went off—and Nick looked on with horror as blood splashed, bits of bone flew... Then he saw with relief that it wasn't Monroe who'd been shot. The bullets had smashed up under the Icy Touch Blutbad's jaw, and out through the top of his head.

Another gunshot made him turn—he saw Hank struggling with the Hasslich, his arms pinioned in the creature's talons, gun firing uselessly into the ceiling.

Nick swung his gun hard, cracking the Hasslich in the head with all his strength.

The troll roared, shook his head, stunned, and Hank jerked his gun hand free and fired four times, point blank, into the Hasslich's chest.

Nick sighed, as the troll staggered backwards, and fell. Another possible interrogation subject gone to meet the devil.

"Fellas, don't shoot me, don't shoot me, I didn't want to do any of this stuff!" whimpered the man lying face down by the bricks of powder. Nick looked at him, saw his Drang-zorn appearance showing in his distress.

"Take it easy, no one's gonna hurt you if you don't resist," Nick said. "What's your name?"

"Doug. I mean—Douglas Zelinski."

"Your hand's bleeding, Nick," Hank said, holstering his gun.

Nick looked at his left hand. There were only a couple of fang marks on it but Monroe had broken the skin.

"Yeah, sorry about that, Nick," Monroe said, getting to his feet. He was back in human form, brushing blood and brains from his shirt with evident distaste. "You stuck your hand too close to my mouth when I was in full Blutbad fighting mode… kind of a reflex… A little antiseptic and it'll be fine. I'm gonna need some too. This scumbag's blood is all over me… ugh."

The Icy Touch Blutbad had shifted back to human form in death.

"You know that guy, Monroe?" Nick asked.

"Naw. Out of town Wesen, be my guess."

Nick grimaced, rubbing his wrists. He nodded towards the body of the troll.

"Man that son of a bitch was *strong*. Nearly cracked my bones."

"He would've, in another second or two," Monroe said.

"Fast too. Rushed right past my gun. Thanks, Nick," Hank said.

"Sure, Hank but—you have to kill him? I wanted to question him."

"You kidding me? He was about to eat my face!"

Nick shrugged. "Probably tear out your throat instead."

"Oh well, that'd be *fine* then."

"You're not going to kill me?" The Drang-zorn asked again.

"No," Nick said. He knelt to cuff the man's hands behind his back.

"They will, though, you know. They'll get to me in jail," the man said sadly.

"We'll protect you," Nick said, feeling a stab of guilt as he said it because he wasn't sure he could guarantee the guy's safety at all. "What's the stuff in the bricks here? Heroin?"

"Nah, I don't think so. But I don't know what it is. They called it *Seele Dicht* something. I don't know what that means. I don't speak German."

Monroe perked up at that.

"Seele Dichtungsmittel?"

"Yeah, I think that was it. How long I got to lay here on my stomach?"

Nick helped him to his feet.

"What's this *Seele* stuff?" he asked.

"Did he say seal dicks?" Hank asked.

"No, I didn't," Monroe said, picking a chunk of brain matter off his shirt. "I said *Seele Dichtungsmittel*. Soul sealant. Legendary. Didn't know if it was real… I don't know that much about it. Rosalee'd know more."

Nick took an evidence bag from his jacket pocket, got out a pen knife and cut into a powder brick. He scooped a couple of grams into the bag, sealed it, careful not to get any on his hands, and tucked it away.

"We'll have Rosalee look this stuff over…" he said.

"Not going to look good if anybody finds out you took that kind of evidence in advance of forensics," Hank pointed out.

"Just one of several things we're going to have to keep quiet about on this one," Nick said. "We'll have to get our stories straight now… And then you go up and call for forensics and the bodybaggers."

"They're gonna *love* coming down here…" Hank muttered.

CHAPTER SEVEN

It was dark out and Monroe was wearing his second best pair of loafers as he walked up the side street to the shady little cul de sac where the Perkins family lived. Dorine Perkins, Lily Perkins, Alvin Perkins, Jr., residents of 1300 Shady Court. Alvin Perkins Senior was dead. He'd died in a forest, at the base of Mt. Hood, some considerable time back. Years now. He'd died out there with his throat torn out.

Died just trying to do his job. Leaving a widow and two children.

Monroe reached the corner and paused, half hidden by a rhododendron bush hanging over a broken down fence from an overgrown yard to his right. Hands in his pockets against the growing chill, he gazed at the cottage across the cul de sac. The lattice on the front of the little white building was dark with thick ivy and honeysuckle; a sugar maple, gone orange, was slowly shedding leaves over the mossy roof. The front windows glowed with yellow light. It was like a cottage in a fairy tale.

And the big bad wolf *had* attacked someone from that fairy tale cottage. But not here. It had happened in a forest miles away, on the clay bank of a small creek, with ferns all around...

The front door opened, and a girl came out. Lily Perkins. She was fourteen, Monroe knew, though he'd never met her. He knew her birthday—he knew her mother's birthday, and her brother's too. He'd never met any of them. They didn't know who he was.

Lily had brown-blond hair bobbed at her jawline. Monroe smiled, seeing she'd added some neon-pink highlights to its tips.

Stylin'. You go, girl.

She was wearing a coat trimmed with faux rabbit fur. It looked a little too small for her, like the family was short on money for clothes. Maybe it was time he found another way to get the Perkins family some extra money. He could manage a thousand dollars. Last time he'd arranged for them to be told they'd won a contest. Time before that, he'd made it look like a gift from a dotty, aging relative. A scribbled note in the mail, with a money order. The dotty relative gag would work again, he decided.

He watched Lily walk down the sidewalk in her scuffed white boots, picking her way carefully across the places cracked by tree roots. She had makeup on. Going to meet friends at the mall. She did that sometimes, Monroe knew.

Be careful, kid. There are wolves out there. All kinds of predators. Watch where you go. Stay alert...

Be careful, Lily. For your father's sake...

Monroe took a long, deep breath, then turned away, and walked back up the sidewalk.

He needed to see Nick. Right away. He owed it to Smitty...

He turned right at the next corner, and walked up to his truck.

Behind him, someone started a van.

When Monroe's truck drove off, the van followed.

* * *

It was eight-thirty in the morning. Hank was still sipping coffee, yawning between sips. He and Nick sat across from Renard, in the captain's corner office. The blinds were shut on the big office window. Renard looked like he was angry and didn't want to say why.

"That scene in the tunnel was messy," Renard said, at last, his voice sharp with disapproval. "Very messy. If we'd had some kind of set up for a raid or..."

"I knew they were down there," Nick said. "I didn't want to lose them."

Hank looked at him. "You *knew*? How?"

Nick shrugged. "I could feel it."

Renard waved his hand dismissively. "I can't put that in a report. And keeping this Monroe pal of yours out of the report's not so easy either."

"How about the Drang-zorn we booked?" Nick asked.

"We'll do what we can to protect him. He doesn't seem to have much to tell us. Seems like the guys he knew were the ones you killed."

He opened a folder on his desk, spun some slick color photos around so the two detectives could see them.

"Speaking of a messy scene," Hank said, looking at the photos. "Somebody else made one. Who are they?"

"Dead gangbangers," Renard said. "*Sombra Corazón*— Shadow Heart. Found dumped in a field out near Canby. Killed elsewhere. We don't know where yet."

"This make the news?" Nick asked. This was clearly the work of Wesen. He wanted to keep this investigation as under wraps as possible.

It was funny—he was a Grimm, and traditionally Grimms killed Wesen. At best they policed the Wesen world, winnowing out the ones who were most dangerous.

But often he found himself trying to *protect* Wesen. He wondered if his Grimm ancestors would approve. Probably not.

"It will," Renard said. "These guys were pretty much torn apart. Shredded. Heads ripped off. We'll claim chainsaws, and whatever. But the Wesen will know…"

"But what about—" Hank began.

But he broke off, sharply, as there was a quick knock on the door.

Sergeant Wu then opened it without being told to, and came in carrying a report. He stopped in the middle of the room and looked from face to face.

"Wow, everybody stops talking the minute I come in? This some kind of internal affairs thing I'm not supposed to know about?"

"No," Hank said. "Captain was giving Nick advice on his love life. Told him to give up on it completely."

"I've considered that," Nick said dryly.

"Very funny," Wu said, dropping the papers on Renard's desk. "I'll tell you a real joke. A cop sees a woman who's knitting while she's driving. He figures that's dangerous, so he shouts at her, 'Pull over!' And she yells back, 'No, it's a pair of socks!'"

You could have heard a pin drop in the room.

"Wu, you need some time off?" Renard asked, finally.

"Me? No Captain, I'm okay."

"Then why're you wasting time in here?"

"I—okay, fine. Just… wanted to drop that off. And tell you we got the report on that substance that was smuggled in. If they were smuggling it in—maybe they were smuggling it out…"

He passed the paper over to Renard, who scanned it.

"Scopolamine?"

"Lots of weird toxic goodies in it," Wu said. "But lab

says that's probably the active ingredient. That grade of scopolamine's illegal. But what they were going to do with it is anyone's guess."

He turned and walked out, muttering as he closed the door behind him.

"Pullover. Socks. Seemed funny to me."

The moment he was gone, Hank chuckled.

"Ha. Not a pullover, socks."

Nick looked at him. "You thought that was funny?"

"Sure. But I didn't want Wu to know that."

Nick took the analysis paper from the lab from Renard and peered at it.

"Scopolamine. That works with what Rosalee told me," he said.

"Which is what?" Renard asked.

"She says it's *Seele Dichtungsmittel*. Soul Sealant. Supposed to enslave people."

Renard nodded. "Lot of stories out of South America about scopolamine making people passive. Dose somebody with it, ask them to bring you their money and jewels and they do it, and cheerfully."

Hank looked at him skeptically. "Is that really true, Captain?"

"Seems like some exaggeration's involved but… With the other ingredients from Hexenbiest recipes, it could work."

"There an antidote to that?" Nick asked. He figured the captain might know, since he was half Hexenbiest himself—a witch-like Wesen.

"Not sure. I never got into the, ah, pharmaceutical side of it all," Renard replied.

Nick looked at the photo of the mutilated gangbangers.

"Killed with real panache," he said. He showed the photo to Hank. "Shadow Heart was into drugs, and prostitution. Suggests that The Icy Touch is moving in on them."

Renard nodded. "They want to sell conventional drugs, they can get them from cartel types like this. And send a message doing it: No one gets in their way. They want to get into sex slavery... and maybe turning Wesen who'd be resistant to them... That's where the scopolamine comes in."

Nick shook his head slowly. "I don't know. Seems kind of... small time for a crime outfit made up of Wesen."

Renard took the photo back, flicked it into a folder.

"It is relatively small time. That's what worries me. They have to have a bigger agenda..."

"Seems to me," Hank said thoughtfully, "for now, it's something that's got to grow. Building up to something powerful. Going to be damned hard to stop. Captain— maybe the time's come to tell the feds about this. If they don't already know."

"The feds are working on Icy Touch already," Renard said.

"I mean—give them the full facts."

Nick stared. "About the Wesen?"

Hank shrugged. "Yeah. Look, how responsible is it *not* to tell them? They don't know what they're up against, they could get killed. You go after one of those ogre things..."

"Siegbarsten," Nick said.

"Right, Siegbarsten. You think you can take one of those down with a .45? You're going to die, because you don't have the facts. Or one of those dragon guys. The agent thinks they're unarmed—and they burn his face off. That's what the FBI could be up against. They're *law officers*—these guys are trying to do their job without the facts. It's not right for us to hold back on them."

Nick could understand where his partner was coming from. But there were other considerations...

Renard leaned back in his chair.

"Are you serious?" he asked. "First of all, the feds wouldn't believe us."

"We could *prove* it. Monroe could woge for them. Get the Drang-zorn to woge for them too. Let them run some tests."

"And bust the Wesen thing open?" Nick shook his head. "Can you imagine the public reaction—the hysteria? There'd be some kind of persecution of Wesen. Witch hunts. Maybe…" He looked at Renard, thinking of Hexenbiests, his mind rapidly calculating the full consequences of what Hank was suggesting. "*Literal* witch hunts."

"They don't have to tell everyone. Who knows what secrets they keep already?" Hank said.

"What, you think the Men in Black are real?" Nick said.

"No. But—maybe there's a department that knows all about Wesen and keeps it under wraps. We could work with them. But surely any agent working on this has a right to know what they're getting into."

"I've sometimes wondered if they know more than we think they do," Renard admitted. "But here's the bottom line, Detective Griffin. You take orders from me. Or you fight me. I decide who knows about the Wesen, not you. Not Burkhardt. And I don't want the feds knowing. Are we clear?"

"I could resign," Hank said, looking back at Renard with cold, flat defiance.

"You don't get it, Griffin," Renard said. He leant forward, deadly serious. "It's not just about your job. It's about *your life*. There's the Verrat to consider. And there are others out there—including a lot of dangerous Wesen, who don't want you talking about this out of school. There's a code. And it doesn't just apply to Wesen—it applies to those who *talk* about Wesen. Close as you can get is… fairy tales. You let anyone know that some of the fairy tale is real, you put Wesen in danger. And someone might just shut you up—with real finality."

Hank's jaw muscles clenched. He looked directly at Renard.

"That a *threat* from you, Captain?"

Renard looked at Hank for a moment longer, then he shook his head.

"No. It's a warning—about what's out there. You've only seen the tip of the iceberg. There's a *whole hidden world*, Griffin." He picked up a pen and toyed with it, all the time watching Hank's face. "The world of the Wesen. And in that world, you've got to move very, very carefully." He pointed the pen at Hank like a magician pointing a wand. "Or you'll stumble into a den of wolves, Detective Griffin—and you won't come out alive."

CHAPTER EIGHT

"Nick? Can we get some lunch?" Juliette asked. "I need to talk something out..."

"Sure," he said, walking out of the morgue, cell phone pressed to his ear. It seemed a strange time for his girlfriend to ask for a heart to heart—right after he'd seen a heart lying next to the corpse it had been torn out of. He'd had a look at the bodies, and parts of bodies, found in that field near Canby. Perhaps they'd torn out some hearts because the gang under attack was called *Sombra Corazón*—Shadow Heart. The Icy Touch mocking the gang it was displacing.

"Nick? You still there?"

"Yeah, sorry, Juliette. Just came out of the morgue. Kind of distracted."

"The morgue? Sounds like it's not a good time for lunch."

"Hey, in my job—if I let stuff like that put me off my food, I'd never eat. Let's meet at Jake's Deli..."

He felt like he wasn't entirely there even as he walked through the door. He kept trying to focus on meeting Juliette, but thoughts of The Icy Touch... *La Caresse Glacée*... kept intruding. His thoughts filled with the inspection of the big container ship that morning.

La Conquete, another worrisome French name: *The Conquest.* Sinister, given the context. It was owned by a French-German shipping consortium. They found nothing on the ship to connect to scopolamine, nothing illegal at all. The shipping containers seemed filled with Toshiba televisions, and ramen noodles. All the manifests seemed in order.

They had only the late Smitty's word for it that the ship had been used to smuggle the mind control drug. The Drang-zorn insisted he didn't have any personal experience of the ship's use in smuggling...

"Nick!"

He looked around, saw Juliette at a small table by the window, just to his right. She did look beautiful. Her long auburn hair shone, her hazel-green eyes were solemn but gleaming with life. Her wide red lips were parted in an uncertain smile. Lovely—but she always was. Even lying in that hospital bed, with those lips parched, hair barely combed, recovering from the memory-damage potion— even there, she'd shone like a jewel. Today she wore an emerald-colored dress, cut low but not too low, a gold necklace he'd given her, with a little cat on the chain, to celebrate the success of her surgery on the cat she kept at the vet's office. She'd saved its life. She saved a great many small, precious lives. Her tenderness toward animals touched him. He wished he could watch her working as a veterinarian. He wished, today, he weren't a detective. He wished he weren't a Grimm.

It is what it is...

He sat across from her, feeling, for some reason, almost as nervous as he had on their first date. Maybe it was the look of mingled fondness and uncertainty in her eyes...

"You ordered yet?" he asked.

"Nope. Here's the menu."

He glanced at the menu and asked, "How're your furry charges?"

"We had a scaly one today. A boa constrictor, in for a checkup. I had to look up its vital signs."

"You like snakes?"

She smiled ruefully. "You know me. I like pretty much all animals."

"But you don't have a pet at home. I was thinking of getting you a puppy..."

"I have to spend so much time at work I don't feel like I can be there enough for a pet at home..." She shook her head. "And we've got two office pets anyway. You know, that cat someone never came to pick up, for three years now, and my assistant's little Yorkie. They keep each other company. The Yorkie sits on my lap when I'm reading lab reports. The cat likes to walk on my keyboard."

He sensed that she was chatting while she tried to work out how to discuss something else. Something serious.

The waitress came over. They ordered deli sandwiches, coffee for Nick and chai tea for Juliette.

Once the waitress had moved away, Juliette leaned toward him, and asked, "Nick... what are we going to *do*?"

He reached out, took her hands in his, held them across the table.

"We could start with holding hands. Then later, at home..." he began.

She squeezed his hands.

"I'm serious," she continued solemnly. "Every time I think we're going to have some kind of stable love life... maybe even a real life together..."

"I know," he said.

The Grimm thing comes between us.

A thought came to him, then—and it stabbed him through the heart.

"Wait—you're not breaking up with me, are you?"

She pursed her lips. He could tell breaking up was at least a possibility. But then she smiled and shook her head.

"I don't seem to be able to. First you kept me in the dark all that time…"

"I was trying to protect you. Without losing you. I guess it was selfish…"

"It was. And then I nearly got killed… and I was hospitalized and lost part of my memory…"

He wanted to say, *Most of your memory came back.* But he knew that wasn't much consolation for what she'd gone through.

Instead, he said, "And now…?"

"And now, sometimes, when we're together—it's like you're not there."

He nodded. "Might be that way for a while. There's something going down now. An investigation. Something… kind of hard to deal with."

"You can't talk about it?"

"Not really."

"Something to do with those bodies they found out by Canby?"

"How'd you know that?"

"The description in the newspaper—the way the bodies were…"

"Oh. Yeah." She knew about Wesen—she knew what the reports of "animal clawmarks" might mean.

Their sandwiches came and they ate, not saying much. Nick looked out the rain-blurred window at people passing by, the colors of their umbrellas blending one into the next…

Juliette pushed her sandwich aside, half eaten, and sipped her chai.

"Maybe… just check in with me now and then. Until

this one's over. If you think it's going to be kind of… all consuming?" she said gently.

"You don't want to see me?"

"I do. Not sure I should, Nick."

"Hank wants us to double date. He's got tickets for Princess."

"You really think you'll be free to go to anything like that?"

He sighed. "Not sure I'll be free to do much… except my job. And a lot of stuff that's not my job. But…"

"Nick? Don't tell me. Right now… I don't want to hear about that side of things." She reached out and took his hand again. "I want to pretend, just for right now, that I never visited your aunt's trailer…"

The old Airstream trailer was cold that evening. Nick sat at the table, looking through the old books. He'd only found one mention in the ornate, yellowed pages, of *Seele Dichtungsmittel*. "Soul sealant"—a term that gave him a chill whenever he heard it. The only reference seemed to have been written by an eighteenth-century British Grimm:

"Of the many potions, nostrums and anti-nostrums, poisons and antidotes, and concoctions of delusions associated with the Hexenbiest, Seele Dichtungsmittel is perhaps the most troubling. What would God have us do but choose good over evil? Free will is the light of the human soul. Yet Seele Dichtungsmittel consumes free will, as a flame consumes a wick until the candle has melted to a puddle…"

How far would they go, using the soul sealant, he wondered. Maybe the organized crime agenda was just the beginning; just the framework for something bigger.

He set the book aside, and looked through two more—

but found nothing more on *Seele Dichtungsmittel*, and no references to The Icy Touch.

Perhaps if he looked under...

A hammering came on the door of the Airstream. Nick pushed back from the table, and drew his side arm. But he holstered it a moment later when he heard Monroe's voice; a hoarse whisper but clearly Monroe.

"Nick? Hey yo, bro, you going to open up?"

Nick let Monroe in. His hair was slick from the rain, his eyes distracted, troubled.

"Thanks. Thought you'd be here. Your cell phone turned off?"

"No." Nick shut the door behind Monroe. "Maybe needs to be charged." He tossed Monroe a towel. "Here, dry off. So—what's up?"

"I don't know... exactly." He sat down in the only other chair, across from Nick, drying his hair.

"Yeah, well, you've got the look of a guy on a mission," Nick said. "Something you want to tell me?"

"Dude—something's gotta be done."

"Always. You want to be more specific?"

Monroe draped the towel around his neck and smoothed his hair back with his hands.

"About Smitty," he said. "I want to *do* something... Make sure there's some payback for what happened to him. I failed him, Nick."

"Couple of the guys from the outfit that took him out are dead, and you helped with that, Monroe. You have to leave the rest to us. That's what I'm here working on."

Monroe hesitated, then nodded toward the open book. "What'd you come up with?"

"Looked up *Seele Dichtungsmittel*, didn't find much. Except the stuff is bad news."

"We knew that from Rosalee."

"How about Rosalee? She hear from this Icy Touch bunch?"

Monroe sat up straight and stared.

"Whoa, hold on, hit the brakes. You think they'll go after her?"

"Take it easy, Monroe. I just know these guys are kinda proactive and… I'm worried about every Wesen in town."

Monroe swore and jumped up, overturning the chair.

"Oh man oh man oh man."

"Monroe—calm down!"

But Monroe was already going out the door.

"I just need to know she's safe!" he called.

Nick sighed. "Wait a minute! I'll come with you!" He got up and hurried after Monroe. "Left the door open and ran off with my towel, too…"

CHAPTER NINE

Doug Zelinski lay on his prison bunk, hands behind his head, staring at the ceiling and thinking about his coming of age as a Drang-zorn. Thirteen years old. Earlier than most Wesen. *Something to do with urges*, Mom had said, and adolescence and hormones and... *Just being badger*. Drang-zorn, after all, meant *urge to wrath*—or stress leading to wrath. And that's what it was like for Doug. Stress... and a *fury* came on him. Most of the time he was peaceful, craved peace even. But The Icy Touch had come, and showed him what happened to Drang-zorn who fought them.

He'd known Buddy Clement for ten years. They'd gone camping together, digging dens for the family, up on the slopes of Mt. Hood. Doug had scooped a den out for his nephew Sammy. No kids of his own, not yet. Hadn't met the right badgerina. Drang-zorn women were scarce. Of course, he could marry a human, it was done, but... It was hard on a Drang-zorn, keeping secrets. Just more stress. He'd lose his temper with his wife and he'd woge in front of her and she'd run in horror...

Even now, he was thumping his right knee against the wall of the cell, once per second, thump... thump...

thump... thump... thump... Just trying to burn off the stress. Sometimes it helped him to gnaw on a knuckle, almost break the skin.

Anything to keep control.

If he lost it and got pissed off, he'd woge, and start raging around the cell. The guards would see him and he'd be in trouble with a whole new set of people. Not enough to be in danger from The Icy Touch. Not enough to have that Grimm sniff him out. No, if *humans* found out about him...

He knew the drill. *Pretend it's a freakish medical condition,* he'd been told. *Talk about growing up in sideshows.*

But the word would get out. The Verrat would know. And they would punish him...

Stay. Calm. Stay. In. Control.

But it was hard, in here. He was trapped in this cell, alone, feeling like he was boiling under a heavy lid, and the pressure was building up, and the lid was going to fly off.

It must be dark out by now, Doug figured. He wished he could just go to sleep. Fat chance. Lot of noise in the city jail. Prisoners jabbering, clattering around, laughing, the crazy ones babbling. One of them on that "bath salts" drug, hallucinating about monsters. "Creatures coming after me, after me, after me," he gibbered. Purely imaginary. And it was ironic. Just two cells down from his, was a *real* creature who could turn into a were badger.

That's what comes of being here, Doug thought angrily. *Think of yourself as a monster.*

When was that damned Grimm going to move him out of here? He'd done his part, recited the story they'd agreed on to Sergeant Wu. Thugs threatening him with guns, forcing him to work in the tunnel. Wu had seemed surprised that Nick and Hank believed the story about being forced into the gang. The sergeant would be even more surprised if he knew the *real* story.

Detective Burkhardt had promised to get him released or turned over to witness protection. But the wheels moved slowly in a place like this...

He couldn't take much more. Couldn't bear it if...

A clang made him twitch. He looked at the old-fashioned jail cell door, saw it shutting behind a new prisoner.

What the hell? Burkhardt promised I'd be alone...

The new guy in fresh orange jail-cell togs had an exotic look to his face, like he was maybe Egyptian or something. Dark eyes, high cheekbones. Looked like a bust Doug had seen of a pharaoh once. He looked like he might be about forty years old, with short black hair. There was something about the guy...

The new prisoner had a big bright smile as he noticed Doug on the top bunk.

"Hi! I'm Colney. What you in for?"

"Oh, got mixed up in a gang. Wasn't my idea." Doug sat up, dangled his legs over the side of the mattress. At least this guy was someone to talk to. Might help keep him calm. A distraction. "You?"

"Shoplifting jewelry." The man laughed softly at his own foolishness. "Trying to impress a girl when I didn't have any money. Picked expensive jewelry—felony stuff." He sighed. "Might have to do some time in the state pen."

Doug nodded sympathetically. "Tough luck. You missed dinner, too."

"Oh, they fed me when I was being processed. Hey—that a deck of cards? You wanta play some hearts?"

"Where? I didn't see any cards. I'd be playing solitaire..."

"On the lower bunk there..."

Doug jumped down off the top bunk, turned to look, saw there was nothing on the lower bunk...

And then he smelled it. Reptile musk.

Snake.

He'd detected something earlier—but all the anxiety had blurred his senses. This guy was Wesen. This guy was…

Doug felt the damp, teasing probe of a forked tongue on the back of his neck.

He snarled, hands balling into fists, he started to woge—but rough scaly fingers jerked his prison shirt up from behind and, before he could turn, fangs sank into the meat of his back, between his shoulder blades.

He shrieked and thrashed, feeling the burning venom pump into him. His back arched, going rigid of its own accord, as if his flesh was itself revolted at the depraved contact.

As the fangs let go and as the room went all murky red, Doug managed to half turn before he fell, so that he tipped onto his back. So rigid his body was like a statue that had lost its base. He struck the floor, but hardly felt it, he was so suffused with pain—and then the pain melted into something even more petrifying: the numbness that was spreading out from the bite.

Venom was invading his nervous system, its icy touch closing over his heart, tightening, squeezing.

Stopping it in mid beat.

He just had time to see the *Königschlange* in full woge as it stood triumphantly over him. Its cobra's hood spread out, the diamond patterning of its scales seeming to pulse with malevolence; its scaly hide, the color of old Greek coins, rippling as it shifted; its fangs still dripping venom; its slitted yellow eyes gleaming with sick delight. Where before he'd resembled a pharaoh, now the creature looked like some ancient snake god.

And the god's forked tongue darted out from its grinning mouth.

"Sssssuffer and despair," the creature hissed. *"Sssssshake and ssssssuffer and die, traitoroussss Drang-Zorrrrrnnn…"*

Then it began to transform back into the form of a normal man.

Doug didn't see the transformation finish—darkness fell like a blizzard of jet black snow, drawing a funereal curtain over the scene. But he was still able to hear for a few moments more.

"Guard!" shouted the Wesen who called himself Colney. "I think this man's had a heart attack! We need help in here! Hey! This man's having a heart attack, for real! Hey!"

It didn't matter what lies the cobra Wesen told. Not now. They both knew that Doug would be dead long before medical help came.

The pain receded into an endless night. It was a relief to let the darkness enfold him…

Nick pushed through the door of Rosalee's shop in time to hear her say, "Monroe, calm down! You can *see* I'm okay."

She and Monroe were standing by the front counter, Rosalee smiling and patting his cheek. She did a little pirouette, whimsically showing herself off.

"See? I'm fine. New dress even," she said smiling.

"I…yeah," Monroe said, looking at her shapely form in the clinging gray silk dress. "I like the dress. Very, very… nice. It's like… really *tight*. Not that, uh, *that* is all I like about it. I mean, it's a great dress. It's got real… Sorry. I'm not a fashion guy." He nodded at Nick, then looked back at her more seriously. "But… Rosalee…"

"But what?" she asked.

Nick leant on the counter, looking at a twisted, blackened homunculus in a half-gallon jar. What *was* that, dried dwarf fetus?

Monroe went on, all in a rush, "But all I can think about is—I don't think you're safe here alone right now."

"Oh you are so full of it. You get so— Nick, tell him!"

Nick smiled at Rosalee.

"She's not in any imminent danger that we know of, Monroe," he said.

Monroe snorted. "'Not in *imminent* danger.' Oh, hey, dude that's *so* reassuring." Monroe turned to Rosalee and took her in his arms. "Rosie, you don't understand. If you knew what was going on… Stuff that would make your head explode… Well, my head hasn't literally *exploded*, no, but—"

"It's *all right*, baby," she said softly, returning his embrace. He nuzzled her neck.

Nick suddenly felt a bit awkward.

"I should go," he said. "I just wanted to suggest— maybe you should go see a relative, or something, Rosalee. Just for a few days. Take a trip, till this Icy Touch thing is over. They've been forcibly recruiting Wesen. Monroe can call you when it's all clear…"

"What?" She drew back from Monroe. "No! I just got back from a trip, I'm behind on the bills; I've got work to do! No one's going to want me to join a gang! Do I look like a gangbanger?"

Nick pretended to look her over doubtfully.

"Um… I guess not." To Nick she looked like sweet-faced, brown-haired Rosalee Calvert, in a new blue silk dress. Nick had seen her fox-faced Fuchsbau form—and it was almost as sweet as her human form. "But—they make a point of recruiting a certain number of people you wouldn't expect in a crime cartel. And you'd be valuable." He nodded toward the crowded shelves of her herbal apothecary shop. "Those skills—your herbal knowledge, your Wesen lore, all the supplies. This shop used to be…

kind of shady. Before your time here, I mean. You know? Wesen working the dark side of the street are going to remember that."

"Oh, look, no one's going to make me do anything I don't want to…"

"Rosie, honey," Monroe said, taking her hand. "They have a policy about people who don't want to play along. They make an example of them."

"Well… stay here with me, watch my back, then, Monroe."

"Hey—I'll camp outside the door if I have to."

"That won't be necessary. I *might* just find a spot for you with me…"

Nick's phone buzzed.

"Your pants are ringing again," Rosalee said. "You ought to get that looked at, Nick."

He laughed and fished the phone out of his pocket.

"Burkhardt."

"Nick…" Hank's voice said. "That Drang-zorn of yours?"

"Yeah?" Nick felt a sinking sensation.

"He's dead. Looks kinda like a heart attack but… he had some marks on his back."

"Two marks, about fang distance apart?"

"You guessed it."

"Shit. Königschlange."

"Don't speak German to me, man. Just—get over here."

"I seem to be spending a lot of time in morgues lately," Renard remarked.

Renard, Hank and Nick were standing around the body of the Drang-zorn. The morgue was cold, and smelt medical. The odor of the place, a mix of chemicals and decay, always made Nick's stomach twist.

He was bent over the body, a ruler in his hand, measuring the distance between the puckered bite marks on Doug Zelinski's back.

"Just right for a Königschlange," he said after a moment, shaking his head. He stepped back, and stared at the dead body lying face down on the steel table. "Juliette says she likes pretty much all animals. Königschlange— even she'd find that one a challenge."

"*Are* they animals?" Hank asked. "They're people, who can shift to…" He glanced at the door to make sure it was closed, and no one was listening. "…to become more… animal."

"Yes and no," Renard said. "But then ordinary human beings are animals—they're primates. Related to apes. Human beings are animals and something higher than animals all at once."

Nick set the ruler down on the steel table.

"Lot of people turn into beasts without having to be Wesen. Serial killers. The worst kind of drug dealers—all the basest of animals."

"True," Hank admitted, frowning at the body. After a moment he asked, "The transformational thing Wesen do, the woge thing… Is it magic? Or evolution?"

"I don't know," Renard said. "Maybe it's mutational, but… no one's done any real thorough biological study of Wesen that I know of." He looked at Nick, his eyes going flinty. "Not even Grimm. They mostly research how to kill them."

Nick noticed that Renard never spoke of Wesen as "we" or "us," though he was part Wesen himself. But maybe that was only because he happened to be talking to a Grimm. Renard was stuck with Nick, for now—but it seemed he could never fully trust him. *Well*, Nick figured, *that feeling is pretty mutual.*

"How did the Königschlange get into the cell?" he asked. "Who booked him in? We gave an order that nobody but Zelinski was supposed to be in that cell."

Renard rubbed his chin. "Technically, it was Brian Murphy. But Murphy says he *can't remember* who gave him the paperwork to book the Königschlange into the cell…"

"He can't remember?" Hank said, in disbelief. "Murphy's not that flaky."

"Hexenbiest, maybe, controlling him while the assassin was booked in," Nick said. "Possibly using *Seele Dichtungsmittel*—so Murphy just goes with it."

"Hexenbiest?" Renard looked coldly at him for a moment, then he conceded. "Maybe. Murphy booked Colney out, too—but he doesn't remember that either. And Colney's nowhere to be found now."

"Colney's the cobra guy?" Hank asked.

Nick nodded. "That's what he called himself when they booked him in." He felt bad about Zelinski's death. He'd thought the Drang-zorn would be safe in custody until something else had been worked out.

Don't assume.

"So—any documentation on this Colney? Fingerprints in the cell, rap sheet, *anything*?" he asked.

Renard shook his head.

"He was careful. And Murphy's got nothing. Not one sheet of paper. Being pretty defensive about it. Claiming someone broke into his files. Maybe he thought he saw paperwork that wasn't there."

Hank looked at Renard, eyebrows raised.

"This *Seele Dichtungsmittel*—it can do that?"

"It could."

"Not a lot they couldn't get away with, using that stuff…"

"What bothers me most," Nick said, turning away from the corpse, "is how many different kinds of dangerous

Wesen are turning up in this town. It's like a convention of the nastiest barrel scrapings of Wesen-kind."

"We done here?" Renard asked.

The detectives nodded, and the three of them left the corpse, heading gratefully into the warmth of the corridor.

"What's their next move?" Hank wondered, as they walked.

"We need prisoners to interrogate," Renard replied, glancing down the hall. Sergeant Wu was coming toward them. In an undertone, Renard added, "If we have to use *Seele Dichtungsmittel* ourselves… so be it."

CHAPTER TEN

Monroe lay shirtless on Rosalee's bed, as she fussed over him. He enjoyed the attention as she changed the dressing on the Blutbad bitemarks. She'd put the bandage on a few hours earlier, after they'd gotten undressed—he'd hardly noticed the wound on his shoulder, hadn't even mentioned it to Nick after the fight in the tunnel, or done much for it besides spraying a little Bactine on it. He'd been thinking more about how he'd bitten Nick's hand while his friend was trying to help him.

"You're lucky this didn't get infected," Rosalee said, tightening the bandage. "Ignoring it like that."

"I'm lucky I didn't give *Nick* an infection. You know I bit him?"

"What? On *purpose*?"

"No, of course not. His hand got in the way when I was fighting the other guy. Nick was just trying to help me. Wasn't that bad a bite but… it worries me that I'd bite him at all. I was woged, feeling about as Blutbad as I ever have, and there was a hand in front of my choppers and maybe I thought it was the creep I was fighting—or maybe I didn't care."

"I don't believe you wouldn't care, Monroe. Not you."

He smiled sadly. "You haven't known me very long."

"If you feel bad about nipping Nick, apologize to him."

"I did. But see—it's not just that, Rosie. I'm worried that being involved in all this stuff with Nick, advising him, getting caught up in investigations... that it might be making me, I don't know... prone to *relapse*. To falling back into what I was. It's like—you ever feel like something's coming to a head in your life, kind of bubbling up in the back of your mind, and you're seeing it everywhere? Maybe stuff you haven't dealt with completely?"

She patted his belly. "Yep. Been there. Felt that."

"That's how it is now. The other day I was on my porch, checking out the smells from the woods. It was like the forest was calling to me."

She smiled. "It *was*. It calls to me all the time."

"But this was like it was saying, *Let go. Go full on Blutbad! Let the wolf out and let the chips fall where they may*. And I was tempted."

"So... head for the mountains, take off your shoes and have a good run."

He shook his head.

"You're Fuchsbau. You can do that." He sighed with envy. "You can go all fox-woman out there. Me..."

A thought struck him.

"Maybe if you were with me. You know, like a chaperone! I can't go by myself or with another Blutbad. You Fuchsbau—you might nip a human being. But you wouldn't... *kill* one."

She seemed to consider.

"Well... no," she said. "It's not very likely we'd kill anyone, as Fuchsbau. But I wouldn't say it's never happened."

"If it did, it was probably the human in the Fuchsbau, not the fox that did the killing. But with Blutbaden—in the old days we preyed on anything that came along. Including people. Most of us know we can't do that anymore. So, people like me, and Smitty, we work the Twelve Steps, we work on our recovery."

She looked at him expectantly.

"Seems like there's been something you've wanted to tell me for a while, Monroe…"

He let out a long slow breath.

"Yeah. I mean—you're Wesen, you had drug problems, you've got your dark side. But it's not like this. And maybe you should know. All of it…"

"I'll get us some wine. And you can tell me…"

It didn't start with Angelina. But she brought out the predator in me. Big time…

You remember hearing about Angelina. Kind of a tough Blutbad bitch. I used to take her out on my motorcycle— you didn't know I had a motorcycle, did you Rosie? I used to love that old rebuilt Indian bike so much I could kiss her. She ran like a fine Swiss watch. It was a Chief, with a 105ci PowerPlus, two-into-one stainless steel exhaust, really stripped down and beautiful. Angelina loved it even more than I did, and I gave it to her, eventually, as a good-bye present. Anyway, we'd take it out into the mountains for long rides, her holding onto me behind, and we'd wear those full-head helmets that cover you right up… and we'd woge during the ride, right? Just go all 'full moon werewolf' astride this motorcycle, barreling along at sixty miles an hour on a mountain road. But our Blutbaden state was hidden beneath our jackets and helmets and inside our gloves and boots. People would drive right by us in their RVs and not guess those bikers had fangs and fur.

See, the whole ride was different, that way, when you're woged and riding a motorcycle. It was something really savage. Talk about "Born to be Wild!"

And then come sundown, I'd drive it up some old gravel fire road, way into the woods, park it off road somewhere, and we'd take off our helmets and gloves and boots and just...woge. We'd go looking for dinner. You know, al fresco, and I mean truly fresh. *Raw*. We'd chase down a couple of rabbits, even a small deer, and we'd... *kill*. And feed! And then we'd get crazy, make love all bloody from our prey. Don't get that *look*, Rosalee, I'm not going to go into it. I don't miss her at all. Really. No, I really don't. And you probably had some experience like that as a Fuchsbau.

So anyway—sometimes we'd encounter a bear, or a wildcat, and we'd have to drive it off. Those critters could be pretty territorial. We were hyper aware of the dangers out there and we got even more savage because of that.

One night we'd slept out in the wild, and next morning we woged, drank from a stream, went hunting for breakfast—you know how it can be, out there. You get almost drunk on the smells and the textures and the sheer *life-force* of the forest. You go all primeval—you almost forget words! We pretty much used no spoken language, on these trips. We were just in this almost frenzied state of alertness—and then one time we encountered a cougar. Or he encountered us. The old canine versus feline, wolf versus wildcat thing was in the air. It was hissing and roaring and slashing at us with its claws and we were snarling and growling and snapping back at it. I finally drove him off but it was touch and go there for a while and we were, like, *so* adrenalized, after that. Our blood was up.

And then Angelina ran into the forest ranger.

The ranger was just hiking up a creek, doing his job. I think he wanted to drag out some dead elk supposed to be polluting it, farther upstream. Angelina was a little ways away from me, sniffing for prey—she just blundered into him, while she was still in this hot blood state. She slashed at him and snarled. Later on she claimed he was reaching for a pistol.

I heard her yip like she was in danger, I ran over there with my pulse just *slamming*. And when I saw the two of them facing off, I guess I lost it.

I leaped off a boulder, and attacked the guy.

Maybe I had in mind I'd just knock him down and we'd run off and he wouldn't know what had hit him, but he'd gotten hold of his gun, and it went off. It didn't hit me, he was just twitching his finger on the trigger… But I guess it freaked me out.

And I…

Rosie, I ripped out his throat with my teeth.

Let me have a glass of that white wine. No, definitely not the red wine, not right now.

Okay. I bit through his jugular—and he died. You can say, natural mistake. Angelina said as much. I *tried* to think of it that way. But I know if I had come upon the scene when I wasn't all worked up in full-on woge, if I wasn't in that *state*, I'd have handled it differently. And the guy would still be alive.

I had a sick physical reaction, afterward, when I spit out the flesh of his neck, spat out his blood, brought myself back to a default human state… and saw what I'd done. I threw up. And then I wanted to run, to just leave him there and try to pretend it hadn't happened. But I made myself kneel beside him, and go through his pockets, try to get a sense of who he was. Angelina all the time urging me to just turn away, to let it go.

My hands were shaking so much I barely managed to find his wallet. I memorized his name, his address from his ID. And I found something else in his wallet—pictures of his wife and kids. I memorized those faces.

"You're just beating yourself up, staring at that stuff," Angelina said.

I didn't respond to that. I wiped my fingerprints off the ID and pictures, and put them back in the wallet, put the wallet back in his pocket. He had a map of the area in his jacket, and I worked out exactly where his body was on the map. I took the ranger's cell phone so I could call it in on that. Then we got rid of all trace of our being there, as much as we could. We literally covered our tracks. And we walked back to my bike. All the way there, Angelina was telling me it wasn't my fault, I'd saved her life and we were in a wild place and a ranger takes his chances in a place like that. She said it was part of his job to risk encountering dangerous wildlife and that's what we were.

When I didn't respond to that she said something that really ticked me off.

"He's just one of them, anyway. A human. He's not *Wesen*."

"You're a sick little wolf bitch," I told her. "We're *all* humans. We're just a different branch of the human race."

She said, "Not all Wesen agree with that."

"It doesn't matter anyway," I said. "I have to take responsibility for this."

At this point I started to think maybe I should turn myself in. I wouldn't have to break the code of silence. I could say I'd been on drugs or something. Like that "Bath Salts" stuff. Tell 'em I tore out his neck in a state of insanity and they could go ahead and incarcerate me.

But there was too much risk that Angelina would be dragged into it. And anyway, I couldn't face jail or a mental hospital. I'd probably kill myself in there.

So I found another way to live with it.

First I called the rangers, gave them a phony name, and said I was a hiker, and I'd come upon a dead ranger. I gave them an exact description of where he was. The creek was on a map and they had no trouble finding his body. I used his cell phone and then tossed it away. I checked the news that evening, and sure enough they found his body before the scavengers had gotten to it. Authorities figured a cougar had killed the guy. They didn't look too closely at the wound. What else could they conclude? They don't know about Blutbaden.

I broke up with Angelina over this. But I gave her the motorcycle. I wanted her to know I didn't blame her for what happened. I just couldn't be with her. She was too feral.

I waited, trying to concentrate on rebuilding old timepieces, and then a couple days later the local news guys interviewed the ranger's colleagues, and people were really, *really* sincere about what a great guy he was. Of course! Naturally I'd hoped that maybe he had a shady past, something I could use to ease my aching guilt. But nope. He just had to be a paragon. A family man. Wife, kids and friends adored him. A terrible tragedy, and so on.

I knew where his family was. The family of Alvin Richard Perkins. I checked on their situation. Not too bad, but not great either. I started to save up money so I could get it to them anonymously, under one pretense or another. I made up a long-lost cousin of Alvin's to be the donor, someone too far away to see personally. "Cousin Jeff." And cousin Jeff, wanting to help out dear cousin Alvin's family, has supplemented their income. Plus, I've kept an eye on the kids in my free time, in case they were being bullied or threatened or victimized: I waited to see how I could help them. I go there at night, look the place over. They're under my protection. They don't know, of course...

But the biggest thing I did for them, and for myself, was to go into recovery as a Blutbad predator. It wasn't enough to just go all Wieder, and swear it off. I'd tasted too much blood in my time.

I asked around, found the meetings for predators in recovery, and started going. That was for the Perkins' family... but it was for me, too. I had to be in command of myself. I had to *master* myself. The wolf in me had to be domesticated. I respect Blutbad nature, Fuchsbau nature—most Wesen have my respect. It's a wonderful thing, feeling that authentically close to nature. Nothing wrong with our animal natures in themselves but... they have to be kept in their place. Something higher has got to be in charge.

So, I had to make it really decisive, make it a lifestyle change. That's why I went vegetarian. And I don't regret it.

But sometimes, the Blutbad side calls to me. The other day, in that tunnel, I had to woge and use my Blutbad side to survive a fight. Nick was there and, like I told you—I bit him. I didn't mind taking an Icy Touch guy out—these are bad Wesen. But still... the whole thing brought up memories of Alvin Perkins. And his wife, his kids...

Anyway, that's the story. You're Fuchsbau, not Blutbad, and Fuchsbau—I mean, a fox will *bite,* but... you aren't so likely to be a physical danger to people. So I worry that you won't, you know, feel good about being with me now, Rosalee. I felt like I had to tell you and...

"Monroe—it's all right." Rosalee touched his face, the caress whisper soft.

He took her hand and kissed it.

"It's all right? Really? Because it doesn't *have* to be all right, if you need time to decide if I'm this awful guy or not... I mean not that I *am* an awful guy, but you have the right to make up your own mind—"

Rosalee silenced him with a finger on his lips.

"Monroe—I'm an ex drug addict. I'm not likely to be all crazy judgmental about your past. And I knew you were a Blutbad when we got involved. You made a mistake and you learned from it. And you changed the direction of your life. You're a good man, Monroe."

He felt as if a hundred pound weight had been lifted from his heart.

"Thanks, Rosie."

"I think it's sweet that you go and check on them."

"Sweet, not creepy?"

"Not at all. You're, like, their Zorro, watching over them from the shadows. You go there a lot?"

"Just now and then. Sometimes I get a feeling I should look in on them, see how the kids look. They're doing pretty good. I just wish... their dad was there."

She leaned back and frowned.

"Monroe—you said you went Blutbad to help Nick?"

"Yeah. Not the first time."

"But—you said someone was *killed*? Did you have to attack someone *as a Wesen*? I mean..."

"It wasn't quite like that. I was wrestling around with the guy, trying to get the gun from him, and he squeezed the trigger. He ended up shooting himself."

"Oh. So you didn't, um... you didn't *bite* the guy who was killed. Like you bit the ranger."

"No. But... I bit *Nick*!"

"You didn't really hurt him."

"That's true. I didn't." He shrugged. "He didn't hold it against me. The bite hardly broke the skin."

"Hardly? It's a good thing that old werewolf stuff about spreading it to regular people isn't true..."

"Hey, Blutbaden aren't werewolves anyway. We're probably the source of the legend, and sometimes we *talk* about 'going werewolf' but that's not a literal thing..."

"I know, but…" She kissed him lightly. "…you're still my wolfy guy."

He took her in his arms.

"And you're my foxy lady."

CHAPTER ELEVEN

Albert Denswoz walked into the meeting with other West Coast bosses of *La Caresse Glacée* with his mind made up.

The Icy Touch would step up its *Vernichten*—the assassinations he'd long contemplated would go ahead...

Federico Malo was already seated and waiting patiently, a dark-eyed young man from Los Angeles, in a tautly tailored black-and-white Italian suit. He had long curly black hair and a neatly trimmed black mustache—a *Hundjager* and eager to follow Denswoz into Hell. *Or so he'd like me to think.*

Beside him was Danielle Lanive, a Hexenbiest who appeared to be about thirty years old, thanks to Hexenbiest potions, but was probably closer to fifty. She was a queenly, tanned woman in a tight white dress; she had long golden hair tied back into one immaculate braid. She was French but with German antecedents, like him—and she was totally loyal to him. There was a physical intimacy between them, when they were alone; they were careful not to show it around the others.

Marque Garnick sat at the other end of the oblong table in the office conference room, tapping his fingers on the oak finish with irritation. Garnick was an ambitious *Steinadler Wesen* in his early forties. The eagle-like Steinadler were proud, magisterial creatures, to the point where some felt themselves above other Wesen. Garnick didn't like to be kept waiting for a mere Hundjager. So Denswoz made sure to keep him waiting a little more. He paused deliberately to look out the big window of the conference room.

Below the rented office suite, just on the other side of a parking garage, Denswoz could see a tugboat pushing a barge up the Willamette River. He took his time admiring the view.

As a Hundjager, Albert Denswoz thought of *La Caresse Glacée* as his "extended pack," and he was very conscious of pack leadership. A pack leader frequently had to let the others know who was boss...

Finally, he gave the room his attention.

"Garnick—do you have the report I asked you for?" Denswoz demanded, as he put his briefcase on the table.

Garnick's scowl deepened.

"Naturally," he replied.

Denswoz would have growled at him, had he been woged. Instead, he merely glared.

"Don't take that tone with me," he said coldly. "You're as fallible as anyone else, Garnick. Let's have the report."

Garnick tossed the folder on the table disdainfully.

Denswoz wished for a moment that he had the coins with him. Garnick would melt, would fall entirely under his sway, if he used the Coins of Zakynthos. That would change the arrogant Steinadler's attitude. But Denswoz had used them only once since he'd had them stolen from Grimm safekeeping, a few months earlier. They'd given him power over *La Caresse Glacée* ritualists—a sublime authority he'd never experienced before.

He was determined to use the coins sparingly. He knew

they could destroy the fool who overused them. They were empowering—but they were dangerous.

Denswoz decided to let Garnick's bad attitude slide for now.

"Danielle—could you set up a paper shredder?"

"*Mais oui*," she said mildly. She got up, went to the corner, and pushed a wheeled paper shredder over to the table.

"As usual," Denswoz said, "we will practice information hygiene. All these documents are to be shredded—computer files are to be kept as encrypted as possible. Has the room been swept for bugs, Danielle?"

"*Bien sur*. It is clean."

He looked around. "Where is Grogan?"

"Here," a voice said.

Jase Grogan was just coming in the door. He was a big, red-haired man with a wide sunburned face, green eyes, a mild Dublin accent. His hair had receded well back from his freckled forehead but he let it grow past his collar to his broad shoulders. He wore a rumpled brown suit that barely contained his hulking barrel-chested frame. There was a peculiar tattoo involving a mermaid and a Christian cross on the back of his right hand. Grogan was a *Mordstier* Wesen, and a bull-like man he was.

"You're late, Grogan," Denswoz told him. "Sit down."

"Rather do that than stand," Grogan said, typically facetious.

He sat to Denswoz's left, leaned back, laced his fingers and cradled the back of his head. He liked to appear above it all, to the point of seeming almost to ooze contempt.

Grogan was a valuable man; had trained their primary West Coast enforcers. His people had taken out the Shadow Heart gangsters working in Canby. He'd made his point.

"I have decided," Denswoz said, "that we will move

ahead with the *Vernichten* list. And I suspect we'll add a few more to it."

"I'm all for removing those people," Garnick said. "But I think we should wait for the right moment—the right chance. You're talking about assassinating the governor of Oregon, for starters."

"We'll use our cobra-hooded *ami*," Danielle said. "The governor has had some heart trouble. They'll call it a heart attack."

Denswoz nodded. "Good. He has to go. The man is going to sign this new law enforcement bill. The lieutenant governor is… a friend of ours. He'll veto the bill, once he's governor. We don't want Oregon overrun with police. And we want a new governor we'll have in our pocket."

"There have been a *lot* of targets lately," Garnick said, chewing the inside of his cheek.

"Things getting too hot for you?" Denswoz asked, calmly. "There is an expression about kitchens—when they're too hot."

"That's unfair, Denswoz," Garnick said. For a moment irritation made him drop his mask and his eagle-like Steinadler visage showed through. Then his face snapped back to human. "We should vote on this."

"Pointless, man," Malo said. "Mr. Denswoz has the final word."

"To put it on the record. For the council bosses."

"I *am* one of the council bosses," Denswoz pointed out. "I'll let them know how you feel. We'll wait a few weeks on the governor, however. He won't sign the thing for more than a month. Now, as for that private investigator in San Francisco…"

"*Him* you can kill as soon as you like," Garnick said, dismissively.

"Good. Why don't you take him out?"

"Me? I'll have it done, if you like."

"Don't like to get your hands dirty?"

"I did my share in my time," Garnick said, his voice tense, creaking with eagle-like overtones. "And I think those three should be moved up your list." He pointed at the file he'd tossed on the table.

Denswoz opened the folder and read out the names.

"Nick Burkhardt, Portland PD detective. Hank Griffin. Partner. And a Blutbad named... Monroe? Where's the rest of his name? That first or last?"

"Ah, we haven't yet secured that information," Garnick said. "He was seen leaving the late Lemuel Smith's place with the two cops who found the body—Burkhardt and Griffin. And our Wesen watching the place said he recognized the guy with the cops as a Blutbad named Monroe. But that was all he could tell us. Our guy then followed him to a house... the address is there in the briefing. Apparently he watched the place for a while. Must have some kind of connection with the people in that house. Name of Perkins..."

"We need to find this guy, lure him out in the open," Malo said. "If he's working with the cops, he's got to go down. Hard."

Grogan chuckled. "Federico, you've been watching too many mafia movies."

Malo's cheeks reddened. "I just mean—if ever we had to make an example, this is the time. These guys took half a ton of *Seele Dichtungsmittel* off us. That much scopolamine... took a long time to get that much pure enough."

"Talk to our friend in the PD, get it back," Denswoz said. "We have more coming in. There are already three pounds here, in town."

"What about Griffin and Burkhardt?" Grogan asked.

"It's risky, eliminating cops," Denswoz admitted. "But

add them to the list. We just wait to implement their *Vernichten* till the time is right—ideally we can take them out together. Grogan—think of something. Now, what can we do to provoke this Monroe character into coming out into the open?"

Grogan straightened up, stretching his arms.

"I get a good moment to take the cops out, maybe their car ran into that river out there—you want me to just go for it?"

"Check with me first—unless it's too perfect to wait on, then it's your call. Sooner or later I want these detectives…" He looked at the report. "…Griffin and Burkhardt… to be thoroughly done for and gone. They're sticking their snouts into way too much. Malo's right. They hurt us already—and the word will get around."

Grogan nodded. "There's something else. They might've seen our boys flying their Wesen colors."

Steinadler looked startled.

"What makes you think that?"

"Couple of our guys were staying woged while guarding the shipment, down in the tunnel. They didn't expect to see anyone but Wesen and if they did see anyone who *wasn't* Wesen, they figured to just, you know, kill 'em. Thing is— this Burkhardt might be the guy we've been hearing about. Some of our Wesen connections say there's a Grimm in the Portland PD."

"A Grimm!" Steinadler exclaimed. "And…does the Verrat know about him, I wonder?"

"Chances are they do."

"You think he's working with the *Gegengewicht*? Supposedly they're making contact with Grimms…"

"I don't know. Not even sure this Gegengewicht thing is for real."

"Oh they're real all right."

Burkhardt. That name...

Denswoz knew that name from somewhere. It troubled him. Hadn't he seen it in his documentation on the Kessler family?

Burkhardt.

Kessler...

CHAPTER TWELVE
LONDON, ENGLAND, 1843

Early in a foggy autumn afternoon, in the first years of the reign of Queen Victoria, a young gentlemen strode along a particularly narrow, crooked, and malodorous London byway in search of a murderer. The young man was David Kaspar Kessler, and the murderer was known only as "the Sacker."

"The Sacker" was the vulgar term, used by prostitutes and wine shop keepers. David's father had suggested that the moniker derived from the state in which the victims were found: the bodies resembling an empty leather sack shaped vaguely like a human being, their guts mysteriously emptied out of them. The victims were men and only men. The killer was thought to be female, but David had his doubts.

David Kessler had hopes, too—he wished to be a detective in Sir Robert Peel's new police force. The new force of "bobbies" didn't have a good reputation with the ruck of the populace, since many of the constables were much too free with their truncheons. In fact, most of them were brutes. Still, the bobbies were more comprehensive than Fieldings' Bow Street Runners. David assumed that, in time, the Peelers would become the framework of a better police force. And being his father's son, David knew he'd find many an opportunity to turn his police work to double duty.

For he had another duty, already—that of a Grimm.

David stepped over a puddle of filth, and paused to put his perfumed kerchief to his mouth. He was not over-nice about smells, though he'd been raised on a country estate far from the worst of London's odorous excess, but he'd learned to keep the scented linen with him in some parts of the great city. If one was occupied with vomiting from the reek of raw sewage, rotting offal, and the disgustingly befouled old River Thames, one could scarcely do one's duty.

Turning a sharp corner in the street—and what street was it?—David stumbled over a gin-soaked drunk, perhaps a woman, he wasn't sure. Though it was but three of the clock in the afternoon, he wished he'd thought to bring a lantern. Coal fires darkened the sky, so that a man didn't know, often enough, if the cloud would yield rain or ash. The cobbled lane was so narrow, its three-and four story structures of blackened brick leaning so ponderously over the alley, it might have been an hour past dusk here. The only light was from lamps shining weakly through grimy windows, and the occasional muted ray of sunlight struggling between the clouds.

"Turn here, ginnelsor," the old procurer had told him. *"Walk ye back and yet back till yer heart dies in ye and ye'll come to the Sacker's ground. May God protect ye."* It had taken David a moment to understand that what sounded like "ginnelsor" meant "gentle sir."

David wondered if his half crown had indeed bought him the right directions, or was the old pimp now sitting having a hearty laugh over a pint with his cronies back in his rancid alehouse? *"Ooh, I wonder wut is down that reeking skulk of an alley! Damn me if I know!"* Quite possibly.

He came, then, to a small common area between the houses, not so much a courtyard as a widening of the way. Here, there was a bit more light and air.

Fifteen long steps across the cobbles was the streaked back wall of a house, where an old man and a young woman sat on a back stoop, in front of a cracked wooden door. The man was a toothless costermonger in a half-crushed hat, his basket on the cobbles beside him; the rather dirty young woman wore a grime-gray bodice and skirt, which might've once been white or yellow, and curious wooden sandals. Her black hair was piled on her head, held in place with small wooden pins; it tufted out here and there over her ears. But it was her slenderness that first struck him, and then something else—her eyes. They were the dark brown, almond-shaped eyes of an Asian, something one only rarely saw in London.

Her gaze was expressionless as it settled on him. In her slender hands was a brown stoneware gin bottle, without label or mark. David found himself staring at her fingers—she had unusually long fingernails. She passed the stone bottle to the toothless costermonger who cocked his eye at David and made a croaking sound that might've been an invitation to buy whatever wares he kept in his basket.

David smiled, and shook his head at the old man.

"If I may be so bold as to observe," David said, walking closer, widening his smile for the young lady. "You, madame are far from—"

But the old man interrupted him with a raw sputum-thick noise that must have been laughter.

"Eff 'e may be so bold! Why, they're all bold with *'er!"*

The girl gave a tinkling laugh and jabbed the old man with her elbow.

"Don't listen to him, sir," she said to David. She had a soft accent he could not place. "I am perhaps wayward, but I do not permit boldness—not of just anyone."

"I… I am gratified to hear it," David said. The young woman fascinated him. "May I ask where…?"

"I hail from Japan, sir," she said. Her voice was high pitched, lilting. Her lips were curiously rouged so that they appeared to be forever pouting. He could see no other makeup on her.

The old costermonger creaked out something else, unintelligible. After mentally processing the remark, David decided he'd said something about the young woman having been away for "nigh to five year or more."

"Five years away from here, and soon going away for five more," the woman said, her voice sounding dreamy.

"And did you return to Japan, in those five years, madame?" David asked.

"Ooh 'e's got fine airs wif his 'madame,'" the old man muttered, gin dribbling from the corner of his mouth.

"Return to Japan?" She looked at him in something like surprise. "No, I cannot travel so far alone, sir. There is one who has given me shelter, in Normandy… to that one I return. But, now and then, I must…" She shrugged and waved a hand to indicate the grubby vicinity.

"May I ask your name?" David inquired.

"Akemi, sir."

"And how came you to Britain when first you arrived? Was it your benefactor who brought you?"

"Why, so it was."

"May I ask his name?"

She gazed vaguely up at him and reached up to twist one of her errant hairs.

"His name? I don't suppose it will matter, now that I have chosen you. His name is… Denswoz."

"A Frenchman?"

"Just so. He was impressed with *geisha,* on a visit to Japan, and wished for one of his own. He bought me from a geisha house. Sometimes I remain with him and sometimes I do not." She shrugged. "He rarely beats me."

"He is to be commended for that." David cleared his throat. "I am making inquiries... there was a young gentleman, by the name of *Perdue*—Roger Perdue. His remains were discovered not far from here two nights ago. Had either of you encountered the gentleman before his passing? He was a young man, running to stout, with curly blond hair and a rather extravagant mustache. He hailed from Glasgow, where he lived with his mother, who had married a Frenchman. I can pay for fruitful information regarding his... demise."

She just stared at him, still twining her hair around a finger.

The old costermonger said, "'Ere, ye'll *pay* for talk? But what is this fruitful? I do not sell fruit but me brother Dim, '*e* does—"

"I mean—the information must bear fruit. I must discover something of use to the... to my inquiries."

The girl's lips parted. He saw that her teeth were a dark brown, and very small, like a row of dirty pearls.

After a moment she asked, "Are you a... Peeler?"

"I am not a constable, madame." Not yet. "I am merely making inquiries for... the family of Mr. Perdue."

She stood with a suddenness that made him take a step back.

"I will take you to a girl who knew him," she said. "But you must pay."

"Certainly. Half a crown?"

"That is not enough."

"A crown, then."

"Two!" she declared, eyes glinting.

He saw she would not be swayed.

"So be it!" He agreed and paid it over.

"'Ere, what about me?" the costermonger demanded, shoving a blackened hand out to him.

Annoyed, since the old reprobate had done nothing for him, David nonetheless tossed him a shilling.

"Miss? Shall we…" He indicated for her to lead the way.

Akemi headed to a passage David hadn't seen, a short alley between two buildings, with scarcely enough room to pass through in single file. He stepped carefully over the usual muck, and suddenly found they were on a fairly wide lane.

"Why, that rascal!" David said. "This is Grumman's Lane! Just where I was when I asked for directions! It could not have been more than a hundred steps from here that he sent me into that labyrinthine warren…"

"Me, I never go the way you came here," Akemi said. "So bad, that way. You're lucky someone didn't murder you. I only go to that stoop to drink and then I come back out here…"

She led him down a hill to a pub. The wooden sign, waving in the coal-darkened breeze, read, "The Ill-Favoured Captain's Inn."

"Come along…" she said.

He ducked his head to step through the door and into the gloomy pub interior. Soot-blackened beams further lowered the already low ceiling. A sagging bar lay at the other end of the narrow room. Several tattooed, sunburnt men, their hair tied back in long, greased, and braided sailor's cues, glanced up from a table where they played at mumblety pegs. They struck David as unemployed deckhands of the King's Navy. One of them leered at Akemi and removed the clay pipe from his mouth to call an improper invitation to her, the words accompanied by tobacco smoke.

"I have a gentleman," she answered simply, walking by the sailor.

Embarrassed, David followed her to the bar.

"Really, I don't think we need give the impression that... ah... well... no matter."

The barmaid was a blowsy red-faced Irish woman with a cast in one eye.

"Eef yer want a room, that's two shillings in advance," she said.

Akemi looked at him expectantly.

David bit off the automatic protest. His uncle had warned him that the work would entail disguise, *"Both disguise of appearance, at times, and purpose."* So David dug for the money in his waistcoat, and laid it on the sticky bar. When he turned to Akemi she was already starting up the narrow, twisting staircase to one side of the bar.

David followed, feeling an odd, premonitory fluttering in his breast. He reached into his sash to see if he still had the small muzzle loaded pistol tucked away.

One shot only... Best hope there's only one of them...

He frowned to himself. His uncle had coached him to be respectful of his instincts as a Grimm. But surely it was his own fear whispering to him, and not a Grimm's insight...

When he got to the constricted hallway at the top of the stairs he stopped—the girl had gone.

He swallowed, wondering why his mouth was so dry, and took several steps more—then found that a door along the left side of the passage was open.

She waited within, sitting on a bed, its ticking scarcely wide enough for one, let alone two. At the foot of the bed was a chamber pot. There was a small curtained window, and little more.

He stepped into the room but left the door behind him open.

"Miss—Madame… perhaps you have misunderstood." He cleared his throat. "I am not here for your—your services. Perhaps you thought my enquiries a pretense. You said you knew a girl who knew him. I am, truly, looking for information about Mr. Perdue and his…"

"His demise?" She was leaning back on the bed, propped up by one hand, the other toying once more with her hair.

"Yes."

"That is what I offer you. I mean—what you seek to find out. I am the girl I spoke of. I was with the gentleman when he died."

"Were you indeed?" He opened his coat, and put a hand, as if casually, on the grip of his pistol. "And who killed him?"

"He was killed by…" She spoke a Japanese word. It sounded like *Jorogumo*.

"And that is the person's name?"

"Ah, no. That is the person's *nature*. I will tell you more. But only if you come to me."

"I… you have told me quite a lot, really. I will give you another crown, and perhaps we might go downstairs to…"

"You can pay me later. You shall give me all you have and willingly…"

"…to have a glass of… of wine and talk a bit…"

His words seemed to evaporate from his lips, to drift away before he could speak them.

It was her eyes. He couldn't look away from them. They'd gone so very dark. They glittered and drew him closer.

Somehow he crossed the room, and took her in his arms.

They kissed. A strange smell seeped up from her mouth, but he didn't care. She was a fountain of ecstasy; the touch of her lips, her shoulders, overflowed with a glory that seemed to flow into his hands.

He drew back to look into her eyes again…

And he froze.

Her eyes bulged, and, as he watched, they became jet black, without any whites at all; dark rings encircled them. Her mouth was parted, and he couldn't see her teeth at all. Instead, from her mouth emerged something he'd only seen under a magnifying glass at one of his uncle's lectures on natural history.

Mandibles. The incisor fangs—yellow and black and coarse—of a spider.

Her face was transforming, too, becoming bristly around the edges. Her hands also became taloned and black…

He drew back, the trance broken. Stumbling, he plucked at his gun.

Then something struck the back of his head and a burst of light was followed by whirling gray dimness…

It must have been but a few moments later that he opened his eyes, and found that he was lying on his back, in the same room, gazing up at the smug face of a man he'd never seen before. And yet the man seemed indefinably familiar.

"He is mine, the last I will need," Akemi said, her voice changed, clicking and distorted. "Five years, and he is the last… until five years once more pass by…"

"You shall have him, my dear," said the man. "The flesh of one of those sailors will feed me, before the night is done. I merely wished to look into his face… Truly a poor excuse for a Grimm, this one…"

"If he had seen you first, perhaps you might be lying here, instead," said the odd, clicking voice.

"Perhaps. When their instincts are aroused they're fast, and dangerous."

"Who are you?" David asked. With one hand he felt for his gun...

The man leaning over him smiled nastily.

"Looking for this?" He held David's gun where he could see it—and then pointed it at him. "Do not move. I also have your knife. You would be dead already, but... I wanted you to *know*. Since you are a Kessler."

"Wanted me... to know...?"

"To know that I am Benjamine Denswoz. I am the son of Lukas Denswoz. Your granduncle shot Lukas, whereupon Lukas lost the use of his arm. But that is not the worst crime to be laid at the feet of your line. The Grimm who shot him killed my grandfather and stole the coins that rightly belong to *us*. And my father swore an oath that your family would forever pay for that perfidy. And so I have lured you here, and given you to my mistress to feed upon. I only wished you to know... the *why* of it."

David looked at Akemi.

"To...feed?"

"Yes. She will liquefy your insides, and she will drink them down—and as you are the final young man needed, her youth will be restored for another five years. She is a rare Wesen, I assure you. And you? Your line will become very rare indeed when we are through..."

"The Sacker..."

"Quite so." He bared his teeth in grinning triumph and drew back.

Before David could move, Akemi pounced, and drove her mandibles into his throat...

The Spinnetod venom paralyzed him before he could do more than thrash a little...

And then she put her lips to his... and something flowed from her, hot and thick, gurgling into his mouth...

To burn its way down to his core.

"Detective Burkhardt, Detective Griffin," Captain Renard said, "this is Agent Don Bloom."

Nick and Hank shook hands with the visitor as a morning rain pattered on the louvered window.

"Have a seat, gentlemen," Bloom said, booting up his laptop.

They sat at the dark wood table in the briefing room in the offices of the Portland Federal Bureau of Investigation. Bloom remained standing at the end of the table.

Nick tried not to let his nerves show. The tension between his life as a cop and his duties as a Grimm was pretty stressful as it was. Walking that line wasn't easy. But this... facing the feds...

Nick smiled, hoping he was coming off as a genial, helpful colleague, and cleared his throat as Agent Bloom tapped his PowerBook, bringing up relevant profiles.

Bloom was a middle-aged man in a neat gray suit and tie. He had thinning black hair, wire-rim glasses over watery blue eyes, and a dour face. He chewed his thin lower lip as he looked for the files he wanted.

"Ah. There it is. The Icy Touch, aka *La Caresse Glacée*.

Quite a dramatic bunch, this particular cartel."

"Dramatic?" Renard asked, pouring a glass of water from a pitcher.

Bloom glanced up. "This thing in Canby. These guys like to leave a calling card. Big bloody mess. They seem to want to call attention to themselves. Maybe that reflects the involvement of Mexican cartel elements. It's kind of like the mutilated bodies that turn up down there. Corpses left hanging from bridges with signs on them, that kind of thing."

"They're tied in with the Mexican cartels?" Hank asked. "The Zetas, Sinaloa, those guys?"

"Tied in? Yes and no," Bloom said thoughtfully, sitting back and tenting his fingers. He squinted at the ceiling as if he could decode the enigma of The Icy Touch from the random hole patterns punched in the acoustic tile. "More like they overlap in some ways. But this is a European-based operation. It's just… they seem to be moving in on the Zetas, for example, in Guadalajara, and recruiting some of them."

"You'd think the Zetas would go to war with them over that," Nick observed. "Seems like they go to war with other cartels as a regular thing."

Bloom looked sharply at him and Nick got a flash impression of the agent—the fruit of a Grimm's insight into human nature. Bloom was not a man to be trifled with. He was not imposing; he was of bland appearance and slightly fussy mannerisms and probably a family man. Not exactly a hard-core field agent. But the FBI agent's eyes flickered with intelligence and Nick was quite sure that Bloom didn't miss much. He hoped to God that, for now, Bloom hadn't spotted the patterns that might lead him to Wesen. If the Feds found out about Wesen, there'd be hell to pay.

At last Bloom nodded.

"The Zetas would go to war with Icy if they could find them. As you know, this organization is damned hard to find. Every time we think we've got them, the source either clams up, disappears—or we find them dead. It's something like what happens with inner city gangs—that fear of 'snitching,' the fear of retaliation—but writ large, across three continents. And there's a whole mythology around these people…" He shook his head.

Renard raised his eyebrows.

"Mythology?"

Bloom nodded toward the PowerBook.

"Stories about wolf people, snake people—I assume it's some kind of shamanistic conceit. Could be that Icy Touch itself is spreading this story about their having some supernatural advantage." He shrugged. "The ignorant are easily bamboozled."

Renard nodded. "Wolves and snakes—real fantasy stuff, huh? They'll be saying they're space aliens next."

Bloom chuckled. "The stuff we put up with at the bureau. We get every kind of eccentric pounding on our doors. People going on about how the Queen of England is a reptilian alien. I figure The Icy Touch is exploiting all the crazier rumor mills out there."

"But—The Icy Touch is real," Renard said, coolly.

Nick and Hank exchanged glances.

Renard smiled thinly. "It's a *real* crime cartel. And it's got *real* ambition. Question is, Don—what do we do about it?"

"The Bureau is hoping to correlate information with Portland PD," Bloom said. "Then work up a strategy to find these guys and nail them under the RICO statutes. Homeland Security is interested too." He sniffed, nose wrinkling as if something smelled bad.

"Why Homeland Security?" Hank asked. "The international angle?"

"That, and the stuff they were trying to smuggle in," Bloom said. He turned the PowerBook around so they could see the screen. "You see that analysis? The most active ingredient seems to be the scopolamine. Which has mind control potential, at least. The other stuff in the mix is obscure. We're still working on it. Seems like it's drawn from some kind of herbal mixture. But it's sure as hell not hippie shampoo. All the compounds seem to affect the nervous system. And there was so much of it—maybe they wanted to dump it in a reservoir somewhere, create chaos in some big city. I doubt it, though, they seem to be more about money than terror; Homeland Security's not so sure." He shrugged. "So if we can figure out what they plan on using it for, maybe we can stop them from putting it into effect."

"I take it we didn't get all they had," Hank said.

"I'm sure that wasn't their only supply. But by the way…" He nodded toward Nick and Hank. "Good work, interdicting that stuff. God knows what they might've done with it here in town…"

"That mythology you mentioned," Renard said thoughtfully. "Could it relate to this use of scopolamine, and the other stuff in the mix?"

Bloom pulled on his chin.

"Could be! Interesting thought. You mean those stories about beast people, monsters—could be hallucinations induced by this stuff? Like they're using some kind of hallucinogenic programming to make people even more afraid of crossing them?"

Picking up on what Renard was up to, Nick nodded in agreement.

"Scopolamine, from what I read, makes people extremely suggestible," he said. "Dose 'em with it, tell them they're seeing a monster—and they'll see one."

Bloom tapped his keyboard.

"I'm going to put that in the file as a possible angle on their hold over people…"

Renard was silent as they left the briefing room and walked down the hall together. In the elevator to the street, alone with Hank and Nick, he said softly, "Let's talk in my car."

The shower had eased off, but the car's windows were glazed with rainwater. Nick waited for Renard to speak. The captain sat behind the wheel of his new Renault, frowning in thought, and saying nothing.

In the end it was Hank who spoke first.

"Nick—remember when you and Monroe were talking about that council, a Wesen outfit that enforces a code of some kind…"

Nick nodded. "Council of Walenstadt, 1521. 'Guidelines to ensure the safety and well-being of the Wesen community.' The Code of Schwaben."

Renard turned to look at Nick, his frown deepening.

"Was it necessary to talk out of school about that, Burkhardt?"

Nick shrugged. "You forget. I'm not Wesen. I'm a Grimm. I don't have the same set of rules. I told Hank about it because it's information he needs. He's in the loop. And he's a useful man. He's done a lot of the Council's work, really. Even before he knew it…"

Renard turned to Hank.

"Why do you bring up the Council?"

"Because, Captain—maybe *they* should be handling this, not us. They sent in that outside shooter to take out those Wesen who were robbing banks with their natural fright masks hanging out. So let them handle this. Then— it wouldn't be on us. It just bothers me that we can't clue the rest of law enforcement in on the Wesen side of The

Icy Touch. We shouldn't be keeping information back from the feds—or from the rest of the department. It's not even *legal*."

Nick winced. "You're right—but it is what it is, Hank. Long as I'm a Grimm I'm going to walk the edge of the legal. And I'll probably step over it sometimes. I'm sorry you get dragged over it too, man. I really am. But I figure you're a detective partly because you like to solve mysteries. This hidden world is a whole new level of mystery. Once you're in on it… you're in."

Renard cleared his throat. "I don't know if there is a file on Wesen at the CIA, or MI6, or the DIA. Or even the FBI. But—I know there are Wesen tucked away in some of those agencies. My guess is, they suppress clues that could lead investigators to the Wesen. So if you decide to break this open, Hank—you'd have them after you too. *And* the Council.

"And me."

"Another threat, Captain?"

"Doesn't have to be. You can work with us."

"I'm playing by your rules," Hank said, "because right now it seems to be the best way to make sure I can stop these sons of bitches. And because Nick's a good man. I've been his partner for a long time. That's why I'm doing it. Not because I'm scared of the Wesen council. Or you."

The interior of the windows was steaming up with their breath. But to Nick it almost seemed as if the simmering anger between Renard and Hank was steaming up the glass by itself. He could feel the tension humming in the air.

"You didn't answer my question," Hank went on. "What about the Council closing down The Icy Touch?"

"They'll be kept informed," Renard said. "But I don't know if they're likely to take any action. First of all, we don't know specifically who we're dealing with. We've got no names to give them. And it's not clear to me that the cartel has broken the Code. They haven't exposed Wesen to the world. They've only threatened other Wesen."

"Seems to me they're putting all Wesen at risk," Nick said. "They're taking over human organizations using Wesen powers. The risk of it all coming out, in that kind of fight… seems pretty strong to me. Could be explosive. It could blow up the whole Wesen community."

Renard grunted. "We'll see." He paused, then added, "There's someone else who might be interested. The Gegengewicht."

"The who?" Hank asked.

"Gegengewicht. It means 'the counterweight,'" Renard replied. "A secretive Wesen organization. I don't know much about them. I have a second cousin, Beatrice, in France— she tried to recruit me into it, a few years ago. They seem to be a Wesen counterweight to the Royals—they think the Royals are a danger to Wesen, and they've got some kind of agenda of their own to counter Wesen criminality."

Renard started the car, ran the wipers, and drove out onto the street.

"I'll research it," he said. "Right now, you two need to start sifting through Portland Wesen. Someone out there has to have some connection to The Icy Touch… Find them!"

Last guy we found with a connection is dead now, Nick thought, as the rain picked up again. *Who else are we going to sacrifice to this investigation? Who else is going to die?*

Ten-thirty-nine p.m. Lillian Perkins, Lily to her friends, was pretty sure she was in trouble. Lily chewed it over in her mind as she walked across the wet asphalt circle of Shady Court, carrying her backpack loosely over one shoulder. She'd agreed she would come home and check in with her mom before going out, and that she wouldn't stay out after ten even when she had permission. It was *way* after ten—and she didn't have permission.

Mom, it was like this… We were just hanging out at Celia's and then someone came over with this DVD and I always wanted to see the movie and…

No, that wouldn't work.

How about, *We got to talking about our homework and geography was so interesting that…*

No, even worse. She'd definitely never believe that.

Lily was almost at her doorway when the man stepped out from behind the bushes and grabbed her arms from behind.

He moved so fast she had only a glimpse of his bearded face, his wild eyes. She tried to scream but he clamped a big, rough hand painfully hard over her mouth.

Lily was lifted off her feet. It sounded like the guy was growling like an animal, which threw gasoline on the fire of her terror, and she wriggled and bit down as hard as she could.

The man yelped and jerked his hand away from her.

She shouted hoarsely for her mom and twisted loose, stumbled toward the front door, fell—and her falling was the only thing that saved her from being struck when he slashed at her with something…

Something rippled at the white-painted wooden column on the corner of the front porch, just over her head—something that seemed to dig long grooves into the wood, like *claws* slashing into the post.

Then she was crawling, and her mom was shouting from the front window, and the growling man had her by the ankles, was dragging her off to the left; toward the bushes and toward the darkness.

"Raise her up and then hold her for me," said a gruff voice.

She was grabbed under the armpits, lifted off her feet—and someone raised a syringe without a needle into view, and squirted it between her lips.

A sickening taste filled her mouth, fumes rose into her nose… and then a strange cloudiness rolled over her.

"You're going to come quietly," one of the men said.

And at that moment coming quietly seemed the most natural thing in the world.

It was as if she was floating a little above and behind, watching herself walking passively between two men, climbing willingly into their van.

Somewhere her mother was calling her name. But she didn't care. Because the cloudiness was warm and safe and spreading…

So that she felt nothing at all.

CHAPTER FOURTEEN

Maybe it was Blutbad instinct. Monroe had brought the Perkins family under his protection—it was the only way he could even begin to make up for killing Alvin Perkins—and once he'd done that, it made their home part of his protected territory. Anyway, that's how it felt, in some primeval part of him. And that instinct was telling him: *Check on Lily.*

Something's wrong...

Monroe parked his truck several blocks away and then walked the rest of the way to Shady Court. The rain had let up. Crickets sawed away. A half moon edged out between two clouds, not far above the Portland skyline. There was a good smell of fallen rose petals and wet earth in the night air.

When he was a half block from Shady Court, he knew for sure that something ugly had gone down.

Sirens, flashing lights up ahead. Cops—at the Perkins house.

He started to run, then slowed to a fast walk, realizing that he didn't want to call attention to himself. For years he'd gone out of his way to make sure the Perkins family didn't know about him.

When he got to the corner he played nosy bystander, hands stuck in his pockets, gawping at the police cars, the take-down lights on the cruisers alternately painting the scene blue and red. Two uniformed officers, one male, one female, no one he recognized, were talking to the weeping Dorine Perkins on the front porch. A third cop, a young Latino guy, was stretching out the yellow police investigation tape. Disembodied voices crackled from the radios in the cop cruisers. *"Five six four, do you read…"*

Two plainclothes guys wearing latex gloves, probably forensic technicians, were using tiny brushes and bottles, trying to take samples from a fresh mark on a wooden post. Even from a distance, Monroe could see what it was.

Claw marks—the distinctive marks of a Blutbad's slashing talons.

Monroe felt a long rippling chill go through him. His mind raced…

Maybe they'd seen him with Nick and Hank at Smitty's place. Maybe they'd been following him—he'd suspected someone was following him, more than once, these past few days. They'd figured out the connection between him and the Perkins…

He'd been so worried about Rosalee, he'd not thought he'd need to protect them as well.

He saw the backpack, its strap broken, lying in the yard. The forensic techs were turning their attention to it now.

Monroe recognized that backpack.

It was Lily's.

Have to know more. Just have to.

He saw Sergeant Wu walking up to the front porch. Monroe was tempted to try to get Wu aside, see if he could draw him out on this.

No. He couldn't just walk up and ask. Too many cops around here. He didn't know every cop on the force and

Nick didn't want anyone to know about their friendship who didn't absolutely have to.

Monroe yawned, as if he was losing interest in the scene, turned, and walked off as if he were continuing his stroll, around the police cars, to the left of the cul de sac. He kept going, hands in pockets, and turned a corner.

The house on the corner was dark, unlit—he could sense it was currently unoccupied. He glanced around to see if he was unobserved, then darted quickly from the sidewalk between the two houses, moving into shadow as quickly as he could. He had an urge to woge, to get into his Blutbad form with its full animal sensitivity, but he repressed it. If the cops even caught a glimpse of him in that state... bad scene, dude.

He climbed over a redwood fence into a backyard, sniffing the air for dogs. He didn't want to have to pry the slavering jaws of someone's pitbull from his ankle. There were dogs barking a couple of houses behind him, but he couldn't sense any up ahead.

Monroe vaulted over a low picket fence, and came down on someone's flowerbed, crushing their perennials. It bothered him—he had a real householder's sense of orderliness, and he hated to violate someone else's. Worse, he was putting his bootprints here in the soft dirt of the flowerbed. That could confuse the investigation, if the cops checked back here—and they probably would. But it was too late to do anything about it now; probably leave more traces if he tried to cover it up. He'd have to toss the boots in the Willamette, later. Damn, they were nearly new...

He crossed to a low fence between the backyard he was in and the Perkins' yard. A flashlight was bobbing along, pointed away from him, behind the Perkins' house. He could see the silhouette of the cop holding it. Looked like

Wu was checking the backyard for traces of the intruder, any other evidence.

How were they going to explain away the fresh claw marks on the post? Vandalism? Some psycho using a gardening tool to leave his special sign?

Wu stepped around the farther corner of the Perkins house, out of sight. The other cops were busy out front.

This is my chance.

Monroe vaulted over the fence, and ran in a crouch, up to the nearest back corner of the Perkins' house.

He went very still, hunkered down, sniffing...

He smelled cat piss. Not Wesen cat. House cat.

He sniffed farther along the edge of the house.

"Shady Court," said a radio voice. *"Confirm a negative on ambulance at this time."*

Monroe smelled turned earth, worms... and there. A rich, strong, distinctive Wesen smell. A Blutbad had urinated here. He sniffed at it again. A male.

The Blutbad had left his scent—and Monroe suspected he'd done it on purpose. Could be he'd left it for Monroe himself to find...

Monroe glanced toward the front, hearing cop voices approaching. One was definitely Wu.

"Sure it looks like claw marks, kinda like on the bodies we found in Canby but, hey, I'm not saying there's a connection. Probably not the same perp. Maybe they both got a crying need for a manicure... I hope that girl's okay..."

Monroe moved deeper into the dark shadow of the backyard. Behind the house was a strip of trees, just past a dilapidated wooden fence. He took two quick running steps, jumped over the fence, slipped into the trees, then turned, ducked low, wondering if he'd been seen.

No. The cops weren't turned his way—they were running flashlights over the back wall of the house. If they kept looking around they might find his footprints...

He turned and hurried off through the trees, to the nearest street. He had to get to his truck, get rid of these boots, get to Rosalee.

Oh God. Lily. They've got her. They've got the ranger's daughter.

And it was his fault...

CHAPTER FIFTEEN

It tumbled breathlessly out of Monroe all at once.

"Nick... They were following me, then they lost me—and taking the girl is supposed to be one of their cute little messages." Monroe paused to catch his breath. "They've got her—and she might turn up dead."

They were in the back room of Rosalee's Spice Shop early the following morning. Rosalee was half sitting on the edge of a work table, with her arms folded over her chest. Nick sat in a chair while Monroe paced the room restlessly.

"How'd you come to know this family?" Nick asked.

Monroe looked startled. "I *don't* know them. I mean... I do. But I don't. I don't know them *know them*, but..."

"Monroe?"

"Nick, I never *met* the girl or her mom, or her brother. Their dad is dead. I... had an encounter with him. But that's really all I can tell you."

"Hey. You're going to hold out on me?"

"Nick," Rosalee said softly.

He looked at her. "Yeah?"

"He really can't tell you. And... this would be a good time

to remember what he's done for you. For the department. For everyone. He's taken a lot of chances, helping a Grimm."

Nick nodded. *Fair enough*, he owed Monroe.

"Okay. Monroe—what makes you so sure Icy Touch took her? Or even Wesen…"

"That claw mark was fresh—the cops were doing a forensic test on it, Nick. And it was definitely what you see when a woged Blutbad slashes wood. But—oh, I didn't tell you! *Piss*, Nick! Piss!"

"What? You have to go now?"

"No, I mean—the guy marked the place! He urinated against the side of the Perkins' house. He put that scent there for me! It's a Blutbad thing."

"Still not necessarily Icy Touch," Rosalee pointed out.

Monroe looked at her. "After what happened to Smitty, and me being mixed up with that—and the Perkins family too? Hel-*lo*! It's got their frozen fingerprints all over it!"

The front door jangled as someone entered the shop, and Rosalee went out to wait on the customer. Looking through the passage to the front, Nick could see a squat man with a round face and slightly prominent front teeth crossing to the counter. The Grimm vision kicked in, and he saw it was an Eisbiber. Beaver Wesen.

Nick leaned back so his face was hidden from the view. A lot of Eisbiber knew about his Grimm status, and he preferred they didn't know he was here. They had a way of chattering too much to other Wesen. Rosalee was already at risk. Speaking of which…

"Monroe," Nick said, keeping his voice down, "you two need to stay someplace else. Not your place, not here. Rosalee needs to take some time off from the shop. If they went after Lily Perkins…" He shrugged. "Maybe Rosalee's next. Chances are they want to put some kind of pressure on you."

Monroe slapped his forehead.

"Oh Jeez. Wow. Crap. You're right!"

The door jangled again, announcing the departure of the Eisbiber, and Rosalee returned to the back room.

"Just an Eisbiber needing a birth control lotion," she said with a shrug.

Monroe grimaced. "An Eisbiber birth control lotion? How does that work? No, never mind, I don't want to know. Rosalee—Nick thinks you ought to lie low for a few days, someplace else. Not my place, not here. Just to be safe."

"You too, Monroe," Nick said, standing up. "You've been a big help. I'll see what I can find out about the abduction—"

His phone chimed. He took it from his coat, saw Renard's name on the display.

"Captain?"

"They definitely have more *Seele Dichtungsmittel*," Renard told him. "Forensics found traces of scopolamine at the site of that abduction on Shady Court. We also got a partial on the license plate used—neighborhood watch saw it peeling out. The partial and vehicle description led to a stolen van, abandoned in North precinct."

"What neighborhood?"

Renard snorted. "Guess."

"Oh. Northeast Salem?"

Northeast Salem Boulevard, along with its side streets, was the worst neighborhood in NE Portland. A series of raids had cleaned it up somewhat, a year earlier, but that just left a power vacuum, long as no one invested in a better quality of life for people there. And no one did.

"Northeast Salem Boulevard it is. Pick Griffin up on the way, and check it out ASAP."

"You got it, Captain."

Nick put the phone away.

"Got something, Monroe. *Seele Dichtungsmittel* found at the Perkins place. And maybe a lead in the North precinct—we might have the van that was used over there. Could be they took her to the area, dumped the van..." He didn't go on speculating aloud. But panderers in the area were known to use young girls. "I'm going to pick up Hank, see what we can find out..."

"I'm going with you," Monroe said, jumping to his feet. He started for the door.

Nick caught him by the shoulder.

"Uh—no. You're not."

Monroe turned to him, mouth open, eyes wild.

"I have to, Nick. If she's over there I can find her. Hey dude, I can sniff the guy out who took her—literally. I have to go."

"And I said no. Not this time. You two need to keep a low profile. And we don't know what we have here, for sure. If I need you, I'll call. Find another place to stay. Motel, friend's house. Somewhere out of town. Call me if you think anyone's on your tail."

"Nick—!"

"I said *no*, Monroe."

"Monroe, he's right!" Rosalee put in.

"No—he doesn't understand!"

Nick hurried out of the shop, leaving Monroe and Rosalee behind him heatedly discussing what they should do—and what Monroe shouldn't do.

Sergeant Wu was already there, on the side street off NE Salem Boulevard, keeping an eye on the van as the forensics team swept it. The yellow tape was up, the rain was drifting by in thin veils, and Wu had his police cap on with the plastic rain cover over it.

At the corner of the street was a bar called The

Flyover, the name written in red neon, with a blue neon airplane flying at the top of the sign. The rain-slick streets reflected the neon with the distorted vividness of an expressionist painting.

"Detectives Griffin and Burkhardt in person, so early in all this?" Wu said, as they walked up to him.

"Could be related to another case we're working on," Hank said. "What you got here?"

"Not a lot," Wu said. "Not a goose egg but not a grown goose either." He hooked a thumb toward the van. "Vehicle stolen from a J. Baldwin, over in Southeast. Seems like a random theft. Likely the vehicle used in the abduction. We found strands of hair matching the mother's description of the girl's in the back—the strand was tipped with hot pink, like teenagers do. Found some powder too, we don't know what it is—we got a good guess, though. Looking for prints now."

"Blood?" Nick asked.

"Not so far. 'Course, in this 'hood, you might find blood anywhere, including the bottom of your shoes if you take a short walk. You guys want some coffee? I brought along a couple extra cups."

"Did it come from that machine at the department?" Hank asked.

"Yeah."

"Then no. Call us if you come up with anything interesting."

Wu nodded toward the bar.

"The watering hole over there might have some beasties at it."

Nick and Hank looked at one another, then at Wu.

"'Beasties?'" Nick asked.

"Get it? Waterhole, beasties? Local thugs hang out there. Neighborhood's once more chockablock with 'em. Like the raids happened a century back instead of a year ago."

Nick nodded, relieved.

"Thanks, Wu."

"How do they look?" Denswoz asked. "Not like a bunch of zombies, I hope."

"Nope. Nice and fresh and fully alive, boss," Malo said. The young man smoothed back his mane of long black curly hair as they walked past the rooms where the girls awaited a call. There were four such rooms, in this particular "massage parlor." Two girls waited listlessly in each of the first three.

"I don't mean *that* kind of zombie, Federico," Denswoz said impatiently. "I mean are they, you know… like somebody gave them a roofie or something?"

"Nah, the Seele's not that heavy. Have a look…"

They stopped at the fourth room. Inside four lingerie-clad girls waited seated on bunk beds, all gazing benignly into space. One of them hummed to the old Rick James song that piped through the brothel.

"What's up with the bunk beds?" Denswoz asked.

"These are the teens. It's part of the whole, you know, *thing* the clients go for, like they're teens at a slumber party or something."

"One of these is that new girl Hergden brought in?"

"The Perkins kid. Top right, there."

Denswoz and Malo stood in the open door, just steps from the girls, but none of the young women looked their way. They'd been told not to, and the *Seele Dichtungsmittel* was in full effect. The girl on the top bunk to the right trembled in her translucent purple lingerie, her face twitched like she was fighting the drug.

"Looks like she's coming out of it," Malo muttered. "I'll have them give her a booster."

Denswoz felt a momentary twinge of something like conscience, looking at the girl, but he pushed it away, dismissed it with ease. They were, after all, just ordinary *Homo sapiens*, these girls. They were not *Duo homo* as he and his followers thought of the Wesen. *Homo sapiens*— ordinary humans— had only a partial nature. They were only half there. The deeper, more vital form was absent. Non-Wesen were *merely* human.

And of course the irony was that their limited and feeble human type had persecuted Duo Man for thousands of years, using the Grimms as their assassins. *Deny your true selves!* the humans seemed to say. *Do you feel the need to prey on human beings, to eat their flesh? Deny your true nature! Destroy yourselves, monsters!*

And yet humanity butchered, murdered one another— they feasted on animal flesh and some of them ate human flesh…

No. He would feel no guilt for enslaving humanity. When The Icy Touch moved on to its final phase, many centuries of oppression would be repaid. And every Grimm in the world would be hunted down… and put to death, the way human beings slaughtered pigs.

Or the way some human beings killed dogs. As a Hundjager, he hated the human practice of forcing dogs to fight one another; of exterminating them in kill shelters. They even *ate* them, in Korea, and China. One day Icy Touch would take over Asia. Then there'd be payback for that, too.

And payback is a bitch…

They turned away from the girls, headed down the hall toward the store front of the supposed massage parlor. A Blutbad sentry walked down the hall, nodding respectfully to Denswoz as he passed.

"All right, Malo," Denswoz said, when they reached

the entrance. "Give them their boosters. We want this place open tomorrow night. Grogan'll probably come by with a few guys to try them out tonight. To check out the full service. But keep an eye out. This neighborhood was raided last year, it could happen again."

"We're aware. We've got a couple of *Geiers* up on the roofs, here and across the street. They're watching the whole block real close. Not much gets past the vulture brothers. And we won't be in this building more than a month. This place is a dump anyway—wait'll you see how we're fixing up the new place. Nice!" Malo clapped his hands together once in his enthusiasm. "Red velvet, porn on big screen TV, full bar, the works. It's in an old warehouse out by the airport, right across the street from the runways. No housing there, no neighbors to complain, not much city police patrolling at all. And Homeland Security won't be interested in us."

"Yeah—about those HSA guys. You set up our Wesen in airport security?"

Malo grinned proudly. "Two in every major airport on the West Coast."

"I need somebody they know. We've got some new captains coming over from Europe. They're going to have clean passports, beautiful IDs, can't tell them from the real thing. But even so—anybody gets suspicious, detains them, it could get ugly. We'll give you the flight numbers, you talk to our Wesen in HSA."

"Just email me the itineraries, boss, I'm all over it."

Denswoz nodded and walked out to where his driver awaited him on NE Salem Boulevard.

Monroe hadn't followed Nick and Hank this time. But he'd bought a Bearcat police scanner a while back, and he was listening to it while he was packing a bag. Right away he heard chatter about "Burkhardt and Griffin" requesting Sergeant Wu remain on site for them out at the abandoned stolen vehicle. Must be what Nick had gone to look into. And he figured Nick would following up on the Perkins abduction.

Of course, Monroe thought, as he stowed his bag in the truck, *I'm just supposed to be home packing up a few things so I can drive back to meet Rosalee at the hotel.* But she was doing some errands too, so what's a little delay— it was no more than a mere, minor, infinitesimal teensy-weensy little side trip...

Monroe sighed. She was going to be mad when she found out.

But he felt a connection to the Perkins. He felt a responsibility toward the ranger's family and Lily was... He sort of thought of her as a daughter. Silly, he supposed, as he climbed behind the wheel, since they'd never even *met*.

He was worried about the Perkins boy, too, and Mrs. Perkins. Would they be abducted next?

He had to do *something*...

"Guilt, Monroe," he muttered aloud as he started the car. "Maybe that's all it is."

Guilt? It wasn't that simple...

A few minutes later he was switching off his windshield wipers as he drove up NE Halsey toward Salem Boulevard. The rain had stopped and the wet cars parked along Halsey gleamed colorfully in the neon light of taverns and a late-night grocery.

He had a bad feeling about this little side trip. But he didn't have to *do* anything. He could just have a look around. Wouldn't have to get in Nick's way. Wouldn't have to actually *confront* anyone... probably.

He turned left onto NE Salem and drove along till he

got to a block where the streetlamps had been shot out, and the only light came from a storefront with blanked out front windows and no sign, and the feeble yellow moon occasionally looking through the clouds, like a sick old man peeking through curtains.

He drove on, up to the corner and around it, half expecting to see police cars, maybe Nick and Hank standing around. But he saw nothing like that. Just a burned out abandoned car, a vacant lot, trash, and a wino asleep in the doorway of a boarded-over building.

He parked, switched the lights off, licked his lips, and thought, *What if Rosalee calls? I'd have to lie to her or get in an argument on a street where I don't want to draw attention to myself.*

He took out his cell phone, and switched it off.

"Come on, do it or don't," he told his worried reflection in the rearview.

He climbed out of the truck, locked it, stuck his hands in his pockets and headed down the street.

A ways down, a couple blocks, was what looked like a neon sign at some tavern. Were there police lights blinking, down there? Maybe so.

Those guys were doing their job. Trained police personnel. What did he hope to find, here, by himself?

A short walk couldn't hurt.

He strode quickly along the cracked, weedy sidewalk, approaching the storefront. It was one story, sticking out from a three-story building. The taller building behind was dark. There were lights behind the brown-paper that covered the windows of the storefront. He could see the stretched out silhouettes of people, shadows from the other side of the brown paper. What went on in there? One of those "private social clubs" that were fronts for local gangs? Or just somebody's low-rent crash pad?

A big dude emerged from the building; he had bushy black hair and a beard, and was clothed in worn blue jeans, steel-toe boots and a sleeveless Levi jacket. His arms were blue with old prison tattoos. He paused to look up at the roof. The man was still about a hundred feet away but it seemed like he was talking to someone up there; to a dark shape on the roof.

Don't stare, Monroe. Just keep walking and stay alert.

Monroe continued on, noticing the bushy-bearded guy crossing the sidewalk to a dented, heavy Ford pickup. It was the kind of truck used by wildcat contractors, guys who fixed roofs and fences, or claimed to, without having a contractor's license. The bed was lined with locked metal toolboxes; the rear piled with odds and ends of plasterboard and paint-splashed two-by-fours.

Bushy beard climbed up in back, opened a tool kit—then straightened to glower down at Monroe.

Monroe hastily lowered his eyes and tried to look casual as he walked by, not meeting bushy-beard's eyes.

Monroe could smell the guy, though. He didn't bathe too often. And there was a particular tang he recognized…

It was the scent left by the Blutbaden at Lily Perkins' house.

Monroe slowed, almost turned, was close to going full-on woge; was ready to jump the guy.

Don't do it. Be smart. Get Nick.

He felt someone else to his left, on that roof. Someone up there was watching him. He caught an acrid smell from that direction, too. Was that the reek of… carrion?

Monroe walked a little faster.

He heard someone talking behind him, but they didn't follow him. He hurried on, down toward that neon sign and the police lights. A drunk staggered past him, asked him for something. He ignored the guy and kept going.

What if he had to take a couple of these Blutbaden down himself? Could he do it?

He found himself remembering something Rosalee had said, right before they'd gone to do their separate errands. *"Monroe—I'm kind of worried about how far you've gotten involved in police work. I like to help Nick too but… I mean, you were wrestling a man for a gun and the man got his head shot off. Now you're talking about tracking down gangsters. I mean—where are you going with this, Monroe?"*

Good question. Where in fact *was* he going with this?

He just kept walking.

Monroe came to the bar, saw it was called The Flyover. Someone slammed a car door to his right and he turned, saw a tow truck starting up, pulling a van away. Was that Sergeant Wu, just down the side street, waving to a couple of guys in a cruiser?

Yeah. It was Wu.

He couldn't see Nick, or Hank. Monroe decided not to ask Wu where the detectives were.

He'd go into The Flyover, think things over. Find a quiet spot to call Nick…

CHAPTER SIXTEEN

Nick and Hank stood at The Flyover's dingy bar talking to a couple of droopy mouthed plug-uglies in stained football jerseys. Nick had already made sure: definitely not Wesen.

It was a well-worn drinking establishment, a lot of dark wood and designs stamped on the old, brown-painted sheet metal ceiling. The inevitable big screen TV was tuned to ESPN and the usual electric beer signs and posters showed winking, leggy girls offering brimming shot glasses of Jack Daniels and Maker's Mark. A leather-clad biker at a green-felt table broke a delta of pool balls with a resounding clack and a bark of, "Ha!"

"Look, fellas," Hank said, "We're just curious about anybody new operating out here on the street. Whatever it might be. Just any kind of sense of it at all. Especially… *where*. We don't need names."

"Don't know of anything going on except what's alla time here," said the larger of the two men. "Which is nothin'."

"Yeah!" the other guy said, laughing and hiccuping at the same time. "Nothin'!"

The plug-uglies bumped fists.

Nick did sense a Wesen in the room, then. Somewhere

behind him. He looked around—and saw Monroe, coming in the door. He nudged his partner with an elbow.

"Hank, look who's here."

Hank glanced over. "Monroe. He better have a damned good reason for showing up here."

"Our idea of a good reason and his aren't likely to be the same."

Monroe had spotted them, was pointing, across his stomach, in a way he thought was sly, to a corner booth. He raised an eyebrow as he looked directly at Nick and Hank. Everyone in the room, of course, knew that he was signaling the two cops to meet him there.

"The man is just not a good candidate for undercover work," Hank murmured, as they crossed over to the booth.

"You got that right."

They sat down across from Monroe.

"What's up, Monroe?" Hank asked.

Monroe licked his lips. "Maybe I should order a beer to look normal and casual, and, you know, for cover."

"I wouldn't bother with cover at this point," Nick said. "What're you doing out here?"

Monroe shrugged expansively as if to say, *No big deal*.

"Hey, I just... I heard a reference to you doing something out here, uh, heard it on my scanner and, um, just thought I'd swing by and see if there was anything I could, you know, sniff out, and there *was*, actually..."

Just then, someone played the internet jukebox, a Metallica song, "Wherever I May Roam," came on and they had to lean closer to one another to be heard.

"Someone sniff *you* out, in the process, Monroe?" Nick asked.

"Me? No! No, I'm sure... well, I'm not sure, but I'm *pretty* sure... mostly... that he didn't sniff me out as a Blutbad..."

"You're saying you ran into another Blutbad on the

street around here?" Hank asked.

Nick glanced around the room. He noticed a woman he hadn't seen before, coming out of the men's room. She was an attractive Hispanic woman, black hair flipped smoothly to one side; she wore a black leather designer blazer, a white silk blouse, black leather pants, spike-heeled red boots. There was a glint of pure hostility in her eyes as she returned his look—and then her face went blank when she saw the gold badge clipped to his belt. But before the careful blankness, he glimpsed the disfiguring Hexenbiest decay spread across her face, corrupting her lips and eyes. The flicker of Grimm insight passed and she was once more the pretty but hard-faced Latina.

"You know her?" Hank asked, noticing Nick's stare as the woman hurried out.

"No. But she's a Hexenbiest." Nick looked at Monroe.

Monroe shook his head. "I don't know her." Then he leaned way toward them like he wanted to climb over the table. "But I know what I scented on the street out there—the same urine marker I found at the Perkins' house."

Hank stared at him. "What? You're going around a crime scene on your hands and knees and, like, smelling the ground?"

"No! I didn't have to get down on my hands and knees. I just… hunched down a little. Well, I squatted…"

"You're lucky you weren't arrested," Nick said. "Where was this guy you… sniffed out?"

"Right down Salem Boulevard, dude!" Monroe replied.

The song ended but then a plane taking off from the nearby airport rumbled over, so low the building shook slightly.

Monroe glanced at the ceiling. "Wow. So that's why they call that it The Flyover. Yeah, the guy had the scent marker on him… I didn't actually notice the address up there but it's a storefront, windows papered over. The only building with any lights on in that whole block down there. Where the streetlights are busted out. You totally cannot miss it."

Hank shook his head. "Wonder how long those streetlights have been out. This happened over in Northwest, those people with money would get their streetlights back on right away."

Nick pulled his phone out, then decided not to make the call in the bar.

"Come on," he said.

He led the way outside. A mist of evaporating rainwater rose from the sidewalk, taking on the hot neon colors of the bar sign. He looked for the Hexenbiest in black leather, and didn't see her.

They walked down the side street to Hank's car, which chirped in response to his key signal. They got in, Hank behind the wheel, Monroe in back.

Nick speed-dialed Renard, and got the answering machine.

"Dammit! Uh, Captain, it's Burkhardt, we've got a tip out here, a *hot* tip, that the perp who snatched the Perkins girl is within a few blocks of that abandoned van. It's not quite probable cause but close enough for a warrant. Be faster if you get it for us… Call me, please."

He broke the connection, sighed with frustration.

"Might be faster for us to get the warrant," Hank suggested. "Email Judge Bernstein yourself, he takes night warrant requests. He'll email us a warrant."

"They *email* warrants now?" Monroe asked, sounding surprised.

"They do. We get 'em on our phones."

Nick thought about it. "It would still be faster if the Renard does it. He works pretty closely with Bernstein. I'll try texting the Captain…"

Hank grunted and shook his head.

"Wait—I just realized that Bernstein is out sick."

"Great. This might have to wait till tomorrow…"

Monroe leaned forward from the back seat.

"Come on—Lily is *in there,* dude, right now! I know she is!"

"You don't *know* that, Monroe," Hank said.

"It's… I can *sense* it. I've got a kind of paternal connection with that girl. Blutbaden can sense things. She's *in that building.*"

"Connection with a girl you never met?" Hank said. "Getting kind of creepy, Monroe."

Monroe went very still… then snarled at Hank.

"Take that back."

"Whoa!" Hank laughed nervously. "I didn't mean it. Chill out. But you're going to have to wait for us to raid the place. We can set up surveillance on it."

Monroe made a visible effort to calm down, but his eyes were narrowed and his lips compressed. He was close to going Blutbad.

"Hank, if you put some cops out there watching the place, then they'll spot them—they got some guys on the roof. They'll make her a hostage or something."

"Guys on the roof? You mean Icy Touch gangsters?" Nick asked.

"I'm guessing. I don't know what kind of Wesen they are but they gave me the heebie jeebies." Monroe pointed at Hank. "And don't say *I* give you the heebie jeebies."

Hank shrugged. "Okay, I won't say it."

"If they've got lookouts on the roof," Nick said, thinking aloud, "all the more reason we need a warrant. We can get a major raid going and really surround the area."

Hank ran the edge of his thumb along his close-clipped goatee.

"What happens if a lot of cops run in there and these guys are, like, woged?"

Nick shrugged. "They'll know when someone's busting in on them. They'll change to human form. So far The Icy Touch has kept to that part of the code. They show themselves to other Wesen—not to anyone else. Not that they're necessarily going to come along like good boys."

Monroe shook his head in disgust.

"Let's just move in on these guys. Hey—maybe I can provoke them and you can come to my defense? Like, 'We were driving by and saw them attacking this poor helpless citizen.'"

Hank snorted. "*No*, Monroe." He turned to Nick. "You're not going to play that game, are you? Because I'm already bothered we're skirting the law three or four ways on all this. We're holding stuff back from the feds. From the department. We need to do this by the book for once."

"She's a fourteen-year-old girl!" Monroe said, desperately. "They could be raping her right now!"

"*If* she's even in there," Nick said. "I know how you feel, Monroe, but…"

"No, Nick, you don't know."

"Well, then maybe you could tell me what happened, between you and the Perkins family."

"I…" Monroe swallowed. "…cannot do that. You're going to wait till tomorrow, really?"

"We have to. Unless we can get a raid organized tonight. There might be another judge available. I can call around."

Nick saw Monroe's Blutbad face come and go, as he struggled with his emotions.

"Okay," he said at last. "I'm… going back to my truck. Assuming it hasn't been stolen."

"I wouldn't assume that, around here," Hank said.

Monroe grunted in response. "Call me if you need me."

He got out of the car, and stalked away down the street toward Salem Boulevard.

"You think we should go after him, drive him to his truck?" Nick asked, looking after his friend. Monroe's anger and frustration was clearly visible in the way he was walking, his shoulders stiff as he marched along. Not good.

"Naw, let him walk, he'll cool off. No call back from Renard? Let's try Bernstein anyway, he might answer..."

"Hey bro," Monroe said, as the bushy-bearded Blutbad came out of the papered-up storefront. He glanced around, as if to make sure the cops weren't around, then flashed his Blutbad face at the guy. The bestial visage was there, and gone again, in a second. "You know where I can get any... work?"

"Why?" the Blutbad asked, stopping to look him up and down.

"Why do I need work?" Monroe replied. "I like to eat! I'm not a big eater but I do need to sometimes..."

"No, dumbass. Why you asking *me*?"

"Just heard... there might be some on this street. For us, I mean. Our people. Noticed a fellow Blutbad. Thought I'd ask." There was a scraping, rattling sound from overhead. Monroe glanced up. "You got birds up there, or something? Damned pigeons, right?"

"Why you care what we got up there?" Bushy-beard stepped closer to Monroe, squaring his shoulders.

"Me? I don't care. I just thought... you might know where there's some work. But... if you don't... Hey... that's a big whatever."

Okay, Monroe figured, the guy wasn't going to spill anything here on the sidewalk and he wasn't going to invite him inside. Maybe he could sneak around back...

The Blutbad just glared at him.

Monroe cleared his throat.

"All righty then. I'll get outta your fur, bro. Good hunting."

Monroe turned away, whistling "Werewolves of London"—then he heard a high-pitched squawk from above, a truly horrid sound like a seagull being crushed in a vice.

"Sure thing," he heard the Blutbad say—and suddenly Monroe felt himself grabbed by the back of his neck and belt, and shoved into the darkness around the edge of the storefront. The Blutbad heaved him hard face down, and Monroe slid in what felt like old broken beer bottles and gravel and, judging from the smell, dried up dog mess.

Well, that's just great.

He was woged and snarling as he rolled over on his back. The Blutbad stood over him, the thug's right side in silhouette against the partial light from the storefront, left side blending almost seamlessly with the darkness.

"I don't know if you can see this gun in my hand," the Blutbad said. "It's a Beretta .44. We decided you're going to be screened, pal. If you don't want a bullet in your head. You're Blutbad—and you're either snooping way too much, or you're just a stupid son of a bitch. If it's the first one, we'll kill you. If it's the second one, and if you're lucky—then you've been drafted."

"Drafted…" Monroe sat up slowly, leaning forward, getting his feet under him. "…into what?"

"The Icy Touch," the Blutbad said. "Only personally—I think you're too damn dumb for it. 'Specially as I didn't tell you to move. And you just moved."

"I did? Oh. So I did. But you know—it's pretty nasty on the ground here. I think there's dog poop. How about if I just… walk away." Monroe adjusted his crouching posture minutely, shifting his weight to the balls of his feet. He could see that nickel-plated .44 in the Blutbad's hand now that he was woged. His eyes were adjusting quickly. The Icy Touch thug held the gun out in front of him, just high up enough...

A rough cawing voice spoke from the roof overhead and the bushy-bearded Blutbad turned his head toward the sound.

"Get him inside," came the raucous voice.

Monroe had a half-second to act while the Blutbad was looking away.

He used it.

He launched himself forward with all his Blutbad strength and fury, springing hard and fast under the gun. It boomed over his back, the sounds of the shot echoing down the street, as Monroe slammed his right shoulder into the Blutbad's waist, knocking the snarling beast-man onto the sidewalk.

It was like wrestling a live power cable. The Blutbad writhed loose, rolling on top of Monroe.

But Monroe kept the roll going, throwing his weight to the left, biting the Blutbad hard in the bicep of his gun arm.

The Blutbad howled, wrenched free, and the gun went clattering away.

Monroe was on his feet, then, ready to jump at the Blutbad again, his blood up, his clawed fingers arched for ripping...

Then he heard a whirring sound, smelled that acrid stench again, turned to see a dark shape coming at him from above. A beaked nose ended in a sharp hook; two beady red eyes, small and unnaturally round, glared out of a demonically vulturine face.

Geier. Vulture Wesen, Monroe realized.

The Wesen was backlit, claws outstretched. But the bared feet of the creature came at him first, thrusting and ripping with heel-claws. Monroe felt a piercing agony in his stomach, as the talons ripped into him, and an unstoppable momentum slammed him back onto the sidewalk. The breath came out of him… and with it came blood, bubbling up hot and thick.

CHAPTER SEVENTEEN

"I don't see him, Nick. He must've gotten to his truck already."

Hank drove along Salem Boulevard, while Nick stared out the side window. The street looked deserted.

"Yeah. Maybe," Nick replied.

He didn't feel good about letting Monroe walk off angry. In this neighborhood, anything could happen.

There was that storefront Monroe had mentioned, its two front windows covered with brown paper, glowing sullenly from lights inside. He saw movement...

"Wait, Hank—hold on. Slow down."

Hank slowed. Nick stared. Two dark shapes stood over a third in the deep shadow to one side of the storefront.

"Pull up," Nick said. "No, screw that, just stop the car, draw your weapon, and get out."

Nick grabbed the flashlight clipped to the dashboard with his left hand, his right already opening the car door.

Hank went immediately into backup mode. He stopped the car and got out after Nick, his gun in his hand but held down at his side.

"You! Police officer!" Nick yelled, gun in one hand,

flashlight in the other. "Freeze right there!"

Nick clicked on the flashlight, spotlighting two strange figures standing over a man lying on the ground. One of the figures, Nick saw immediately, was a Blutbad; the other had blood-dripping hands, bare feet, a hooked beaklike nose…

Geier, Nick thought. A particularly dangerous Wesen.

The Geier was just picking up a nickel-plated handgun.

At his yell, the two Wesen turned toward Nick—the Blutbad snarled, and the Geier hissed and leaped straight upwards, grabbed the edge of the building, and swung up acrobatically onto the roof.

"Hold it right there!" Hank shouted—and snapped off a shot at the vulturine creature on the roof. The shot went wild and the Geier slipped back into the darkness.

The other Wesen turned toward Nick and hunkered down, ready to charge, in full Blutbad woge.

"Hold your fire, Hank!" Nick yelled. He put away his flashlight and gun and braced for the attack. They needed a live prisoner—someone they could question about The Icy Touch.

The Blutbad leaped at him and Nick jumped neatly to the right, let the Blutbad slam into the car door. Nick spun and aimed a wheeling kick at the creature, catching it in the ribs as the dazed Blutbad straightened up.

The Blutbad staggered under the impact, then got to his feet and launched himself through the air toward Nick.

Nick ducked down, letting the Blutbad pass overhead, then grabbed the creature's ankles before he'd struck the ground, flipping him over onto his back.

Nick turned and placed his boot on The Icy Touch gangster's neck.

"Don't move or I'll crush your windpipe."

The Blutbad lay very still and shifted back into human appearance.

"Kind of weirds me out when you move that fast, Nick," Hank said softly. "I can't quite see what you're doing…"

"Are you the Grimm?" the Blutbad asked, voice hoarse.

"Shut up," Nick said. He drew his gun and pointed it at the Blutbad, lifting his boot off the gangster's neck. "Turn over on your stomach."

The thug's jaw muscles worked, but after a moment he turned over and Nick handcuffed him.

He'd just snapped the cuffs shut and straightened up when he heard the crack of Hank firing his Glock. Something squawked in pain.

Nick turned to see Hank aiming up at the roof.

"Guy up there was pointing his weapon your way, Nick."

Nick nodded. "Thanks." He looked up at the roof. "You hit him?"

"Think so."

"Keep an eye on this one for me?"

"Sure." Hank came around the car, pointed his gun at the prisoner.

Nick took out his flashlight, and strode over to the figure lying in the shadows by the storefront.

It was Monroe.

Monroe lay on his back, limp, torn, inert. Blood was pooled around him.

"Hank! Monroe's down over here!" Nick called, rushing to his friend. "We need an ambulance out here fast! And backup around the building! Cars on the street behind it!"

"You got it!" Hank dragged the Blutbad to his feet and shoved him headfirst into the back seat of the car. Then he pulled the hand-radio from his belt and called in a request for backup and an ambulance.

Someone opened the front door of the storefront a crack and peered out, only a sliver of face visible. Nick opened his mouth to tell them to surrender, but the door slammed shut.

"Seems like probable cause to me," Hank said. "Guns out front. Man down."

"Hell yeah."

Nick knelt by Monroe.

"Hey, dude. You still with us?"

No response.

Monroe's eyes were closed. He was in his default human appearance. The blood had stopped flowing from his wounds but he seemed completely motionless and limp. Nick had a sickening feeling Monroe was close to death.

He sprinted back to the car, and Hank, anticipating him, opened the trunk. Nick grabbed the white plastic first-aid box, and raced back to Monroe. He was half expecting to be shot at from the roof or the front door, but he heard only arguing voices inside the building and, he thought, the sound of a girl sobbing.

He knelt beside Monroe, his knees in Monroe's blood, and popped the box open. His hands went expertly through the motions, improvising pressure bandages on visible wounds as fast as he could.

When he'd done what he could to stop the bleeding, Nick felt Monroe's wrist, and thought he detected a faint pulse.

"Come on, Monroe," Nick murmured, hoping for a response. "Hang out with us here, man. Rosalee's waiting for you. Don't bug out on me, man."

Still no response.

A patrol cruiser roared up and screeched to a halt, two cops jumped out. One of them was Officer Warren, a young black cop Nick knew pretty well.

"Warren! It's Burkhardt! Over here! Can you stay with Monroe here?"

"Yeah, detective, I got this," came the reply.

Nick stood up. He was so adrenalized and angry that he pushed past Warren, almost knocking him over as he headed to the front door of the storefront.

Nick pocketed the flashlight, drew his side arm, and banged on the front door with the muzzle.

"Police! Open the door!"

Silence.

He tried the doorknob. It was locked.

Nick stepped to the left, in case someone fired through the door, and waited.

Come on, you bastards, open up.

Still no response. Then he thought he heard a scrabbling sound.

"Nick!" Hank called. "Wait up!"

Nick saw that Hank was helping one of the uniformed officers transfer the prisoner to the patrol car.

They're getting away, Nick thought. *No time to run around the back. I'm not waiting.*

Nick stepped back, raised the gun in readiness, then kicked the door, hard, close to the lock. It smashed open, swinging crookedly inward. He scanned the room beyond it.

No one there.

It was a kind of improvised waiting room, with plastic chairs around the walls, and one lamp, a red-painted door leading beyond.

He stepped inside, swinging his gun to make certain the room was clear.

Nick continued onward to the next door, found it unlocked. He flung it open, revealing a long hallway stretching toward the back of the low building. To the left were four doors, all of them open. He rushed down the hall, gun at the ready, swung it into the nearest doorway, and saw a room with two sets of bunk beds. Empty. There was a girl's shoe lying on the floor, and a rumpled pair of silk underwear. Nothing else.

He hurried on to the next room, but found nothing but

cots, a smell of perfume, and some torn lingerie.

It was the same in the next two rooms. When he emerged from the last room, he saw an open closet across from the doorway—there was a raw earthy smell emanating from it.

He pushed through the door at the end of the hallway. It opened onto a small kitchen. There were liquor bottles on a kitchen table, partly drained. A few Styrofoam cups were scattered on the floor and dishes were piled in the sink.

The back door of the kitchen led to a stairway, up into the taller building behind the storefront. But he doubted they'd gone up there. They'd be trying to get to the street.

Then he saw the blood on the floor: a trail of scarlet splashes leading down a narrow hallway past the stairs.

Heart banging in his chest, mouth dry, Nick strode past the stairway, following the trail of blood toward a door at the back of the mold-reeking hallway. The back door was closed, and locked. He kicked it open and stepped onto a ramshackle back porch.

Someone lay on the ground, outside.

It was the Geier—the vulture Wesen—squirming in pain. Hank's gunshot had connected.

Beyond the injured creature was a weedy back lot, littered with empty bottles, and then the next street. There were no police cars there yet; no one at all except the Geier.

Nick approached the Geier, who had transformed back into a fairly ordinary-looking man, gaunt and bald. He clutched his wounded belly, eyes squeezed shut. The Geier wore a brown-leather jacket and jeans, no shoes. The nickel-plated automatic lay next to him. There was blood on the Geier's feet—Nick figured this was the one who'd wounded Monroe.

"Where are they?" Nick demanded, standing over the Wesen.

The Geier opened his eyes.

"You shot me," he said.

"My partner shot you, but I'll shoot you myself unless you tell me where the girls are. They were in there just a few minutes ago, right?"

The Geier's lips moved soundlessly. Then he managed, "Don't know... what you're..."

Nick holstered his gun and went down on one knee. He was literally seeing red—the air seemed suffused with a scarlet tint. This creature had attacked his friend, and Nick wanted him to suffer. He was surprised at the depth of his anger.

Nick grabbed the Wesen by the throat.

"Come on, tell me, Geier. You're dying—maybe if you do the right thing for once you won't go to Hell! Where are they? *Where did they take them?*"

"You're the one who can... go to Hell... Grimm..."

Nick lifted the Wesen up by his neck and slammed him hard onto the ground.

"Where'd they take them? Come on, the guy you just cut to ribbons is not going down for nothing!"

Nick slammed the Wesen on the hard ground again.

"Where are they?"

"Don't... don't..."

The red and blue lights of a patrol car, pulling up behind the building, flashed in Nick's peripheral vision. A car door opened, and police radio voices sounded. He ignored them.

"Where?" he demanded again.

The creature laughed wheezily at him, and he saw the flicker of its repellent Geier features.

Nick shook the Geier, hard.

"Where are they?"

The vulture Wesen gasped—and with that single gasp came a single word.

"Closet…"

Then blood streamed from the Geier's nose, he shuddered, and his eyes rolled back in his head.

As blood ran over his hands, Nick let go and jumped to his feet. He was distantly aware that the red rage had taken over—he was driven by the fury of a Grimm state he'd never felt before.

"Detective!" called the cop who'd gotten out of the cruiser.

Nick turned away, stalked back toward the building, muttering to himself.

"Closet. I'm an idiot. Walked right by it…"

"Detective, hold up!"

Nick ignored the officer and ran into the building, back through the hallway, the kitchen, into the storefront hall, and back to the closet he'd walked by.

An old dull-yellow piece of carpet was thrown sloppily over the back of the empty closet. Nick crouched for a closer look—there was dirt around its edges. He pulled the carpet away, to reveal a square of darkness, a large hole leading downward at a slight angle, past the concrete foundation and into the earth. He got his flashlight out, clicked it on. The dig-marks looked like Drang-zorn work and the dirt was dry, as if long exposed. Probably the tunnel had been here for weeks. He could just make out the petit prints of bare feet, and boot prints beside them.

"Nick!" It was Hank, calling from somewhere behind him. "You find something back there?"

"Yeah," he replied, "they bundled the girls out this way. They can't be far ahead…"

"Nick, wait—"

Nick vaulted into the hole, dropping to the dirt floor. A little dirt pattered down around him. He heard Hank telling a uniformed cop to look for the tunnel's egress.

Nick drew his gun, peering down the tunnel. The flashlight beam showed only a low passage, and, farther down, something glimmering in the dirt.

More earth pattered down around him, and Nick stepped out of Hank's way as his partner clambered down into the hole, cursing under his breath.

"New suit… brand new jacket…" Hank muttered.

He dropped beside Nick, dusted his hands off.

"Second damn time I followed you into a nasty old tunnel. But come to think of it there was that other time too—"

"Come on," Nick interrupted him.

Bent under the low dirt ceiling, the detectives followed the tunnel. After a few steps, Nick stopped to pick up the thing he'd seen glittering: a girl's charm bracelet.

They went about sixty yards, then came to an aluminum carpenter's ladder leading out another hole. Nick looked up as Hank crowded behind him. No one was visible up there. Just a soft yellow light past another old, cracked foundation and a crudely cut square in a wooden floor. They both listened. Nothing except, very distantly, a siren.

Nick pocketed the flashlight, and climbed the ladder, slowly. He held the gun carefully in his right hand, using the heel of his hand to help in climbing.

His eyes came level with the floor, and he peered cautiously over the edge, half expecting to get his head blown off. But there was only an empty room, dust whirling in the light from a naked overhead bulb. Blue paint was flaking off the walls. He climbed up the rest of the way, as quietly as he could. It was an empty bedroom in a decrepit old house.

Hank climbed up after him, gun in his hand.

"Glad to be out of there. Might've collapsed any time," he murmured.

Nick went to the hallway, stepped out gun first, swinging the Glock left and right. The hall was empty; the house was silent. There were dirty footprints on the floor, leading to the back of the building.

Out back, the two detectives found a gravel alley, a burned up '57 Chevy with missing wheels, tire tracks. No Icy Touch thugs; no girls.

Hank squinted at the ground.

"Truck was here recently, looks like. Maybe a cargo truck."

Nick nodded, feeling hollow.

"Yeah. Probably shoved the girls in there and… gone."

Hank got on a hand radio, called for backup, and put out a call for a large truck in the immediate area.

"That's all we can do right now," he said. "Maybe we'll get lucky. Or maybe they got the jump on us."

Nick looked at him. "How's Monroe?"

"On his way to North Portland ER."

"Anybody have an opinion on… Will he make it?"

"Ambulance jockeys said he had a pulse. Blood pressure was dangerously low. They were giving him plasma when the ambulance left."

Nick took a deep breath. "Blutbad are tough. But a Geier gouged him. Vulture Wesen. The guy you shot at… He went down behind the building…"

"I know. I saw the body. Perp is dead. Nick…" Hank cleared his throat and looked away from him. "They said you were, what, hammering the guy on the ground?"

"He was dying. You put a bullet in him. But… yeah. Could be I finished him."

Hank shook his head. "Doesn't sound like you."

"I… had to find out where they took the girls. He told me about the tunnel."

"Okay, but… Nick, in case you didn't get the memo,

the police department doesn't actually torture anyone for information. Take it easy, okay?"

Nick nodded. "I... wasn't thinking of it like that. Like torture." How had he been thinking of it? He didn't know, not right now. His head was aching, his mind full of what had happened.

"That's how it looked to the patrolman. He's already reported it. What happened to you back there?"

"I don't know. I guess... I'm more attached to Monroe than I thought I was. And maybe... maybe a Grimm is more instinctual than I realized. More driven by Grimm genes than I knew. It was like..."

He broke off as a patrol car bumped down the narrow alley, and pulled up behind the old building. Sergeant Wu got out, with a female cop, an Asian American Nick didn't know. She looked at Nick with cold disapproval.

"Nick!" Wu looked pretty uncomfortable. "What'd you find here?"

"Just tracks. Good sized truck. Tunnel in the building back there. They got away. Anybody stop a truck in the area?"

"Not last I heard."

Wu looked at Nick for a long moment, and finally took a deep breath and said, "Nick... I got a call from Lieutenant Jacobs. Internal Affairs. He wants you in his office first thing tomorrow morning. And—he says I've got to take your gun and badge. If you refuse, I'm supposed to put you under arrest."

CHAPTER EIGHTEEN

Nick knew Lieutenant Jacobs only superficially. He had a feeling he was going to get to know him a lot better now.

The Portland Police Department's Internal Affairs Officer had Nick's personnel files open on his computer. He was an older, heavyset, uniformed cop, an African-American with short white hair, a white mustache. He peered at the screen through small reading glasses. He was known to be a guy who did his job, and did it solidly, without being overzealous. He had a reputation for giving an officer on the street the benefit of the doubt.

But Nick had heard that once he pursued a bad cop, he kept going until the guy was either neutralized at a desk or fired.

Jacobs' forehead was crimped with worry, his lips compressed—making Nick suspect he was in trouble.

"You've got a lot of shootings, some kills, some unresolved issues here, Nick," Jacobs said, his voice a deep rumble.

"Shootings went through the routine investigations, Lieutenant. They were all cleared."

Jacobs continued to pore over Nick's personnel records. "Some of these cases... wow. You seem to get the crazy ones. Every time a crackpot sees a werewolf or something, off you go to check it out, huh?"

Nick chuckled. "Just kind of lined up that way for me. Roll of the dice. Mostly I pursue homicides, Lieutenant."

"Yeah. You have a good record of successful convictions. Lot of commendations. But all these shootings. And now this—interrogating a perp by cracking his head on the ground…"

"I didn't exactly do that. I got a little physical with him. But—there's good reason to believe a group of young women, including some teenagers, have been forced into prostitution. And it seemed urgent."

"So all of a sudden you're Dirty Harry? No, that doesn't fly, Detective. There were witnesses." He pointed his finger at Nick and peered at him over the top of his glasses. "And you were out of control."

Nick started to deny it. Then he thought about it a moment, and nodded.

"Yes I was, Lieutenant. But I don't think I killed him. He had been gut shot by another officer already."

"I've got the Coroner's report. They can't be *sure* but right here it says, there was a *good chance* the perp would have lived longer if you hadn't gotten rough with him. Maybe he'd have lived long enough to give some really useful evidence, you ever think of that? All you got from him was a tunnel that led to nothing."

Nick felt like he was sinking in quicksand. And it was his own fault for stepping into it.

"Yes, sir. It was bad judgment. Adrenaline and…"

What else could he tell him? *I'm a Grimm, and I don't have being a Grimm completely under control yet. There are Grimm instincts and they can really take a man over if he's not careful. Oh yeah, let me explain what a Grimm is, Lieutenant Jacobs…*

Yeah, right.

"Adrenaline's the classic excuse, Detective, and I know all about that. When I was a patrolman I fired my gun one time without intending to and the wrong person was shot. I was lucky he wasn't badly hurt. But this was something more than that, Detective Burkhardt."

"Yes, sir."

"I mean—you *shocked* some people who were watching you do this interrogation. And those officers don't shock easy."

Nick just nodded, and waited for the ax to fall.

"Detective Burkhardt, in light of this event and this long history of shootings—cleared shootings or not—" Jacobs glanced at his screen again "—in light of all that, I'm going to have to recommend you be put on suspension pending a full investigation. No gun, no badge. Detective Griffin and Sergeant Wu will take over your duties for now. Are we clear?"

Nick stood up.

"Yes, sir." He cleared his throat, to get the hoarseness out, and kept his face as emotionless as he could. "We're clear."

It was an overcast morning. Nick had slept badly, and was still smarting from his meeting with Jacobs. He was craving coffee as he strode into the hospital, but he had someone to see first. Rosalee had left the hospital room number on his voicemail. Ground floor, toward the back.

"Monroe?"

Monroe opened his eyes a crack, peered up at Nick.

"Hey, dude." His voice was weak, his face pale. His upper body was heavily bandaged and there was an IV tube in his left arm. "Like my new digs?"

Nick nodded, swallowing the lump in his throat.

"Private hospital room. You rate high around here, man."

"Yeah. I'm a big shot." He pushed a button to raise his bed up a little. "You find Lily Perkins?"

Nick shook his head. "Just—confirmed they were there. The gang got them out through a tunnel."

"Drang-zorn hole?"

"Looked like it. We're on it, Monroe. We'll find her."

Or rather *Hank* would find them. Nick was short a badge and a gun, for the moment. He didn't mention that fact. He didn't feel like laying that weight on Monroe right now.

"You come to say 'I told you so'?" Monroe asked.

Nick sat down in the chair by his bed.

"About what?"

"You guys warned me… to wait…"

"You did what you thought was right."

"I was just talking to the guy out front… kind of feeling it out. I didn't go busting in but…" He licked his lips.

"You want some water?"

"Yeah, thanks, Nurse Burkhardt."

Nick smiled, and poured some water from a plastic pitcher into a glass, handed it carefully to Monroe.

Monroe sipped. "You need me to testify?"

"We might."

"Rosalee doesn't want me to."

"I can understand that."

Monroe rubbed his forehead. "The drugs they got me on here, sometimes I worry I might—" he glanced at the door and lowered his voice "—I might woge. Like, in some hallucination. Some guys've been known to woge in their sleep. I never did. That I know of. But…"

"I checked with the doctor. You might not need the morphine for much longer. Good news is, you're… well, you've got tough stomach muscles or something. The Geier didn't cut as deep as it might've. Missed your vitals. It probably doesn't feel that way, but… you've got a good prognosis."

"Definitely doesn't feel that way. But I'm healing." He glanced at the door again. A nurse walked by, in a hurry, ignoring them. "It's a Blutbad thing."

Nick nodded. "I went to the trailer last night, looked it up. Book says Blutbad heal pretty fast."

"Not overnight. But faster than… I don't know about Grimms."

"Where's Rosalee at?"

"Went to get me something to eat that's better than hospital food. You're lucky she's not here, man. She's mad at you. She blames you and Hank for this."

"How's she figure that?" Not that Nick didn't blame himself. He should've made sure Monroe was safely away from Salem Boulevard.

"I don't know, dude. But she's pissed off. She might go all fox lady on you and give you a good nip in the ass."

Nick chuckled. "Sounds like you're on some pretty good stuff in that IV. I better let you rest. We're talking about putting a uniform on the door to keep watch on you. Got to clear it with the Captain."

Monroe shook his head. "That'd just call attention to the room. I don't think the scumbags are looking for me. Question is, bro—are they looking for *you*?"

"You're not supposed to be in here, you know," Hank said, mildly, as Nick joined him in the observation room.

"Just passing through the office. Captain asked me in to talk about what I could say to Internal Affairs…"

"And what you couldn't."

"Yeah. Mostly that. Waste of time. Already knew what not to say."

The hirsute Blutbad they'd taken into custody, who

said his name was Pete Hergden, was sitting sullenly in the interrogation room on the other side of the window. Now and then he glared coldly at the mirror he knew to be transparent from the other side.

"Furry without even being woged," Nick observed. "He's all beard and bushy hair."

"Yeah. You could make a nice coat out of the guy."

"Get anything out of him?"

"Nah. He claims he was just hanging around outside, hoping to score some pot from somebody in the 'hood, buy a joint or something. Then Monroe went off on him—like Monroe was on meth, he says. Claims Monroe knocked him down and some other guy he didn't know came along with a gun and a knife, and cut Monroe up and…"

"Really? *That*'s his story?"

"Sure. Denies being a sentry. Says he doesn't know anything about anybody on the roof, or anybody in the building. Claims he hadn't heard even a rumor about the girls."

"Not allowing polygraph?"

"You guessed it. Prints turn up some priors. Burglary, one assault. Nothing big. Ninety days in county, nothing longer. Probation's long done. Zip on his sheet about a connection to any cartel."

"Says he never heard of Icy Touch?"

"Says he heard it mentioned, doesn't know anything about it. I look at him, he looks at me. We both know he's lying." Hank shrugged. "Doesn't get us anywhere."

"He tried to jump me, that count for anything?"

"Maybe not—we were plainclothes, unmarked car. He says he didn't see any badges. Thought we were going to rob him. No one's going to believe he thought we were jacking him up, but, you know, once he's *in court*… what's the judge going to do?"

"Is he lawyered up?"

"So far just the public defender. If he gets some expensive mouthpiece out of the blue maybe we could figure out who's paying the tab. Doesn't look like he'll need it, though. We don't have much on him. And of course, he's talking about police brutality."

"What!"

"Oh yeah. Because you slammed him against the car. He says he wasn't going to attack you, he was just trying to scare you off. And after what happened to the other guy… the DA might swallow it. As far as Monroe's testimony— he's kind of fuzzy on what he saw. I figured maybe he doesn't *want* to testify…"

"I get the impression Rosalee doesn't want him to. Doesn't want to make him a target. Considering all that's happened…"

Hank nodded. "Yeah. Not sure he could make much difference anyway. It's his word against the other guy's."

Nick glanced at his watch. He had arranged to have coffee with Juliette.

"Think they'll come after Hergden in jail, like they did the Drang-zorn?"

"I don't know. Hergden seems more like an insider. Maybe they trust him. And they know we haven't got much on him. The unregistered gun, yeah—but can we really tie it to him? You found it on the other one. We can't even prove for sure those girls were in that building. Common sense, sure. Some clothing. But—proof? We haven't got any good DNA samples from anything. We don't have a lot to go on."

Nick snorted. "Look… you could turn off the tape recorder in there, let me go in, talk to him as a Grimm to a Wesen…"

"He knows you're a Grimm—he saw you in action.

I doubt you're going to scare this guy. He's much more scared of Icy Touch."

"Let me try."

Hank shook his head.

"Can't do it, Nick. I'm not sure even the Captain would be okay with that. Not till you get your badge back."

If he ever did get it back...

Nick nodded toward the Blutbad on the other side of the glass.

"I'd sure like to get him alone." Then he realized how that sounded. "I didn't mean..."

Hank looked at him evenly.

"Come on—you know what I mean!" Nick exclaimed.

"*I* know you're all right. But maybe you should talk to some old time Grimms. I'm serious. Get some... *advice*. Maybe ask your mom or something? Seems like maybe Grimms have to learn some self control. Just like a Blutbad."

Nick grimaced. "I guess."

"Just talk to her, Nick."

"But what's she going to tell me? 'Stay in control'?" He looked at the Blutbad in the other room. "I already figured that out. My gold shield is gone. I'm not a cop anymore." He went to door, and opened it. "So yeah, Hank. I got the message."

CHAPTER NINETEEN

"Detective? It's Wu. We think we found the truck they used to get the girls out of that building."

"Yeah?" Hank's fingers tightened on his cell phone. He had his other hand on the door of the interrogation room. "Where?"

Twenty minutes later he was driving up to the site of the abandoned truck in Southeast Portland.

It was a white cargo truck, parked crookedly—it had blocked half the narrow street. A thin afternoon rain fell over the two patrol cars securing the scene. An officer started to get out of a cruiser but Wu waved him away.

"We got this, Bill," he said.

Hank and Wu walked around back of the truck.

"Vehicle's registered to a rental outfit, in Beaverton—it was reported stolen two days ago. Patrolman found it open, empty, keys on the floor in the back. But look here..."

The two men climbed up in back and Wu pointed at the scratched white inner wall, near a back corner.

"You see that?"

Hank bent to look closer. Near to the floor, someone had written what looked like, "Lilyhelp" in lipstick and makeup. It was blurred, barely visible; looked as though the makeup had been wiped from her face with a thumb that she had then used like a crayon.

"Patrolman searching the truck noticed it," Wu said.

"Looks like the dope they had her on was wearing off, and she left us a message," Hank said, straightening up. "Smart patrolman. And smart girl. Smart enough to leave it in a spot where the creeps weren't likely to see it. But someone else might. Any fingerprints?"

"Some in the back. None that've turned up in the database yet. Maybe there's something to that idea of getting your kids fingerprinted in case someone snatches them. If I have kids, I'm going to get them fingerprinted, have their pictures on file, get their DNA taken, and maybe train 'em to use a shotgun too."

"Make it a Taser. You come home late sometime, they'll shoot you dead. Anything up front?"

"Haven't had forensics go over it yet," Wu said, as they climbed out of the truck. "Found some powder—could be that same stuff you guys turned up in the tunnel. Scopolamine, with the green specks in it. I sent it for analysis, we'll see. And... I kept this back for you..."

He took a plastic evidence envelope out of his pocket. There was a crumpled piece of paper in it.

"Only thing I found on the truck—it looks like they threw it out the driver's side window but it blew back, got stuck against the cargo container."

Hank took some latex gloves from his pocket, pulled them on, and removed the slip of paper. Wu held his hat over it to keep the rain off.

"Gas station purchase," Hank said. "And if I'm reading the time right—not long after Nick chased them out of that place on Salem. I'm gonna run this."

He returned it to the bag, went back to his car, and

called it in, with Wu standing at the open door.

It took about ten minutes to get the data back. The credit card number on the receipt belonged to a Roger Claymore. It was used at a gas station in Northeast Portland, near the airport.

"My guess," Wu said, "is they dropped off the kids somewhere and had to get rid of the truck. And it was almost out of gas."

Hank nodded. "Sounds about right. They drove it over here, abandoned it. Neighbors see anything?"

"No, it must have been dumped in the wee hours of the morning. Nobody but the raccoons were watching. I can never get much out of raccoons."

Hank looked at him and snorted.

"Okay, I'm going out to that gas station, see what I can find."

It was getting near dark by the time Hank got to the gas station.

The Mexican guy behind the counter shrugged, said he hadn't been there when the purchase was made and they didn't have a working security camera.

Hank returned to his car and drove around. He found a road that skirted the fenced off airport runways. Gigantic passenger jets flew overhead, looking low enough to scratch the paint on your car. He could smell the jet fuel. On the other side of the road were rows of warehouses, all of them shut down at that hour, and one out of business machine shop.

Dead end, maybe. There were those warehouses. But he didn't have enough evidence to get search warrants to go through them.

Eventually Hank drove back to police headquarters, tired, hungry, and wishing he could talk all this over with Nick.

* * *

The rain had cleared up but the wind seemed to think that meant it was time for its moment on the stage, and a north wind blew piercingly across Portland, as Nick arrived at the trailer the next morning. The sky was a destruction derby of racing clouds.

Nick looked around, to make sure no one was lurking about, before unlocking the door of the airstream trailer. When he opened it, the cold wind tried to slam the door against the silvery metal of the trailer's outer skin. Nick winced as it angrily banged it shut behind him when he stepped inside. He'd been feeling jumpy, since seeing Monroe lying on the ground in a puddle of blood.

He sat at the table, his hands on the Grimm books, but he didn't open them. He was thinking about his conversation with Juliette when they'd met for coffee yesterday. He'd tried to explain why he'd been suspended—he hadn't been quite ready to tell her just how his being a Grimm had figured into it.

"… and Monroe was sure this kidnapped girl was in this place and I told him he had to wait till we could get a search warrant. But he went off half cocked and tried to investigate it on his own… Got nailed by one of the thugs."

"Nailed? Oh Nick! They shot him?"

"They… stabbed him. But he's going to be all right. I'm sorry, I should've been clear: he's not going to die. At the time we didn't know how badly hurt he was and I got pretty mad. I caught the guy responsible… the others got away… and I felt like I'd let Monroe down and I couldn't find the girl… I guess I just lost it with the guy. I was trying to get him to say where they took the girls and…"

"What did you do, Nick?"

"I thumped his head on the ground. Kind of. And he did

tell me something useful but... Hank had shot this suspect earlier, and well... The guy died—while I had my hands on him. A patrolman saw me losing it with this perp and busted me for it. Which was probably the right thing to do. I can't say it wasn't."

"Hank had shot him? Maybe the man would've died anyway."

"Maybe. Coroner's not so sure. And it looks pretty bad, shaking a wounded man around."

"That just doesn't sound like you, Nick."

That was his moment. He could've spoken up. He could've been honest, told her about the Grimm factor. And how it could be driven by instinct, how it could bring up powerful feelings, at times overwhelming...

But she was already uncertain about him, after all they'd been through. He couldn't bring himself to give her another reason to leave him.

Maybe he *should* talk to his mother about all this.

What had happened to him out there was something primordial. Almost like the Grimm version of a woge.

He'd always thought of a Grimm as another kind of policeman. A cop for Wesen. But maybe he was just another kind of inhuman *creature*—as inhuman in his way as a Wesen like Monroe was in his.

Maybe he was no kind of cop. He had failed as a detective, failed to keep his cool on the job—and he was failing as a Grimm. The Icy Touch were out there, an organization of shady Wesen—the worst of their kind. He needed to stop them. But they'd slipped through his fingers.

And where was Lily Perkins now? What were they doing to her?

* * *

Hank Griffin felt somewhat jacked up after breakfasting on a double espresso and a large dark-chocolate brownie. Maybe that's what had pushed him into driving out to this godforsaken industrial zone, and around and around these warehouses.

No, it wasn't that. It was Lily Perkins—and the other girls, whoever they might be.

And it was Monroe. It was Nick getting suspended. It was how far these Icy Touch scum were pushing this town.

He turned a corner, drove by the shuttered metal shop, then slowed, catching sight of two men get out of a blue Lincoln Continental, half a block up. One of them had a pretty recognizable silhouette.

That beard. That bushy hair.

Hergden.

Hank turned left into a driveway between two warehouses. He didn't want Hergden to recognize him.

He stopped his car, jumped out—and shivered in the cold wind. He got a trench coat from the trunk of the car, pulled it on, then headed to the corner of the building and peered cautiously around the edge. He could see Hergden and a big bull of a man with red hair walking up to the door of a warehouse just down the street. The bigger man unlocked the door, while Hergden glanced around, to see if they were watched.

Hank drew back and thought about calling for back up, right now.

But he called Renard instead.

He got straight through to his boss. "Captain? Listen, I've got something out here—that area where they gassed up their truck…"

"Griffin? It better be something solid. Bloom's been on the phone to me. He's got word this kidnapping might be Icy Touch. He wants in on this. We need to make some progress before the feds take it away from us."

"This could be what we need. Did that Hergden character get released?"

"He did. After filing a police brutality complaint. We didn't have enough to hold him and the DA said he didn't want to follow up."

"I just watched Pete Hergden walk into a warehouse out here, with a big red-haired guy I've never seen before. Not three blocks from that gas station."

"We can set up a watch, but…"

"I need a warrant and I need back up, Captain. Right away."

Silence. Renard seemed to be thinking about it.

"I'll send out some back up. Give me the exact address. But the warrant, that'll need to wait till you find something more. Maybe if you scout the place out."

Hank ground his teeth. "Okay. But Captain—tell the patrol cars to stay off the street—they need to keep their distance till I give the word. Last time we spooked these guys and lost them." He gave Renard the address.

"Keep me informed, Detective. And keep your head down."

Hank clapped the phone shut and went back to the street. The two men had vanished into the warehouse. It was a one-story aluminum-sided place, neither big nor small, with construction material piled outside. Like someone was doing some building work inside.

Should he call Nick? He wanted to. But he couldn't. This wasn't a good time to call in the Grimm. Especially when the Grimm wasn't carrying a badge just now.

Hank crossed the street, the wind snagging at his trench coat. He buttoned it up, mostly to hide his gun, and hurried past the front of the warehouse that the Wesen had gone into. The place was windowless on the front and there were no business signs on it that he could see.

He sidled past stacks of empty paint cans, piles of torn out wallboard, and an aluminum ladder, and walked down the narrow concrete passage between the building Hergden had gone in and the one on his right, which bore a sign that said "North Portland Imports."

Hank moved as quietly as he could, listening. But he heard nothing but the wind whistling overhead.

He looked up, and saw a long strip of narrow windows well out of reach, stretching horizontally just under the roof overhang. One of the panes was slightly broken, in a lower corner. Brown paper blocked off the window from inside, like the storefront on Salem Boulevard.

Hank hurried back to the front of the building. He saw no one on the street, so he grasped the ladder, and, careful not to bang it on anything, he carried it back along the narrow alley. He set it up under the broken window, and climbed its rungs, trying to make as little sound as possible. When he reached the broken window, he pressed his ear to the papered-up section.

Nothing, for several seconds. Then… faintly… voices. A gruff man's voice.

And then a girl's voice. A fairly young girl.

"Don't, I don't need it—*don't*!" she said; her voice sounded genuinely distressed.

Close enough for a warrant, anyway, along with the gas receipt, and Hergden's being there.

Hank climbed down, wincing when the ladder squeaked, returned the ladder, and headed back to his car. He sat inside, and called Captain Renard.

"Captain? I've got something solid. Young girl in distress. Suspicious persons possibly connected to kidnapping and vehicular theft and the smuggling of…"

"Alright, alright, Griffin. Check your email in ten."

Hank hung up and waited impatiently, phone in one hand, checking his watch, knowing that the Captain had sent some patrol cars out and worried that some overeager rookie would run his siren and alert the gang.

Finally his smartphone signaled to tell him he'd gotten an email. He opened the message, and smiled. The warrant.

Hank backed onto the street, drove to the corner and turned left. He went around the block to where he found four patrol cars waiting, along with a van of vice officers just finishing putting on helmets and bulletproof vests.

Sergeant Wu emerged from a patrol car, returning Hank's wave.

A lanky guy with a blond crewcut nodded to Hank. Aaron Kasacki, the vice lieutenant.

"Detective!" he called. "We're ready when the warrant's here!"

"Already got it. Let's do this."

CHAPTER TWENTY

Standing in the alley across the street from the warehouse, Hank took the digital print out from his shirt pocket, unfolded it, and looked at it again.

It was a photograph of Lily Perkins.

He shook his head, thinking of this young teenager in the hands of these monsters. Not Wesen monsters—he'd come around to Nick's viewpoint, that Wesen differences were sometimes monstrous, like the *Jinnamuru Xunte*, the flylike Wesen who'd temporarily blinded Nick, but others were just people with unusual characteristics. Maybe Wesen weren't exactly human. But they were still people.

No, these guys would be monsters whether they were ordinary humans or not. The Wesen element just made them much trickier to apprehend. And maybe lethal to handle.

He folded the picture up, checked the straps on his Kevlar vest, and spoke into the radio on his shoulder.

"Okay, Lieutenant, let's do this. Just remember, speed matters. These guys have a tendency to use tunnels to escape. We don't know where those tunnels are and where they go, so we need to catch them before they can use one."

"Copy that, Detective. We're moving in."

Moments later a large police van pulled up in front of the warehouse. The van was unmarked—they were going for a "jump out" style raid.

The back of the van popped open, and Kevlar-strapped officers with handguns, helmets, and headsets jumped out, and lined up to one side of the warehouse's front door. Both hands on his semi-auto pistol, Hank hurried over to join them as an officer tried the door. It was locked.

Lieutenant Kasacki nodded to a powerfully built officer carrying the big metal handheld battering ram. The officer slammed the bazooka-shaped steel ram into the door close to the knob and the door flew inward.

The Lieutenant shouted, "Portland Police! Stay where you are!" as the officers streamed into the building, with Hank just a few steps behind the leader.

The door opened into a lobby done in red velvet, with several red velvet plush chairs, presumably for waiting customers.

Hank figured none of the Icy Touch thugs would be woged—they wouldn't risk that in front of a phalanx of police officers. And by now they must know that cops were raiding the warehouse.

He followed the lieutenant and two other officers down the hallway at the back of the lobby. Immediately Hank saw Hergden ahead of them, running away at the other end of the hall, his distinctive bushy hair bobbing as he went. The officers with Hank were already rushing through a side door off the hallway—they'd seen the girls in there.

Hank shouted, "Hergden! Police! Stop!"

Hergden partly turned as he ran, and fired a random shot down the hall with a big revolver. Hank moved to the side and the bullet hummed passed his right ear.

Hank paused, then fired back, aiming carefully and using only two rounds, afraid he might accidentally hit one of the girls. The bullets from his powerful police handgun could punch right through these thin walls.

Hergden was hit, stumbled, then fired again, the shot going into the floor. He fell on his side, doubling up, groaning, then he tossed the gun aside.

"Don't shoot!" he grunted. "I'm not going anywhere!"

Hank moved to him—saw the injured man half woge into a growling wolflike face for a moment, maybe in sheer pain and fury. Then the Blutbad suppressed the woge, gritting his teeth, squeezing his eyes shut.

Hank picked up the discarded revolver and glanced behind him to see if Hergden's shot had hit anyone. Sergeant Wu and the other officers were ushering two girls out of one of the rooms. No one seemed hurt.

He turned back to Hergden.

"Where are the rest of the girls, Hergden? And where's the tunnel?"

"You shot me," Hergden groaned, sounding amazed.

"Yeah. Where's the..."

"Detective?"

Hank turned to see the lieutenant coming toward him. Kasacki opened his visor, revealing a grin.

"We've got the girls. At least some of them—maybe all. And I think we found that tunnel, too. It's another closet setup. The other suspects seemed to have busted ass like rats down a hole already..."

A uniformed African-American female hurried down the hall toward them. She had a stethoscope around her neck and carried a large red and white medical kit.

"Man down?" she asked.

"Suspect, here, took two rounds," Hank said. "I'd like to cuff him if you okay it."

She went down on one knee and examined the now-limp form of Hergden.

"You won't have to, Detective," she said after a moment. "Two hits, one up pretty high in the rib cage—doesn't look like there's any point in trying to resuscitate."

They didn't have a warrant for the adjacent buildings but they had probable cause to follow the tunnel back.

Hank broke out his flashlight. He and Sergeant Wu shared a look of resignation as they approached the tunnel.

"Not this again," Hank murmured. Peering into the opening, he could see the tunnel was pretty poorly shored-up. Nodding to Wu, but wishing it was Nick and his finely honed Grimm instincts following him into the hole and not the sergeant, who knew nothing of the real dangers that lurked inside, Hank climbed down the ladder and began to walk along the grimy passage. Wu shuffled along behind him.

The narrow way soon broke through a curved concrete wall and they found themselves in a large drainage tunnel, full of old silt deposited on the floor by a shallow green stream.

Wu hesitated, looking at the ground.

"That's weird," he said.

"What?"

Wu laughed softly. "Those tracks look almost like hooves. Like someone was really *hoofing* it."

Hank realized he couldn't let the sergeant come any further, not without telling him about the Wesen. And he couldn't do that, not without speaking to Nick.

"Yeah—um, Wu, how about if you head back, get some patrol cars looking wide through the area. Maybe someone can figure out where this tunnel comes out."

"Good call, Detective. You'd better not follow this thing back yourself..."

"Right. I'll be up there pretty soon."

Hank didn't like misleading Wu, but he felt he had no choice. Plus, he'd noticed another track near the hooflike mark. It was the footprint of a girl's shoe.

He was fairly certain the Icy Touch gangsters had taken at least one of the girls with them. It didn't matter which one.

Sergeant Wu went back up the tunnel. Hank stayed, thought about it for a moment. Once again wished he had Nick with him.

This, right now, would be a really handy time to have a Grimm around.

He shook his head and started down the drainage tunnel.

The dripping, cracked ceiling was barely an inch over Hank's head; though he tried to stay quiet his footsteps alternately clacked and squished on the muddy edges of the tunnel floor. Hank walked on about fifty yards, came to a turn and halted; he heard the echo of unintelligible voices. He switched off the flashlight, pocketed it, drew his gun, and craned to look around the corner.

Standing in a pool of light about thirty feet ahead, two figures were at the bottom of a ladder. One was climbing quickly up; the other, with a silhouette almost like a two-legged bull—reminding Hank of a minotaur—was looking up, waiting for his turn.

Hank stepped into view.

"Police! Hold it!"

The minotaur turned, and roared, its guttural voice booming up and down the tunnel. Half bent over, the Icy Touch Wesen charged toward Hank, like a bull charging toward a matador.

Hank raised the pistol, started to shout a warning—the Wesen wasn't showing a weapon and Hank was reluctant to just open up on him. But the creature came at him so quickly, before Hank could pull the trigger he was past Hank's gun muzzle, and on him, driving him back.

Struck in the lower chest, Hank felt like he'd just been hit by a car. He found himself skidding backwards on the slimy floor, water sloshing over the shoulders of his trench coat.

Another perfectly good coat, ruined, he thought dimly.

The breath was knocked out of him and the dark tunnel seemed to spin around the looming outline of the Wesen. But Hank still had the gun—he raised it and fired. The muzzle flash lit a snarling bestial face, exposing a flattened nose, red eyes, downturned bovine ears, and horns.

Mordstier, Hank remembered. He'd seen the entry in one of Nick's Grimm books.

Hank could see blood along the creature's side—his bullet had torn into the Mordstier's shirt, slicing along the ribs.

Hank raised up on an elbow for a better shot—but suddenly the creature was gone, hooves clacking as it moved away.

Hank got to his knees, sucking his breath through his teeth, pain shooting up his side. Seemed like he had a cracked rib.

He struggled to his feet, pushing the pain aside, and moved to the corner just in time to see the Mordstier's bare feet climbing the ladder into the ceiling... The Wesen had shifted back into human form.

"Stop!" Hank shouted, limping closer. But the Wesen climbed out of sight—and before Hank could reach it, the Mordstier was drawing the ladder up after him. Then the light from above abruptly cut off, and Hank was in deep darkness.

Cursing, he got the flashlight out, and directed it upward to the hole in the ceiling.

A wooden trapdoor blocked the exit.

He turned away, and sloshed back to the other tunnel. Remembering that girl's footprint in the mud...

CHAPTER TWENTY-ONE

"Maybe you're the one who should be in a hospital bed," Nick said, as he and Hank walked down the hallway to Monroe's hospital room.

Nick had seen Hank grimacing with pain.

"Rib's just cracked. Not a big deal."

"Hurts like a bitch though, I bet," Nick said, remembering some of his own injuries.

"You win the bet."

"So, no prisoners to interrogate."

"Nope. One shot dead, the others got out. I guess four in all. I had a bullfight with one. And the matador lost."

"The girls been… used by customers?"

"Nah, we got there soon enough. But they weren't much help. Too out of it on that stuff. But we lost the Perkins girl… The other girls said two of these creeps took Lily into the tunnel."

"Why her?"

"Seems like one of the bigshots came around and took an interest in her."

"Crap. Not going to be good, telling Monroe we lost her."

"We'll get her back."

But Hank didn't sound convinced.

Nick knocked on the door to Monroe's hospital room.

Rosalee answered. "Nick! And Hank." She didn't seem terribly happy to see them. She looked at Hank. "You okay?"

"Just a little bruised. Maybe from having to spend a lot of money on dry-cleaning. How's Monroe?"

"See for yourself."

She opened the door for them, and they found Monroe fully dressed, muttering to himself as he packed a small bag.

"Should I take these hospital slippers with me or not?" he said.

"Hey Monroe," Nick called.

He glanced up at them. "There they are. And I don't see good news in those eyes. Please tell me I'm wrong."

Hank shook his head. "It's bad—with some good. Bad news is, Icy Touch still has Lily Perkins. Good news is—we got the others out. And we rolled up that operation, at least for now. Seized a lot of that Seele stuff."

Monroe closed his eyes. "She wasn't there?"

"She was the only one they took with them when they got out," Nick said. "Somebody in the organization took a fancy to her. Maybe that'll keep her safe for a while."

"I'd guess that's not much consolation for her mom."

"No. It isn't. I'll find her, Monroe," Nick said.

"We'll both find her," Monroe said.

Nick looked at him questioningly. "You look better, but…"

"Nick?" Monroe zipped his bag shut and turned him a look that fairly throbbed with emotion. "We. The term is *we*. As in you and me, Detective Burkhardt."

Hank shrugged. "Maybe working outside official channels, you guys can do more than the PD can…"

* * *

Burkhardt... .

Kessler.

There it was. The Icy Touch's documentation on Grimms made the lineage quite clear...

Denswoz leaned back in the leather chair of his den in the Red Lodge, and looked at the family tree for the descendants of Johann Kessler. There were some question marks on the breakdown but what he needed was there. Kelly Kessler had married a Grimm named Burkhardt. Her whereabouts were unknown. But it was she who'd taken the Coins of Zakynthos to other Grimm for safekeeping.

Denswoz grinned at that. "A safe deposit box is really not terribly safe, Mrs. Burkhardt," he murmured.

It was late, and he had been tired, thinking of going to bed. But not now. Now he was energized. He'd been coached by his father about the ancestral vendetta against the descendants of Johann Kessler.

More than once they'd struck down members of the Kessler family. One, he remembered, had been fed to a Spinnetod in London. And then there was another encounter, in the following century. Berlin...

He scowled, remembering that story. Only a partial victory...

So. Kelly Kessler was the mother of Nick Burkhardt, the most troublesome detective in the Portland Police Department. Not only was he related to the Kesslers—Detective Burkhardt was a Grimm.

He heard footsteps outside the door; a soft, familiar knock.

"Come in."

Malo opened the door and entered pushing a disheveled, dazed teenage girl ahead of him. The teenager's wrists were cuffed behind her; there was duct tape over her mouth. She looked around the book-lined den, her reddened eyes finally resting on the ornately barred windows.

"You wanted to see the Perkins kid?" Malo asked.

"Yes. Is she the only one we got out?"

"Afraid so. And Grogan was lucky to get her out. Just her and a couple of our sentries."

"Burkhardt was in on the raid?"

"Nope, Burkhardt's on suspension. It was his partner. The black dude, Griffin. And he was the one asked about the girl, too, when they detained Hergden."

Denswoz nodded thoughtfully. First had come indications that a Wesen connected to Burkhardt had a special interest in this girl. Then Hank Griffin had asked Hergden about the Perkins girl *specifically*. If she was of interest to Burkhardt and Griffin, she was a valuable lure. Denswoz was glad he'd told Grogan to make absolutely sure she was kept out of police hands.

"Keep her under lock and key, downstairs," he told Malo. "Remove the gag and the cuffs, feed her. See she's comfortable but quiet. She'll prove valuable yet…"

He looked the girl over. *Seele Dichtungsmittel* had glazed her eyes—but there was a glint of defiance there, too.

She was a strong one. And that was good.

When it came time to kill and eat her, that would make it all the more delectable.

CHAPTER TWENTY-TWO

About four in the morning, Renard gave up trying to sleep. The greatest challenge of his career was out there in the world, just beyond his reach; The Icy Touch was humming in the darkness like some sinister dynamo, and he didn't have a handle on it. Sleep wasn't an option tonight.

He got out of bed, put on his bathrobe, went to the kitchen. When he turned on the lights the room seemed too bright to his tired eyes, at first. Beyond the window, a distant siren sang mournfully. He might get a call about whatever that was about...

He unlocked the drawer that contained his Hexenbiest essences. He wasn't as up on Hexenbiest "potioning" as most. As he took out the relevant bottles and small jars of rare herbs and dried fungi, he thought wryly that maybe he had half the expertise because he was only half Hexenbiest.

But was there such a thing, really, as half a Hexenbiest? When he woged, he was full Hexenbiest. And the potions seemed to take shape under his fingers with an instinctive, intuitive ease.

Renard quickly concocted the fatigue neutralizer, and drank it down. He felt himself woge as it hit him, his face contorting. He let the woge take its course, for a moment, his back arching with the energy of the transformation, combined with the power of the potion. Then he shook himself and shifted back to ordinary human appearance.

He needed to stay calm, to think…

He made himself a cup of green tea, found some scones, and took this light breakfast into the extra bedroom he used as an office when he was at home.

He sat at the desk, his nervous system buzzing with the Hexenbiest remedy, and his mind riding a white-water course of possibilities. He switched on his computer and checked the time in Europe. Lunchtime in France, now— maybe it was time to talk to Beatrice. Would she feel safe talking on the phone? Probably not. Not the usual way.

He went into his files, looked at the information he'd taken from the last time he'd seen his second cousin in Paris. Where was the code? There it was, in both English and French: *"C'est très jolie après* the wind musses your hair."* Franglais. Nonsense.

He opened his cell phone, and sent her the message as a text.

Then he sipped tea, nibbled scones, and waited.

Just as he was about to call the department to check on major cases, his phone chimed:

"Oui, pour l'éternité," the message said.

He activated the webcam on his computer, and the encryption program. Then he spoke, "Beatrice. Encryption."

He waited.

Another full minute. Then Beatrice's face appeared in a window on his monitor. Her dark blond hair was up in fringe braids and her skin was the color of a well-stirred latte; she had her mother's almost catlike green eyes; she wore a diamond stud in one nostril, and her luscious lower lip was also pierced. She was a lawyer, an assistant prosecutor in Paris—and a Hexenbiest. Even on webcam she looked enticing. It was strange, when she woged from this beauty to Hexenbiest "deformity". But perhaps even stranger, Renard reflected, was the fact that a Hexenbiest couldn't see anything deformed in the contorted witch manifestation. To Renard and other Hexenbiesten, both appearances were beautiful, seductive.

"Sean! It's good to see you," she said in French. "Are you well?"

"Yes and no. Your transmission is fully encrypted?"

"Yes, of course." She sighed with comic theatricality. "I hoped you were calling to flirt with me, but I doubt you would bother to concern yourself about encryption for flirtation."

He smiled. They were cousins but that hadn't stopped them having a fling, five years back. And it had been intense—until their intimacy had been discouraged by the Royals.

"Why do you think I live way over here, Beatrice? It's safer with an ocean and a continent between us. I have only so much willpower."

She laughed. "I'll pretend to believe that bullshit."

"You feel comfortable speaking freely about those friends of yours you told me about?"

"Gegengewicht... ?" She gave a French lilt to the German term for the secretive Wesen organization that worked beyond the reach of the Verrat and the Royals.

"The same."

She nodded. "What's happened?"

"You know about The Icy Touch?"

Beatrice hesitated, a hesitation prolonged even more by intercontinental lag.

"I've heard. Rumors. Some say they are Wesen."

"I can see they've got even you spooked."

"Even me? Lots of people!"

"And the Verrat? They don't think this cartel could be destabilizing for Wesen, to say the least?"

She gave her best Gallic shrug. "They seem to be in denial that Wesen are significantly involved. Some of them don't believe the cartel exists. Some of them… I don't know."

"You think there are Icy Touch agents infiltrating the Verrat?"

"If Icy Touch is indeed a Wesen organization—I suspect it. We haven't confirmed they are Wesen. They're very secretive. And any time that secrecy seems threatened…"

"Someone disappears or someone dies."

"Or both. What have you found out, Sean? We need to know. If the rumors are true, then Wesen of conscience need to stop The Icy Touch—but the Verrat won't move. And this is exactly why Gegengewicht was created! Philippe knew this sort of thing was coming. There are hints that the crime cartel is just the beginning. That it's just a way to finance a bigger agenda."

"I wondered about that."

"There's something else—did you know that the Coins of Zakynthos have once more been stolen?"

A sick chill went through Renard.

"No. I didn't know that." That news gave him a dizzying mixture of feelings. He'd been addicted to the coins, at one point, and altered by them. He had found himself going megalomaniacal, intoning veiled threats in a news conference, under their influence. He'd been relieved when the coins had been taken from him… and at the same time he'd felt wounded at their loss.

"They were in a safety-deposit box," Beatrice said. "Someone in the bank… we think someone under the influence of a Hexenbiest drug… may have taken them."

"A Hexenbiest drug. Soul Sealant?"

"*Seele Dichtungsmittel*, yes."

"We believe Icy Touch is using it right here in Portland. They're using scopolamine—that's not necessarily Hexenbiest. But there are herbs in it associated with Hexenbiest potions."

"Still—that's not proof. But if *La Caresse Glacée* is using the Sealant…" She shook her head, and nervously licked her piercing. "That's very bad. And if they also have the coins…"

Renard nodded. "Exactly. Does your organization have any documentation on The Icy Touch? I mean—not just rumors, or police records. But… anything internal? Something with names?"

"We have exactly one piece. A letter. A man calling himself *Poigne Fermé*. Not a real name obviously. We think it's a name he used when helping form *La Caresse Glacée*— but we're not sure this is about The Icy Touch. We only suspect it. We have a scan of a… it's something like a memo. All their communications since have been encrypted, or destroyed after reading, so far as we can find out."

"Can I see this memo?"

"I'll have to ask Philippe."

Philippe. Renard had never met the alleged leader of Gegengewicht; he didn't even know his last name. After a few glasses of wine Beatrice had once hinted that Philippe was a Blutbad who had some sort of religious conviction— and out of this conviction came a belief that not only were Wesen to be protected from humanity, but good Wesen must protect ordinary humans from the darker Wesen. He had been known to work with certain Grimms, it was said, but didn't trust most of them.

And Philippe, the putative head of Gegengewicht, was as hard to find in person as anyone from The Icy Touch.

"Will I ever meet this Philippe?" Renard asked.

"That depends. Do you wish to join Gegengewicht?"

Renard chuckled. "I think not."

He had so many entanglements with the Royals and Verrat he could hardly swear loyalty to an organization that was so shadowy and independent from them.

"But… perhaps your Philippe, and your other associates… perhaps we can all help one another. A temporary alliance. You could speak to them for me."

"Would you give your word that any interaction with us is confidential to the point of, well…"

"You're not going to go all thirty-third degree Freemason on me, are you?"

She smiled. "We aren't Masons. They don't even know we exist. But… we do swear oaths upon fear of death. As the highest levels of Masonry do."

What was one more oath? He'd sworn many. This was already life or death. In time, The Icy Touch would come for Sean Renard, and they would not care that he was a police captain. They would "invite" him to join them— and they would not take no for an answer. He had to destroy them before they destroyed Portland—and before they destroyed him.

He nodded. "Record my oath, and show it to Philippe. And speak for me. I have known all this time about Gegengewicht. I never went to the Verrat or the Royals with the information."

"Philippe would say, not that we know of! But very well. I am recording."

"I, Sean Renard, on pain of death, swear that my alliance with Gegengewicht will be discreet, that nothing I learn about Gegengewicht will be placed in the public record, offered to police authorities, given to the Verrat— or to any of the Seven Families."

She nodded briskly. "Good. I will consult with him right away, if he is available…"

She broke the connection, and he waited.

He ate a little more, drank tea, and waited. He stared at his cell phone, then the computer. Still no response.

After forty minutes his patience gave out. He considered calling her back, but decided not to. Instead he showered, shaved, dressed, and drove to police headquarters, arriving just after seven. He had been at his desk for ten minutes when he got her text.

It's coming encrypted. Can you access, where you are?

He responded in the affirmative.

Will send as attachment. Destroy utterly after reading. Use tagged computer cleanse.

Within a minute, he received an encrypted attachment on his work email. He decrypted it. It was in French. He read it swiftly.

My Wesen Brothers and Sisters

We are reborn. We are reborn in our renewed determination. We are reborn in our renewed vision. We are reborn in ruthlessness in the service of our kind. We of dualistic biological nature are more than Homo sapiens; *we are twice human. We are twice in power, twice in soul, twice in sapience. Our senses are keener, our loyalties deeper.*

The time of global reckoning is nearly at hand. The time of righteous revenge comes as surely as a storm sweeps across the sea.

We will need all our strength, all our objectivity. We are badly outnumbered. But other resources can be ours: Infiltration, and gold.

Infiltration will in time give us information and the safety of camouflage. Gold will buy weapons; gold buys politicians; gold buys power.

Gold buys an army.

We cannot wait. There is no time for conventional economics.

We will take what we need. We will sell addictive poisons to Homo sapiens; *we will sell their children; we will twist their arms and wring gold from their clenched fists...*

We must be willing to do whatever it takes.

I am your brother. I am,

Poigne Fermé

Renard sat back, stunned by the boldness of it. *Gold buys an army?*

He almost felt drawn to the thing himself...

He chuckled and shook his head. He had chosen another course. He would go his own way.

But there was only a reputed connection between The Icy Touch and this *Poigne Fermé.*

If this the memo *was* about The Icy Touch, then it was imperative that they be stopped at any cost. Because what The Icy Touch intended would destroy either humanity— or all Wesen. And blood would run in the streets.

Pondering, Renard looked out the window of his office, saw Sergeant Wu striding past. Wu nodded to him; Renard nodded back.

Then Renard made up his mind. He sent a quick encrypted email to Beatrice.

Going to need more help, when things come to a head. Gegengewicht in USA?

After a few minutes, she responded.

Yes, some of us in USA too. But as to more help— under advisement. I am told: "Perhaps and perhaps not." We need more data, proof that The Icy Touch is truly Wesen and as widespread as you say. The memo does not directly refer to The Icy Touch. May not indicate that

The Icy Touch is truly dark Wesen.

Renard grunted. Proof? Could he risk sending them internal police reports? And the FBI data that Bloom had given him? If he was found out, he could be prosecuted...

Anyway, there was no proof in those reports that The Icy Touch were Wesen.

But without Gegengewicht who could stop The Icy Touch? The feds? They knew too little about what was going on. And for the sake of decent Wesen the feds had to be kept in the dark.

Round here, there was only himself, really, unless you counted that annoying Blutbad, Monroe. And then there were non-Wesen. Like Hank Griffin...

And one relatively inexperienced Grimm...

Nick jogged along the gray sidewalk, under gray skies. As he ran, he glanced repeatedly over his shoulder, half expecting a van to pull up, maybe with a window rolled down. Some Icy Touch sharpshooter suddenly firing out the window...

He was on suspension, now. There was no Hank to cover him. He wasn't even sure he could call for back up. And he didn't have his police-issued Glock on him. He had a Smith and Wesson at home, of his own—and a concealed carry permit. Maybe he should...

His cell phone rang, just as he drew up in front of his house. Breathing hard, he looked at the screen. He didn't recognize the number, but answered anyway.

"Burkhardt."

"Mr. *Nicholas* Burkhardt?" came a rather crusty voice. Sounded like an elderly man.

"Nick Burkhardt, yeah. Who's this?"

"Nicholas, my name is Chance Weems. I was a friend of your father, Reed, and your mother, Kelly."

Nick blinked. "Weems? I... I don't remembering hearing the name..."

But then again, he hadn't heard that much from his parents. He'd been raised mostly by his Aunt Marie after the car accident that killed his father—the accident that appeared, for a time, to have also killed his mother...

"Nicholas—I have information about your father and mother that you should know. Vital information."

Nick hesitated. Who was this guy? He could be working for some enemy of his mom's.

"What information would that be, Mr. Weems?"

"I am not at liberty to say on the phone, Nicholas. You know that your father and I used to fly kites together?"

Nick was startled. Nick had flown kites with his father as a small boy. Dad had been a member of a kite-flying club. Not many would likely know that.

Still—why should he take a chance on this, right now? It could easily be a set up.

"I'm not sure I'm comfortable meeting you, right now, Mr. Weems. My life is in kind of a holding pattern. I'm dealing with some issues at work. I can give you my office email..."

"No emails, Nicholas. This has to be in person."

"Then it'll have to wait." Nick glanced up and down the street—and saw an old white van coming slowly his way.

Lots of those kinds of vans in town. It was nothing.

But all the same he went quickly inside the house, still talking on his cell phone.

"And—let's say just say, Mr. Weems..."

Nick closed the front door, looked through the blinds. The van drove by, a long-haired guy at the wheel bobbing his head, singing along to something on the radio.

"Let's just say I'm avoiding situations where there are a lot of unknowns."

"We can meet in a public place. There's a roadhouse, out on the Columbia. Place called 'Joey's River Snag.' Do you know it?"

"I've driven past it. That's a ways out of town..."

"If you're worried about problems here in town—might be safer there."

"I didn't say I was worried about..." He blew a long breath out between parted lips. "Okay. But... I'm going to need a little more to go on here, Mr. Weems."

"I have information about how your father died."

"I'm pretty sure I have a handle on that."

Who was this guy? Another Grimm?

"You only know part of the story, Nicholas. Tonight, Joey's River Snag. Let's say eight o'clock. They have a fine venison stew there. You're buying."

Weems cut the connection.

Nick frowned, and headed upstairs. Before hitting the shower, he went to get his personal handgun from the dresser drawer. He took the Smith and Wesson out, and laid it on the bathroom counter by the sink, close to the shower door.

Keeping the gun in reach of the shower? I'm getting seriously paranoid.

He was just pulling off his sweatshirt when the phone clipped to his sweatpants chimed again. He saw the office number, and answered it.

"Captain? Internal Affairs make up its mind?" he said.

"Not yet, Detective. Just a second..." He could hear Renard get up, close his office door. His voice, almost a whisper, he said, "The coins. They've been taken again."

"The coins? Oh. You mean... *our* coins?"

The Coins of Zakynthos.

"That's right. We don't know who's got them, but there's reason to believe it might be The Icy Touch."

CHAPTER TWENTY-THREE

"I'm just—I'm getting antsy, that's all."

"Everyone gets antsy when they're convalescing, Monroe."

"I'm not convalescing, Rosalee. I'm *fine*, just a little… Kinda…"

"A little cranky, is what you are, besides still wounded. And you're convalescing till the doctor and I say you aren't."

Drinking cocoa, bundled in coats and sweaters, they reclined in lounge chairs on a redwood porch hoping the late afternoon drizzle would let up.

"It was almost sunny, about three," Monroe groused. "I thought for sure the clouds were going to bust out with some sun. But then the sky says, 'Naw, let's give 'em some more drizzle.'"

They were staying at a friend's vacation cabin out east of Portland. Monroe's pal Carson was a fellow fanatic about clockwork, and, in Monroe's terminology, "all things that go clickety click." Carson was more about clockwork dolls and automatons; the cabin was eerie with machines that turned their heads and watched you whether or not you wound them up—Carson had them set up with motion detectors to scare burglars.

"Am I ever going to meet Carson?" Rosalee asked.

"Well, not right away," Monroe said, leaning forward to squint at the sky beyond the porch roof. "Carson doesn't even know we're here."

"Monroe!"

"It's okay, he gave me a key, said anytime I wanted to go out here it's cool with him. I don't have to ask permission. He's down in San Francisco half the time anyway. That's where his main collection is."

She frowned, and he could tell she wanted to head him off from talking about clockworks.

"Is he Wesen?" she asked.

"Yep. He's Eisbiber."

"Oh, I like Eisbiber! They're sweet."

"I'm sure they'd like to show you how sweet they can be."

She laughed. "I'm not into them that way. I'm more of a Blutbad girl."

He looked at her with his eyebrows raised.

"You sure you wouldn't just up and give me the old heave-ho for a hot Fuchsbau dude? I mean—what would your family say if you told them you were dating a Blutbad?"

"They wouldn't like it," she admitted. "But Jewish girls date Goyim sometimes and Fuchsbau date Blutbad, and who cares. They can lump it."

Monroe checked his phone yet again, hoping maybe he'd missed a text from Nick.

"Where *is* he?" he growled in frustration. "Nick was supposed to call me. I was kind of thinking of getting you to drive me over to the trailer…"

"You're not going anywhere today. We'll see how healed you are tomorrow."

He pointed a finger at her. "You didn't answer the first question, missy. I mean—I've got to say, I've wondered if some kind of, what, primordial Fuchsbau instinct could draw you to a good-looking Fuchsbau over me, sometime."

"Are you serious?"

"Kind of."

She shrugged. "Of course! When Fuchsbau mating season comes, anything could happen!"

Monroe was appalled. "Fuchsbau *mating season*?"

She laughed. "It's always mating season for a Fuchsbau. I'm *kidding*, Monroe."

"You had me going there. Wait—it's *always* mating season, even right now?"

"Not for you, mister. You're wounded. You're not going to be using those muscles for a while. You want some more cocoa?"

He sighed. "Yeah. Extra marshmallows."

"Okay. Then I'm going to make you that tofu veggie stir-fry you like for dinner." She got up, then turned to him, brows knitted. "Monroe—Nick and Hank can get in touch with you, can't they? And we can call them if anything happens?" She looked out at the fringe of woods past the back yard. "I mean, it's not like we could explain it to a nine-one-one operator." After a moment, still scanning the woods, she murmured, "I feel kind of vulnerable out here."

"Don't worry, got 'em both on speed dial. Good cell phone service out here, phone's all charged up."

"Okay." She kissed him on the cheek and went into the cabin.

He snorted. "Cheek kisses. That's what I get."

He took out his phone again. Why not call Nick right now?

He hit the speed dial for Nick, and waited.

The phone rang, and rang.

Finally the answering service came on. He waited for the beep and said, "Nick? Call me, will you? I need an update…"

He hung up.

Nick wasn't working. What was he doing that kept him from answering the phone? Maybe he was caught up in a private moment with Juliette.

Or maybe not.

Some Blutbad intuition stirred in Monroe, then. He felt a piercing pang of worry about his friend.

Nick? Are you okay?

Nick pulled up on the road's shoulder across the highway from the bar. He cut the lights and the engine, and looked the place over. Last time he'd driven past the roadhouse, months ago, it had looked like it had gone out of business. It didn't appear much livelier now.

Just fifty yards from the broad dark sweep of the Columbia River, the roadhouse was a one-story rectangular building with a false front of half-logs to give it a frontier appearance. It looked run down, paint peeling, the neon Heineken sign in its only window brown with dust. But there was a bigger sign on a pole that was lit up against the night sky, "Joey's River Snag." The sign flickered, and the "N" on "SNAG" went out.

Nick snorted. *S AG.*

There were lights in the curtained window, too. And when he switched off the engine and opened the car door, he could hear Hank Williams on a jukebox. He couldn't see any cars in the gravel parking lot—wait, there was one, a white vehicle of some kind parked around back, on the Columbia River side.

Nick checked that his light-weight polymer S&W was loose in its holster under his coat, and waited as a lumber truck rumbled by, its headlights seeming to turn and take him in as it came around the curve. As it passed he could smell the fresh cut fir strapped to its trailer.

He angled across the highway, heading to the right side of the building, hurrying so he was less likely to be a handy target from that front window. Maybe this guy Weems was on the up and up. But it seemed a pretty big coincidence, this old friend of his parents cropping up just when the Icy Touch trouble was going down.

Nick ignored the front door and headed for the one in the side of the building. His shoes crunched across the gravel as he approached it. He reached for the doorknob... then heard someone walking up behind him.

He spun, and saw an old man with a sparse white beard, a red windbreaker, and a white golf cap.

"I'm Chance Weems," the old man said. He grinned, snaggled teeth, and stuck out his hand.

"You move quietly, and fast," Nick remarked, as he took the man's hand.

Then his Grimm insight showed him Weems' true face. He was a Hundjager.

"You're Wesen!" Nick blurted, starting to pull his hand back.

But Weems gripped it, hard. It was Nick's gun hand and Weems held on tight—and grinned. He woged.

Nick twisted his hand free, reached for his gun—he heard the door to the bar opening behind him. He started to turn toward it.

But he never got completely turned around.

Something heavy hit him the side of the head, hard.

He staggered, then he was struck painfully in the chest... and his back arched as electricity coursed through him.

Taser.

He was in a shining white emptiness. He heard three tentative heartbeats—and his vision faded in.

He was lying on his back, with three Wesen standing over him. Two were Hundjager—Weems and a taller, leaner man in a tailored suit. The leering Hundjager beast-face sprouted out of the suit jacket—a Hundjager with a red silk tie—like something from a bad dream.

The third Wesen was almost a Minotaur. He was a Mordstier, complete with stubby horns, flopping bovine ears, a bull's muzzle, and red eyes.

Weems had Nick's gun in his hand.

"Tell you something, Grimm," Weems growled, pointing the gun at Nick. "I *did* know your mama. She tried to kill me—I got away by the skin of my teeth, but she did kill my son. Seems she objected to something in our diet." He turned to the taller Hundjager. "Denswoz—you promised me I could feed on his flesh."

"You will, when the time comes. After I'm done with him," snarled the Hundjager in the finely tailored suit. He turned to the Mordstier. "Grogan—take care of him. We're too out in the open here."

Nick tried to get up but he was still half paralyzed. The Mordstier dropped his knee on Nick's chest, pinned him down, squeezing the breath out of him. There was something shiny in the Mordstier's inhuman hand—Nick tried to knock it away, but Denswoz, growling, stamped his boot down on Nick's wrist, holding it down, so that the Mordstier could drive the syringe home.

CHAPTER TWENTY-FOUR

Trooper Virgil Vallen was patrolling the I-5 south of Roseburg, wondering when they were going to get around to changing his shift. He'd been almost three years on this night shift. He had commendations. He'd *earned* a day shift. It had been promised to him. But he was still out here on the freeway at close to eleven p.m., wondering if his wife was sleeping okay without him. Marlene was getting hung up on sleeping pills lately.

Vallen had trouble sleeping himself, on this shift, and he was feeling it. Maybe stop for some coffee... At least the rain had let up...

A car whipped past him in the fast lane. Toyota Camry, looked like, heading south—doing at least eighty-five. He glimpsed a male driver.

Fast lane's not quite that fast, pal.

Vallen hit the lights and siren. He floored the accelerator to catch up with the Camry. At first he thought the guy wasn't going to stop and he radioed Trooper Garcia for back up.

"You close, five-seven? I'm just passing the first truck stop south of Roseburg."

"Copy, Virgil. Coming north, less than two miles out."

"Hold on, he's signaling and slowing—looks like he decided to pull over... Be good if you swung by anyway."

"Copy, roger that. Got to get to an overpass..."

The Camry cut so sharply across lanes to the right road shoulder, once more Vallen thought the driver was going to run for it. But the vehicle fishtailed to a dusty stop in the gravel of the shoulder. The car still had its engine on.

Vallen pulled up behind, not too close, pretty sure this driver was out of it. He could be panicked by the police, could be on meth—or something else. He could be dangerous.

He wondered if he ought to wait for Garcia, but the guy in the Camry might flip out and take off during the wait.

Vallen slowly got out of the State Police patrol car, drawing his gun but keeping it low at his side. He approached the car close to its driver's side rear fender, so the driver wouldn't have an easy shooting angle on him.

Two cars drove by, and a semi truck. He could feel the wind of the truck passing. To his right was a shallow ditch with a little running water, and a big, dark field of sedge. Way, way off in the distance were the lights of houses. It was a lonely place on a dark road.

"Sir?" Vallen called. "Can you cut your engine?"

No response. Tailpipe was still spewing exhaust.

"Sir! Cut your engine!" Vallen called louder.

The engine cut. The driver rolled down his side window.

"I have to go," the driver shouted, in accented English. Latino guy.

"You'll have to wait here, sir!"

Vallen returned to his patrol car, holstered his gun, and called in the Camry's plate. Driver was listed as "Santiago Mendoza." Naturalized United States citizen. And... there was a warrant out on him. He was wanted by the FBI for questioning.

Vallen was glad to see Garcia pull up close behind.

"Virgil? Anything I should know?" Garcia radioed.

"Yeah. APB on the guy. Feds want him for questioning. Mexican cartel connections. Naturalized citizen, Latino. Maybe you can talk to him better but he seemed to understand me when I told him to turn the engine off."

"Copy. You want me to come up on the right side, or you want to wait for more back up?"

"Let's see if we can do this. You take the right."

The troopers got out of their vehicles, and Vallen waited for Garcia to come up on his right. Then they approached the car, guns drawn and ready, safeties off. Vehicles whisked by. Vallen could hear a big truck coming up behind.

The two officers stopped just behind the Camry.

"Mr. Mendoza!" Garcia called. "Keep your hands where we can see them, make sure there's nothing in them, and get slowly out of your car!" He repeated the message in Spanish, loudly over the sound of the approaching semi-truck.

"I have to *go!*" the driver wailed. "Icy Touch! *Hombre bestia!* I can't stay! They are coming—"

Something loomed on Vallen's left, gray metal too close for comfort, and he stepped reflexively to his right.

It was as if a giant hammer had slammed into the Camry. A semi-truck without a trailer, as big a cab on it as he'd ever seen, crunched into the Camry at the driver's side door, slamming it at a sharp angle and ramming it across the shoulder. With the Camry pushed lower, half into the ditch, the semi-truck rolled up on top of the Camry, as if it were part of a monster truck show, crushing it, almost flattening it.

Vallen could see blood squirting through a break in the roof of the car.

The truck kept going, into the wet, shallow ditch, water spraying under its wheels, bouncing when it hit the rise of the field, veering out of control—then flipping over on one side.

Vallen stared in amazement at the smashed car, the overturned truck.

Smoke suddenly billowed up from the crushed Camry.

Both troopers turned and ran toward Vallen's cruiser, crouching behind it just in time to hear the Camry's gas tank explode.

Vallen stood up. Flame streaked from the Camry, licking toward the gray sky; smoke billowed to veil the overturned truck.

The two men gaped at each other, Garcia shook his head.

"Holy shit," he said.

They'd come so close to being run down. And the driver, Mendoza, was flattened. Had to be dead.

What was it he'd said?

"They are coming."

Vallen shook his head, laughing softly in disbelief.

The two troopers turned to stare at the overturned semi. The door turned to the sky was open.

It hadn't been a few moments before.

Was that someone running off into the darkness, beyond that barbed wire fence? Vallen wondered. Then the smoke drifted over his view again.

"You see somebody out there?" Vallen asked, nodding toward the field.

"No. Even if I did…"

"Yeah. I'll call this in. Get some firetrucks out here and… Let's wait for back up."

Garcia, staring out into the darkness of the field, just nodded.

* * *

Renard was still in his office, working late, when the text came from Beatrice.

Check email.

He quickly hit refresh on his email, and an encrypted message from his cousin appeared.

He typed in the new password—a mix of Latin and Greek—and read:

> *Sean*
> *Philippe convened the Gegengewicht committee. There is much skepticism. They cannot believe The Icy Touch is truly accomplishing all you claim. Not everyone is convinced the cartel is Wesen. They assume "a few Wesen members." But this claim that it's all predatory Wesen is hard for them to swallow. They need more proof. Something official. Everything you can give us. We will be careful with it.*
>
> B.

Renard clacked the computer mouse on his desk in irritation.

He deleted the message, then picked up his cell to make a phone call.

"Don Bloom here," the FBI agent said crisply.

"It's Sean Renard at Portland PD," Renard said. "Sorry to call so late"

"It's all right, Captain. What can I do for you?"

"First of all, anything new on The Icy Touch?"

"One gangster from the Shadow Heart bunch— *Sombra Corazón*. Guy named Santiago Mendoza. Staties picked him up heading south. We had him on a watch list, State Trooper busted him for speeding. Seemed kind of panicky. Called in his plates and we told him to hold the guy."

"Where was this?"

"Near Roseburg. Mendoza tells 'em he can't stay, someone's after him. Says *Icy Touch*. Says *bestia hombres*, 'beast men'—sounds like that druggy myth stuff going around about The Icy Touch, right?"

"It kind of does," Renard said. If this kept up, Bloom might start suspecting it was more than mythology.

"You have this Mendoza in custody, Don?"

"Nope. That's the bitch of it." Bloom told him the story about Santiago Mendoza's death.

"Crap," Renard muttered.

"Indeed. They're crushing people with semi-trucks right in front of troopers. It was dark out there. There's smoke, then the truck starts burning—the troopers get firemen out on the freeway. When the fire's out... they can't find anybody in the truck. No one! They searched the area. No one around. Just some tracks in the field by the road—too messy to get much from them."

Some Wesen move fast, Renard thought. *Very fast.*

Aloud, Renard said, "Weird. Sounds like whoever it was had to be following this Mendoza in the truck, planning to take him out."

"Yeah. The semi-truck was stolen. No prints. I was about to send you a report. Story's going to be up on the news in the morning. Some of it, anyway. Clearly these bastards have big plans—just wish we knew what the Hell those plans are. They're thorough—they go for the pre-emptive strike when it comes to keeping people quiet."

"About reports—you gave us a pretty good selection on putative Icy Touch activities. But—it's mostly American stuff. We sure could use some background on their European activities. France, say."

Bloom chuckled. "You got wind of a... what was that movie? A French connection?"

"You could say that. Maybe if you've got a friend in the CIA... ?"

"Were you going to share this connection with us?"

"Just something one of the girls heard—the ones we got out of that warehouse out by the airport."

"Well—send me a report. And I'll see what I can find for you. First thing tomorrow. Right now, I've got dinner with some colleagues over here to get to."

"Tomorrow's fine. Thanks, Don."

Renard hung up and stretched. He was hungry and fatigued himself. But he lingered at his desk, thinking.

Whatever the feds might have on The Icy Touch in Europe, it wouldn't directly prove the Wesen connection to Gegengewicht. But maybe there were dots they could connect for themselves.

Still—how could they help him bring down The Icy Touch... Unless someone found out where the Icy Touch leadership was?

Maybe Burkhardt had made some progress on that.

Renard put in a call to the Grimm, and got his voicemail. He left a message.

"Detective, this is Renard. Call me back, ASAP."

Burkhardt. Why aren't you staying in touch?

CHAPTER TWENTY-FIVE

Nick sat on the edge of his cot, started to look at his watch, then remembered it was gone. They'd taken it away along with his gun and wallet and belt. He had no idea what time it was, or how long he'd been unconscious.

The headache was fading—the coffee helped, though it felt like a burning acid in his belly. He hadn't eaten any of the scrambled eggs and toast on the tray he'd found when he'd come to. The sight of the food made him feel sick.

He got up and walked across the brick-walled, windowless room and tried the door again. The heavy steel door was immovable; the lock felt unbreakable. He had nothing to pick it with, not that picking locks was one of his Grimm skills anyway. He wished he had Monroe here—he'd be a natural lock picker.

But then no reason Monroe should die in this place too.

He looked at the dishes and cutlery still on the tray by the door. Stuff was all plastic. Nothing to pry the door with; nothing that would make an effective weapon.

For the fifth time in the last half hour he paced the cell. It was about thirty by thirty-five feet, and contained only a wooden-framed cot, a pitcher of water, a stained toilet, and a sink. The toilet was the kind you saw in airports, with no tank, its pipes going into the floor. There was a blurred set of initials scratched into one of the bricks above the toilet. Someone else had been held here. He looked at the initials again. *L.P.*

Lily Perkins. Where had they moved her to?

Was she dead?

He heard footsteps; saw a shadow at the narrow rectangular space under the door where they had pushed through the tray.

Nick stood, bracing himself, hoping for a chance to rush whomever opened the door.

What about the cot? Wooden frame. Break it up, use pieces for a club. Maybe…

But there was no time for that now. The lock grated and the door creaked open, swinging outward.

Nick found himself staring down the barrels of a twelve-gauge shotgun and an AR15 assault rifle.

"If he so much as twitches," Denswoz said, "blow his head off."

The two Wesen keeping Nick covered were in human form just now; they were muscular, swarthy men wearing jeans, sweatshirts and Kevlar vests, standing to either side of Denswoz. Their weapons never wavered. Nick's Grimm senses told him that one guard was Hundjager, the other a Königschlange—possibly the one who'd killed the Drang-zorn witness.

Denswoz was also in human form. He smiled urbanely, arms crossed over his chest. Just behind Denswoz was the Mordstier, woged. Grogan wore no shoes in his Wesen form. No need when you have hooves.

When he spoke, Grogan's rough voice was barely understandable.

"You cops like putting people in cells," Grogan said.

"How you enjoying this one?"

"Not up to my standards," Nick said.

Denswoz chuckled. "That's it. Keep your spirits up."

"Where's the girl?" Nick asked.

Denswoz shook his head. "Not your business. Not that it matters what you know. It must have occurred to you that since I'm showing you my face... well..."

Nick nodded. "It occurred to me. You're pretty confident you can keep me here."

"I can keep you till you're dead, and torn to pieces, and eaten, and digested."

Nick frowned thoughtfully. "Seems to me most Hundjager don't eat human flesh. The better class of Hundjager wouldn't approve."

"They'll all join us, in time," Denswoz said nonchalantly. "Or we'll kill them."

"You have plans for me, I'm guessing, before you get to the killing and eating?"

Denswoz let his smile fade: his face became stony, his eyes flinty.

"My people... my family... has long had plans for you, Nick Burkhardt. They've had plans for you since the time of Napoleon Bonaparte."

That caught Nick off guard.

"Since Napoleon's time? That's thinking ahead."

"They've had plans for every member of your line, Burkhardt. One of your ancestors... another vile Grimm... committed a crime against one of mine, Alberle Denswoz. Alberle's son swore an oath to punish your family. Destroy it, if he could. Each of his descendants has sworn the same oath. And we have hunted and killed your family ever since. When we have destroyed you, and your mother—I do believe that will end your line of Grimms. You see, my name is Albert Denswoz. I am Alberle's direct descendant."

"I see." Nick's mouth was very dry, all of a sudden. His mother. Denswoz would go after Kelly next.

"Just to make absolutely certain," Denswoz went on musingly, "we'll have to kill your girlfriend too. Juliette is her name, yes? On the off chance that she's pregnant."

Nick tensed—he was close to lunging at Denswoz.

Juliette.

He saw the eyes of the shotgunner narrowing; the one with the AR15 leaned forward, very slightly.

"They're within an eyelash of opening fire, Burkhardt," Denswoz warned. "Don't be foolish. I have plans for you. Please don't spoil them."

"Okay," Nick said, forcing himself to smile. "There are other options, though. You could surrender to me."

Grogan laughed—a kind of bovine coughing sound.

"I have done what I came here to do," Denswoz said. "It is part of my family tradition to inform you scum, before you die, that you are being destroyed as a result of our oath."

"And what was the great crime my ancestor committed?" Nick asked.

"There were several crimes. The murder of Alberle Denswoz. The mutilation of his son. The theft of objects sacred to us."

"Objects…"

Denswoz smiled mysteriously. "Objects which are at last back in our possession. But the crime goes unpunished— until you and your kind are wiped out. Of course, all Grimms will be exterminated, when we're done. But you being a descendant of Johann Kessler—you must die a particularly slow and memorable death."

"Naturally," Nick said calmly. "A sadist loves a rationale for cruelty."

The Hundjager's eyes widened, his hands balled into fists.

"You will not provoke me. I am not the fool you are.

You came into our arms with charming alacrity."

"I knew something was up," Nick said. "I figured it might be a trap. But—here's an old Grimm expression for you: Sometimes, in order to find out where the wasp nest is, you have to kick the tree."

"Won't do you any good, coming here," Grogan rumbled. "And you don't know where you are anyway."

"Chances are," Nick remarked, glancing around, "I'm still somewhere in Oregon. Near the Columbia."

"How'd he—"

"Shut up, Grogan," Denswoz said wearily. "He *didn't* know it. I don't suppose it matters, but—information hygiene in all things. That's our way."

"The Icy Touch's way," Nick said. *"La Caresse Glacée."*

Denswoz sniffed and waved a dismissive hand.

"All will be clear quite soon. Better eat those eggs, Detective. Probably your last meal."

Denswoz stepped back and murmured to the Mordstier, who slammed the door shut with a resounding clang.

The locked turned, and Nick thought ruefully, *I'm not really making a lot of progress here.*

CHAPTER TWENTY-SIX
BERLIN, GERMANY
DECEMBER, 1936

"It seems foolish to move the coins," Jonathan Kessler said in German, as his fellow Grimm worked the combination lock on the office safe. "Suppose we're stopped? The Gestapo have been putting up checkpoints."

"Only within a certain distance of the Reichstag," Berg replied, flicking through the combination that Kessler had given him. "I doubt there'll be one around here. It is the security of this building that worries me. And if Berlin is bombed…"

Kessler reached into his coat, drew out his pocket watch. It was two-ten in the afternoon.

"We must hurry."

"Yes, yes… I got one of the numbers wrong… Let me start over…"

Hans Berg was a young man, no more than thirty, with prematurely thinning blond hair, a long nose to go with his long face and long pale fingers. He was thirty years Kessler's junior, but prone to imagining himself in charge. Like Kessler, Berg wore a heavy overcoat over his suit. The heated room was too warm for their attire, but they intended to leave the building quickly as possible and it was snowing outside. Kessler wore a gray fedora; Berg had a damp woolen watch cap half stuffed in a pocket.

Berg swung the door of the floor safe open, and swiftly began to search through deeds and other church paperwork in the safe.

"The envelope is marked with two circles…" he muttered.

Kessler glanced at the window but there was nothing to see there since he'd pulled the shades. They were in the office of a Lutheran church, behind the chapel. It had been thought that no criminal would bother to break into a minister's safe. The Coins of Zakynthos should have been safe here. But there were rumors that Rudolf Hess was searching for "occult" artifacts and now the decision had been made to move the coins out of Berlin.

The Lutheran minister who officiated at this church was a Grimm—usually the only Grimm in Berlin. At present he was off in Bavaria searching for a certain Hundjager, one he said was "particularly vile." The Reverend Scheller was one of those Grimms who believed that all Wesen should be exterminated. Kessler didn't share that view. But Scheller believed all Wesen demonic; he clung to the old ways.

"Here they are," Berg whispered at last, taking a manila envelope from the safe. He opened it and peered inside, his voice tremulous. "Yes. They are here."

He began to reach into the envelope, and Kessler grabbed his wrist.

"Don't touch them."

Berg glared at Kessler. "The coins don't affect Grimms."

"We're not sure they *never* affect Grimms. The coins are dangerous." Kessler took the envelope from Berg and resealed it.

Berg frowned. "They're dangerous for humans—and Wesen. Not for us."

"The coins are dangerous in other ways," Kessler said.

"For all humanity." He closed the safe, and removed his hat, wiping sweat from his forehead. "If it were up to me, they would be melted down. Destroyed."

Berg's frown deepened. "That could be dangerous in itself. Who knows what would happen if that were tried?"

Kessler replaced his hat on his head.

"They could be sealed in lead and dumped in the deepest trench of the sea. But they should not be where men can get them, no matter what. Napoleon himself misused them." He folded the envelope as small as he could and put it in the inside pocket of his overcoat. "If Hitler got hold of them…"

"They've been used by Wesen—so we need them for Grimm studies," Berg said stiffly. "Herr Kessler—I think you should give me the coins to carry. I am a younger man. Stronger. If we have to run…"

"Don't be absurd," Kessler said. "You are no stronger than I."

The two men left the office, relocking it and going down a hall to the back door. Outside, they paused to look around, blinking in the sudden afternoon light; the snowfall had stopped, and the sun had broken through the clouds. The streets were slushy with wet snow. A delivery truck swished by, sliding a little as the driver fought to keep it on the slippery road.

The lot back of the church was a garden, right now mostly covered in snow; withered brown plants poked through the white covering here and there. Feeling exposed, Kessler led the way along the snow-encrusted path to the street where his silver-painted touring sedan was parked.

"I hope to buy a motorcar soon myself," Berg remarked wistfully. "But, I am a poor lawyer, taking clients I should not take. You, however—a professor must make a good living, to have such a fine motorcar."

"I am no longer a professor," Kessler said. "Eighteen years was enough. And when I inherited my father's estate, I retired. I write papers, I research our… our undertaking. This is my life now."

"Ah. Your father's estate." Berg's bitterness was quite unveiled; he looked as if he'd sunk his teeth into a lemon. "My father killed himself when he lost his business. He left me nothing. I am a poor man."

Kessler remembered Scheller had told him that Berg had a bad gambling habit. Perhaps that was the real source of his poverty.

He unlocked the car and they got in, Kessler nervously starting the vehicle before Berg had even closed his door.

The wheels spun in tractionless frustration for a few moments, and then they gripped the road and the low-slung sedan swished along the slush-filled street with the other cars. Kessler drove past row houses and a beer hall with a taxicab parked in front of it, and then he turned left at the corner.

Not far down the street, three men in long gray Gestapo winter coats had set up a checkpoint beside a large black car, half blocking the road. Behind them stood an SS soldier with a rifle. The Gestapo were checking papers, talking to the driver of a bakery truck, their breath steamed in the cold.

It was too late to turn around now—the Gestapo was looking for someone, perhaps the so-called anarchists Hitler was worried about, and they would pursue in their state-issued black car if Kessler suddenly swung the car about and tried to avoid the checkpoint.

Heart banging in his chest, Kessler looked for a place to pull over. Perhaps he and Berg could pretend they were going somewhere on the street, and wait out the checkpoint. They could act as if they planned to visit one of the lodging houses here…

"Give me the coins," Berg said suddenly. "They will more likely search the driver. Quickly!"

"What? That's not so! If they choose to search at all, both of us will be searched."

"I was to take them, anyway, Herr Scheller told me so," Berg asserted.

Kessler glanced at Berg—he could see he was lying. He'd sensed that Berg was hiding something earlier, and here was an outright lie—Kessler was never wrong in recognizing a liar.

As the delivery truck was waved through, Kessler pulled over in front of a lodging house, as if parking. But they were too close to the checkpoint, and seeing them the tallest of the Gestapo men, in an officer's cap, scowled and gave an order. Another officer and the SS soldier with the rifle strode over to Kessler's car, gesturing for him to roll down the window.

Kessler smiled in a puzzled sort of way as he complied. He kept the touring car's engine running.

"Yes, gentlemen, can I be of assistance?" he asked politely.

"You do not wish to pass through the checkpoint?" said the officer, with a pronounced Austrian accent. He was a tall man with a jutting chin, high cheekbones, and ice-blue eyes.

"Checkpoint?" Kessler replied easily. "No, no, we have no problem with checkpoints. I am simply planning to visit a *lady* at the lodge here. My young friend has not had much experience with women. I believe she will be of service to him."

The young SS soldier leered at that, but the Gestapo officer didn't seem convinced. He scowled—and then Kessler saw it.

The bestial face emerged, for just a moment. The officer was a Hundjager.

The SS soldier saw nothing of this since the officer had not woged.

The Gestapo officer bent over slightly and looked through the window at Berg.

"Your name, and identity papers, please."

"My name is Mueller," Berg said. "I am... *Otto Mueller.*"

Kessler looked at Berg. Otto Mueller? He hadn't mentioned using such a cover name.

The Hundjager officer stared at Berg, his eyes widening.

"Mueller? I did not expect you to be with anyone else!"

Kessler suppressed a gasp. The Hundjager had been waiting for someone going by the name Mueller. And Berg had given that name. Therefore...

He reached down to put the car in gear—but then Berg put the muzzle of a Luger against the side of Kessler's head.

"I am sorry, Herr Professor," Berg said. "But I must have the coins. I have made an arrangement. Herr Hess has offered me a great deal of money. You knew where the coins were; I did not. I am afraid I forged the coded letter..."

Kessler let out a long sigh. The letter had come through the mail, stating the coins must be removed to a safer place. He had a tendency to trust other Grimms implicitly. But they were prone to human failings like anyone else.

The Gestapo officer smacked his hand on the roof of the car.

"If you have the package, give it to me now!" he demanded angrily.

"I shall hand it over to Herr Hess personally, as arranged," Berg said. "That is Herr Hess's wish."

The officer grunted, and straightened up.

"Then take it from him, and come out of the car." He turned to the soldier. "Take this 'Herr Professor' prisoner."

"Kessler!" Berg snapped. "The envelope! Now!"

Kessler reached into his pocket, took out the envelope

with the coins—and tossed it into the back seat.

As he'd hoped, Berg turned to grab at the envelope, looking away for a moment. Kessler's Grimm reflexes came into play and he wrenched the gun from Berg's hand, turned it about and fired the Luger at the officer and the soldier, two shots, all in less than a second.

The bullets struck both men, hitting each one consecutively in the forehead, and they fell back, dead as they hit the snowy ground.

Kessler thrust the gun into his coat, put the car in reverse, slammed on the accelerator, and backed up down the gutter, splashing slush.

The men remaining at the checkpoint shouted. As Kessler shifted gears and spun the wheel, one of the Gestapo fired a gun—a pistol by the sound of it. A bullet pinged off one of the touring car's fenders.

Kessler accelerated as he turned the car to head back off down the street, ignoring Berg—who was ducking down beside him, shouting for him to stop.

I should kill him right now, he thought.

And then he heard the car door open and, turning his head, Kessler saw Berg had the envelope with the coins in it—and was leaping from the moving car, shouting, "Don't shoot, don't shoot!" at the Gestapo. Berg cried out in pain as he struck the road. "No!" he cried out, "I have a package for Herr Hess!"

Another gunshot cracked, and Kessler swore and hit the brakes. The car spun on the slick road, half turning, and stopped. He saw Berg lying face down in the slush, legs twitching, his arms outstretched toward the checkpoint, one of his hands clutching the envelope containing the coins. Blood was pooling around his head. A Gestapo officer was running toward Berg's body.

Kessler ducked down as a side window of the touring

car blew inward with a tinkling sound. They were still firing at Kessler, shouting at him to surrender.

I cannot leave the coins.

Another bullet smacked into the car and then he shifted himself high enough to get the car moving again, turning it toward the Gestapo.

But one of them had the envelope, was running with it toward the black sedan. The other was standing in the middle of the street, aiming with two hands on his gun.

Kessler ducked as a bullet smashed through his windshield, hissing just overhead. Then the officer fired once more, and a tire exploded. His car spun out of control, and thudded into something. He glimpsed the Gestapo officer who'd fired at him flying through the air, struck by the car.

The touring car struck the sidewalk and stopped, radiator spouting steam.

Kessler jumped out, pulling the Luger from his coat. He swung it toward the Gestapo car—but the officer was already at the wheel, starting the vehicle. Kessler fired, striking the car over and over, emptying the Luger, but none of the bullets penetrated to the driver.

Still clutching the gun, Kessler ran clumsily through the snow, toward the car—but the Gestapo officer chose to make certain that the package Herr Rudolf Hess had been waiting for was taken to him, even if it meant letting Kessler escape.

The black car roared away, taking the Coins of Zakynthos with it. As it turned a corner, Kessler noticed the swastika painted neatly on its side.

He stared after it. Shame twisted in his belly like a dirty blood-soaked rag.

I failed, Kessler thought. *I was a fool. I should have killed Berg when I shot the other two.*

He turned, hurried across the street, passing the now still corpse of Berg, and the dying, groaning SS soldier. Skidding in snow, he ran to the corner and around it, then slowed. Up ahead, a heavy man wearing a taxi driver's cap was just leaving the beer hall, walking to his cab, wiping his mouth.

Kessler called out to him.

"Taxi! I am in a hurry!" He forced himself to smile at the man as he waved.

The taxi driver shook his head.

"No, I am going home now!"

"I will give you four times your normal fee and a tip to boot if you take me where I'm going. But you must drive as fast as you can!"

"Speed will be difficult with the snow on the streets but… very well, sir!"

Five minutes later, Kessler was sitting in the back of the taxi, half listening to the driver's inane chatter as they bumped and skidded along. So far there'd been no pursuit. At some point in the next hour the Gestapo would organize a search for him, but by then he would be undercover, and on his way out of town. There were certain well-paid, trustworthy men who did jobs for Grimms, sometimes. Those men would help him escape from the city. With luck he would be safely away. But his failure would go with him, like an unwanted travel companion.

I should have shot Berg and yet—he was a fellow Grimm. My instinct was to preserve another Grimm. He and I should have been brothers.

Brothers? Berg had betrayed all Grimms—for money! Simply for money. And what would happen now?

Hess knew about the coins, clearly. Berg would have confirmed the story, in making the deal to sell them.

Rudolf Hess would likely give the coins to his adored Führer.

Adolf Hitler would have the Coins of Zakynthos.

And where would that take the world?

CHAPTER TWENTY-SEVEN

Juliette marched into the cabin ahead of Hank.

"Monroe—where's Nick?" she demanded.

Monroe winced.

"*Hi Monroe, how are you feeling?* might be a little more appropriate here, Juliette," he said, as he shifted uncomfortably in his easy chair.

"Monroe, she's worried," Hank said, closing the door behind them.

"I'm sorry, Juliette," Rosalee said. "He's a bit cranky. He's stopped taking the painkillers."

"I don't need the pills anymore," Monroe said. But it was true he was feeling on edge. "I'm sorry, Hank's right, I'm out of line. I don't know where Nick is, Juliette. I'm kinda mad at him because he said we'd work together to find Lily and then he vanished on me. You up to speed on Lily?"

"Nick told me some, and Hank told me the rest," Juliette replied. She stared at the floor as she unbuttoned her coat, as though trying to hide how worried she was.

Rosalee took Juliette's coat.

"Let me hang this up. You and Hank sit down, we'll

have some coffee and figure this out."

Juliette went to the sofa, started to sit—then stopped as an automaton on the mantle, shaped like Pinocchio, turned its head to look at her with glassy eyes. She sank slowly onto the sofa, staring at the toddler-sized automaton.

"Did that thing just look at me?" she asked.

"Oh yeah, sorry, should've warned you," Monroe said. "Beautiful machines. He's put motion sensors on them, so that they look at you when you move. 'He' being the guy whose cabin this is... Just ignore Pinocchio and friends. They're very discreet. They listen but they don't talk."

"They *listen*?" Hank said, sitting beside Juliette. "Great. Makes me feel comfortable." He accepted a cup of coffee from Rosalee. "Thanks. So no one's heard from Nick?"

They each shook their heads in turn. Hank put the coffee down.

"That's... I don't want to scare you, Juliette."

"I'm already scared. I know something's wrong."

"Feels that way to me," Hank admitted. "He'd be in touch with one of us. Or at least the Captain—but the Captain hasn't heard from him either. Suspended or not, Nick's still a police detective. There's no way he's going to be out of touch with us."

"Hard to believe he wouldn't call Juliette," Rosalee said.

Monroe sighed. "He seemed really sincere when he said he was going to work with me on this. He's always returned my calls when we..." He broke off, seeing the effect all this was having on Juliette.

Juliette's eyes were bright with unshed tears.

"Hank—do you think he's dead?"

"No. No, I don't. The Icy Touch would've left his body somewhere as a message. That's their whole style."

Juliette squeezed her eyes shut.

"Then they have him prisoner?"

Rosalee sat on the sofa's arm, put a hand on Juliette's shoulder.

"He's a Grimm. He's survived… so much. He'll be alright."

"Thing is, Juliette," Monroe said slowly, "I really, *really* think you and Hank ought to bunk here with us for a few days. We're off the grid enough they won't find us easily, if we don't do anything dumb. We have an extra bedroom here. Hank can sleep on the sofa."

Hank looked at Monroe.

"You saying Juliette's in danger?"

"I… don't know. Don't want to scare anyone. But they must be pissed off about you and Nick getting in their way. These guys are the dark side of Wesen, pure and simple. They're going to hurt you and Nick any way they can. My advice, Hank—get out there and do your job but… might be smarter not to sleep at home for a while. And Juliette should stay here for sure."

"I have tomorrow off," Juliette said, wiping her eyes. "But after that I have to be back at work."

Monroe shrugged. "Maybe… But I mean, if it's not all… uh… worked out by then… see if someone can cover for you. I'm not saying it won't be, you know…"

Noticing Rosalee glaring at him, Monroe shut up.

Juliette accepted a tissue from Rosalee, dabbed at her nose, and looked around the room at the other automatons perching on tables and shelves around the room. A Santa Claus nodded and stroked its beard; a red-nosed old babushka chuckled and lifted a laundry bag onto her shoulder; an American Indian sat on a horse—both the horse and the Indian turned to look at Juliette.

Juliette laughed and shook her head.

"Good luck sleeping in this room, Hank."

Hank snorted. "For real."

She sighed. "Nick told me about the kidnapping, the little girl, how he lost his... his temper. How he questioned that man and got suspended and... I knew he was still holding something back."

Hank cleared his throat. "Maybe he didn't want to talk about the Grimm thing. There are sides of being a Grimm he doesn't necessarily have control of yet."

"He should have told me! He should have trusted me." Unconsciously, Juliette shredded the tissue between trembling fingers. "It took him so long to tell me about being a Grimm—about Wesen. It wasn't right for him to keep it from me. I was scared—things were happening that I just did not understand. I thought I was going crazy."

Monroe nodded. "I hear you. We should have told you... I should've said something, but Wesen are trained to keep it on the lowdown."

"It wasn't your fault, Monroe," Juliette said firmly. "It was Nick's. He just didn't trust me."

Hank sipped his coffee, then said, "I think he was afraid you'd leave him. His being part of the Grimm world—that could be a pretty big deal breaker, for a lot of women."

Monroe laughed dryly. "Ohhhh yeah! As in 'I'm a Grimm, I kill creatures out of *Grimm's Fairy Tales,* so be my Valentine.' Yep. Could *so* be a deal breaker."

Juliette shook her head. "I would have stood by him. I *did*, when he finally told me. But it took him so long. Now he's hiding things from me again. That—just might be the deal breaker..."

Nick had decided he could get more leverage on the sink than the toilet.

He had broken it partway off the wall, pushing the sink a little at a time, with all his strength. It made a squealing noise with every push. Eventually some sentry would check on him and hear the noise. He had to get this done fast.

He could see the pipes in the back, and one of them was already leaking water around the join. If he could get the water flowing and the pipes broken enough to cut flesh…

Nick gave the small sink another strong heave, summoning more strength, and with a creaking wrench the main pipe snapped off. Water gushed onto the floor— and the edge of the broken pipe looked sharp.

He pressed the back of his left arm against the broken edge of the sink's pipe, and began sawing it back and forth. After about ten seconds, the blood started to flow.

He kept sawing.

It hurt. It hurt a lot.

Chance Weems felt like this Nicholas Burkhardt was *his* prisoner, as much as anyone's, and he was going to make sure no one screwed up and let the Grimm get over on them. He owed that to his son Jody, who had been killed by Burkhardt's mother.

And Weems had far more experience with Grimms than the others did. He knew they could be more dangerous than they looked. Faster. More deadly.

So Weems was appalled when he got down to the cell in the basement and found the sentry was gone from the door.

"What the hell!" Weems burst out, as the young Hundjager, Roger, came around the corner, shotgun in hand, whistling to himself.

"Where *the hell* have you been, you damned fool?" Weems demanded.

"Whatya mean?" the young man retorted sullenly. "He can't get through those walls or that steel door. Boss said I could go for a dinner break, so I did. He said a half hour, I'm back in half an hour!"

"Denswoz said you could go off without there being

someone to replace you? Then he's a fool too!"

"You better not let him hear you say that," Roger said, looking over his shoulder.

"You were supposed to get someone to spell you." Weems nodded at the cell holding the Grimm. "You hear anything from him?"

Roger shrugged. "One time he sounded like he was going kinda out of his gourd. Said he was going to kill himself if we didn't let him out. I just laughed at him. I told the boss about it, said not to believe a word the Grimm says."

"Wouldn't bother me if he killed himself. Then I could feast on him all the sooner. Denswoz better keep his promise."

Weems noticed Roger looking intently at the bottom of the steel door.

"There some kind of flood?" the sentry asked.

Weems looked. The low horizontal space they used to push a food trays in was bubbling with water.

"This ain't good. You better…" But when he saw the blood it startled him into a momentary silence. The unmistakable red liquid was swirling with the water, and there was quite a bit of it. The blood was running out from the cell, under the door, and onto the stone flags of the corridor…

"You go get the boss," Weems said. "I'll keep an eye on this."

"Oh shit. I hope nobody blames me if he's dead. Boss'll be mad. He wanted that guy kept alive till he was ready for him. We're still waiting for people for the party."

"Just go get the… Dammit Roger, what are you doing?"

Roger had stretched his key out on the chain that attached it to his belt. To Weems' amazement he was unlocking the door.

"Don't—!" Weems said.

But Roger swung the door open and stepped back, pointing the muzzle of his shotgun toward the cell.

"It's okay, I got it covered. Safety's off, gun's loaded."

Weems shook his head. He drew his pistol—he was still carrying the Smith and Wesson they'd taken off the Grimm—and moved to follow Roger into the cell. He had to admit, he was curious himself...

The Grimm was lying on his back to one side of the fallen, cracked sink. There was blood all over Burkhardt's neck and wrists. His arms were flung out, and he seemed limp, his chest motionless, eyes closed. His mouth, trailing blood, was slightly open. Blood-streaked water bubbled and flowed around him.

"Look at that!" Roger said. "He's dead! He must've cut his throat on that busted piece of metal!"

"If you'd a been here you'd have heard him busting that washstand down!"

"I did hear something—but I figured the guy was having a tantrum, kicking the walls or something."

Roger went in for a closer look.

Then Weems noticed the cot. The wooden frame had been pulled apart, the lumber twisted free of the bolts.

Wait. Oh no...

"Boy, stay back—" Weems warned.

But Roger was already bending over the body of the Grimm. And then Weems spotted the sharply broken-off piece of wood, about the length of a baseball bat, lying next to the Grimm's outstretched arm.

"Get back!" Weems yelled.

He tried to bring the pistol into play but Roger was in the way—and then there was a blur of motion, and the Grimm had thrust the spear of broken frame up, angling it past Roger's ribs and into his heart.

Roger screamed and, half impaled, twisted to fall on his side, writhing on the wood as he died.

Weems stepped to the left and snapped off a shot. But the bullet struck the wall just above Burkhardt as the Grimm pulled the shotgun from the dead sentry's nerveless fingers.

Weems stepped back and tried to aim—but the Grimm was fast, just too fast.

It was almost as if the shotgun, when it went off, was silent. But the truth was, Weems just never heard it blow his brains out.

Nick was hoping the noise of the pistol and the shotgun wouldn't carry past the thick walls. But the door to his cell was open. The Icy Touch Wesen could be coming.

He picked up his Smith and Wesson, stuck it in his waistband, and then turned to the still gushing water pipe, bending over to thrust his cut forearm under the water, trying to clean the wounds a little. The long shallow cuts he'd made had produced enough blood to spread around his body for a good theatrical effect—and enough to run under the door with the water, getting their attention. But the cuts weren't severe enough to do him much harm.

He straightened up, pumped another shell into the shotgun, stepped over the bodies to the door. He stopped at the threshold, and glanced back. Two bloody bodies, water flooding around them. Entrails dangling from the younger one, drifting like seaweed in the outflow from the broken sink.

Quite a mess.

He stepped into the hall and listened. He heard no voices, no sound of anyone coming. He'd had the impression the cell was in a subbasement, under a large building. Maybe it was deep enough down they hadn't heard him.

Especially if there were intervening doors. He returned to the cell, carefully leaned the shotgun against the wall, and removed the keys from the younger Hundjager's body. Not a pleasant task, but there was a whole ring of keys. That could prove useful. He was surprised to find no cell phone on the sentry.

He turned to Weems, searched him for a cell phone. He didn't have one either. Must be that Denswoz restricted them, when the men were out here. *Information hygiene in all things.*

Nick pulled the old Hundjager's jacket and shirt off, and stuffed them into the broken pipe end where the sink had been. It took some adjusting, but he got it plugged up pretty well, stopping the water flow.

He went back to Weems' body.

"Sorry, Weems, don't like to be disrespectful to the dead, but…"

Nick pulled the dead man's pants off, and used them to wipe up the floor outside the door as best he could. Then he tossed the wet, bloodied pants inside, retrieved the shotgun, and went into the hall. He locked the cell door, hoping another sentry might not look inside before taking up his post. The guy would be standing sentry over two dead men.

Nick started slowly up the stone stairs, under naked light bulbs in the ceiling, going as quietly as he could. His shoes and socks were wet, and water dripped down his back.

He climbed six steps, stopped and listened, then went up to the next flight. He listened again. Then he moved on. Two more flights, the rest of the way to the closed steel door at the top of the curved stone staircase.

Nick pressed his ear to the cold metal of the door. He heard nothing. He tried the handle. Locked.

He got the keys from his pocket, looked at the lock, and tried the most likely one. It turned easily.

He gradually opened the heavy steel door, stopping to listen with each small movement. Now he could hear voices, down to his right, too far off to be intelligible. Someone laughing; someone else making a remark.

He peered round the doorway. At the far end of the hall a little light spilled out from a partly open door. They were probably in there.

The voices didn't indicate any alarm. Apparently the thick walls and steel doors had muffled the gunshots.

Nick stepped into the wood-floored hallway; a Persian-style carpet runner went its length. There were pastoral paintings on the walls, and elegant amber-colored light fixtures on the ceiling. He turned, quickly locked the cellar door, then moved down the hall to the left, away from the voices he'd heard. He wanted to keep moving until he was away from whoever was talking behind him.

He kept the shotgun at the ready, willing to shoot almost anyone he encountered, if he had to, but hoping he could bludgeon them from behind instead. A silent kill would be better.

Only... Suppose he killed an ordinary, clueless security guard, or a startled cook? Someone innocent...

But hiring ordinary humans to work in a place like this didn't seem like Icy Touch style. Denswoz was clearly one of the organization's chiefs. He'd be surrounded by Wesen. Probably everyone in the building was a Wesen.

But that brought up another problem. Some of the Wesen recruited into The Icy Touch had been forced into the crime cartel. Did he have the right to kill them? If not—how could he tell one from another?

He couldn't think about that. He had to find the girl, if she was here, and get her out of this place. But along the way, there were other little tasks he could see to...

About twenty strides down the hall, he reached a corner, and stopped to listen. The only sound he heard was the beating of his own heart and the soft click of central heating coming on.

Nick stepped around the corner, coming to a corridor that ran along a series of dark-wood paneled doors.

He stopped and listened at the nearest door. No sound. Maybe there'd be a phone in there...

He reached down, tried a couple of likely keys before finding the right one and unlocking the door. He found himself in a bedroom. He saw no landlines, no phones at all. No luggage to search. The bed was made; the room seemed unused. There was a curtained window, across from him.

He walked quickly across the braided rug, and moved the curtains aside just enough to get a look.

It was night. Security lights and cameras were posted along a high black metal fence beyond a neatly trimmed side yard. He was on the ground floor. On the other side of the fence a large man in a rain coat and baseball cap walked sentry. He carried an AR15, and looked bored. Beyond the sentry was what appeared to be a wood.

Nick figured he could wait for the guard to move on a ways, then escape through the window.

But there was a good chance that Lily Perkins was in this building. And somewhere there had to be a phone, or some other method for contacting Renard and Hank.

He let the curtain drop before the sentry looked his way, and returned to the door. He listened, still silent. He returned to the corridor, softly closing the bedroom door behind him.

Nick tried the next door on the right—same thing. Empty unused bedroom. No phones.

The third door was unlocked and turned out to be a bathroom.

The next door was locked. And there was a sound coming through it—the sound of a girl crying.

CHAPTER TWENTY-EIGHT

Renard was driving down SE Sandy on his way home from the office, when the call came from Internal Affairs. He put the call on speaker.

"Renard."

"Lieutenant Jacobs at IA. About your man Burkhardt…"

"Investigation done?"

"Not quite. A lot of odd stuff in his files. But… I tried to call him, couldn't get him on the line. No answer. Then somebody just told me his car was impounded?"

Renard felt a cold breeze when there wasn't one.

"Really? First I've heard of it. Impounded where and how?"

"Deputy was driving out in the boonies, saw it through the brush. Stuck off a fire road. Somebody had tried to cover it with cut brush but the weather exposed it. Deputy checked the registration, found the car belonged to a Portland cop. He gave the department a call, and we told him to bring it to impound."

"Sounds like someone wanted to get rid of it… I can't see Burkhardt hiding it in the woods, out in the middle of nowhere. Where was this?"

"A few miles from the Columbia, east of The Dalles. Nothing much there. No houses. Nearest business is a bar called Joey's River Snag. Burkhardt taking vacation time out that way?"

"Not a chance," Renard said. "He was waiting for word from you. He might go out there for a few hours, but vacation, no.."

"Any possibility he might be despondent over the investigation and... a suicide risk?"

Renard snorted. "Last guy in the world to commit suicide. Way too tough."

"So where is he, then? Any theories, Captain?"

"I don't know, Lieutenant, but it's... it's worrying. He was investigating a crime cartel and he crossed them up good."

"Yeah. In the tunnel by the docks. More shootings. But your guy's got too many shoots in his jacket."

"He's a good man, Lieutenant. Stopped a lot of ugly stuff going down."

"Seems like a good guy. But a magnet for weird cases."

Renard wasn't going to get into that.

"Any sense of where his Internal Affairs case is going?"

"Can't discuss it yet, Captain. Sheriff's department has some rangers looking for him in the woods. I'll let you know if they turn up anything."

If they turn up anything out there, Renard thought, *it'll be Nick's dead body.* "Okay. I'll get his partner out that way, see if he can locate him."

"You think the cartel took him out?"

"I don't know. It's a possibility. Any blood in that car?"

"Deputy didn't see any. Got to go, Captain. Sorry to bother you after hours but I thought you should know."

"Thanks, Jacobs. And don't worry about the hours. Never have figured out what my hours are."

Jacobs laughed. "I hear you."

Renard cut the connection. Then he speed-dialed Hank Griffin, and got straight to the point.

"It's Renard, Detective. You hear anything about Burkhardt abandoning his car?"

"His car? No!"

"They found it in the woods, out a few miles off the Columbia. Nearest place is some roadhouse past The Dalles."

"Nick would never…"

"Yeah. I know. This is not good. Place was called Joey's River Snag. You know it?"

"Seen it once. Looked closed down. I take it you haven't heard from Nick?"

"Nope. You?"

"Not a word. Monroe hasn't heard from him either. Not even Juliette."

"Juliette hasn't heard from him? Can you head over there, Griffin? See if you can find anything? I'll call the Sheriff out there, ask him to help you out if you need anything."

"Yes, sir. Update me, Captain, if you hear anything."

"Sure. Same here."

Renard cut off the call and then saw heavy raindrops hitting the windshield.

"Dammit," he murmured, switching on the wipers. "Raining again, too."

A couple of minutes into trying to find the key that would unlock the girl's room, Nick heard voices, the sound of two men approaching from around the corner.

He hurried back to the bathroom, and slipped inside, standing to one side, the shotgun butt turned toward the door.

He heard someone say, "… she's probably fine but…"

Then his companion replied, "Gonna hit the can. Be right there."

A few seconds passed.

Then the bathroom door opened, and Grogan stepped in, in his human form, softly singing an old song with an Irish lilt.

"We may have brave men, but we'll never have better, Glory O, Glory O, to the bold Fenian men…"

He walked right by Nick, then seemed to sense something, got halfway turned before Nick pole-axed him with the butt of the shotgun to his forehead, hitting the Mordstier with all his Grimm strength and precision.

"Turnabout's fair lay, Grogan," he murmured.

Grogan grunted, and staggered backwards, blood dripping from a split forehead. Then he went down heavily.

Nick knelt to examine him. He was still alive, but it looked like he'd crushed the front of the Mordstier's skull. Might not stay alive for long.

Nick searched Grogan's coat, and found a cell phone. He smiled.

"Good man, Grogan," he muttered. He pocketed the phone, pulled Grogan's coat off him, and used the sleeves to tie his hands behind his back. He stuffed a half-used toilet-paper roll into the Mordstier's mouth, to keep him quiet should he come to.

Once again he stepped back into the corridor, shotgun at the ready.

The corridor was empty. Nick moved down to the girl's room door and found it unlocked, standing just slightly ajar. He looked through, saw a man facing the girl, who was sitting pressed against the headboard of a bed, hugging her knees. They'd dressed her in an ill-fitting red shift, and sandals.

"You had best do everything he wants," the Wesen was

saying, his voice vibrant with threat. "Or he'll give you to me! Look!"

The man woged—and Nick saw the scaly hood of the Königschlange fanning out from his head as the Wesen transformed.

"I sssshall *bite* into you, and inject you with jusssst enough venom to paralyzzze you. And then—"

Then the girl saw Nick and her eyes widened as she stared past the Königschlange.

The cobra Wesen turned, hissing, and Nick gave him the same pole-ax move with the shotgun butt in the forehead— but with not quite the same effect. Woged and scaly, the creature was more resistant to the blow, and though the Wesen fell backwards, he remained conscious. The creature bared his fangs, reptilian eyes exuding raw hatred.

Nick threw himself onto the Königschlange, using his weight to press the shotgun barrel down hard on the Wesen's throat.

The Königschlange writhed and struck at him with clawed hands; venom dripped from the fangs in his open mouth. Nick kept the pressure on the creature's throat. That red haze was there, again, before Nick's eyes, and his every Grimm instinct told him to kill this Wesen—and it wasn't an instinct he was inclined to fight.

It took several long minutes of pressure to strangle the Königschlange. But at last the creature's struggles subsided, and it went limp. The Wesen's face slipped back into human form, staring in death—and Nick recognized it. He'd seen a print from a security camera outside the city jail, from the night Douglas Zelinski died in his cell. This was the Königschlange who'd killed the Drang-zorn.

Nick got up shakily, went to the door, closed it, then turned to the girl. She looked as scared of him as she'd been of the cobra man.

262

He put a finger to his lips to signify quiet, and whispered. "I'm a police detective. We were looking for you and they caught me. But you're getting out of here, Lily."

"Really?" She sat up straight, eyes lighting up. "Where's your badge?"

"They took it. But believe me—I am who I say I am. My name's Nick Burkhardt. And you're Lily Perkins. I've got your picture in my car—your mom gave it to us."

"I guess I believe you. I can't stand not to." She looked at the dead man on the floor. "What *are* they?"

He approached her, trying to smile reassuringly, keeping the shotgun pointed at the floor.

"Keep your voice down, Lily," he said gently. He looked at the dead Königschlange. "He's... they're called Wesen. They live amongst us. Hiding from us, mostly. There are quite a few kinds. They come in fifty-seven varieties, like Heinz. Well, maybe not that many." He glanced at the door. "It's a long story. I'll tell you about it later."

How much could he tell her? As little as possible—no need to tell her about Grimms. But she knew about Wesen now. He'd just have to swear her to secrecy and hope it stuck.

He offered her a hand.

"Come on. We're going to find our way out."

After a moment's hesitation she took his hand and let him help her off the bed.

He let go of her and patted her shoulder.

"You're pretty damn brave, Lily. But listen—I might have to shoot somebody. If that starts, you flatten down."

"Okay."

"How do you feel? You're not still on the... the drug they've been giving you?"

She shook her head. "No, they haven't dosed me today."

"Good."

She followed him to the door, and he opened it, looked outside. It was clear for the moment. That couldn't last.

He gestured to Lily and they started padding down the corridor. They came to a wooden stairway, with runners and a carved banner shaped roughly like a dragon. The building had the proportions and feel of a mansion.

He led the way up the stairs, shotgun ready.

"Why are we…" she began.

He turned to her, put a finger to his lips, then leaned close and whispered in her ear.

"Need to figure out where we are. The address."

Eyes wide, she nodded, and they climbed to the second floor. Another long corridor. He heard voices from somewhere further down, and then he caught sight of a door ajar, closer, to the right.

Moving swiftly, Nick checked inside the room, then he led Lily through the door. They were in a luxurious office, the walls lined with books. Lily had the good sense to close the door softly behind her.

"I was here before," she whispered.

The office contained a large old-fashioned dark-wood desk—with a computer on it. On a small table beside the desk was a printer.

Nick turned to the girl.

"Lily—do me a favor. Go to the door, press your ear to it. Listen, let me know if anyone's coming."

She nodded, and hurried to the door.

Meanwhile, Nick approached the desk and flipped through the stack of mail he found scattered among the papers on its surface. One letter was a property tax notification. He looked it over, and decided it almost certainly referred to the mansion he was in. Next he turned his attention to the computer, tapping the space bar to wake it up. There was a word processing document open on the screen. Looking it over, Nick decided it was the opening of a speech.

Brothers and Sisters of The Icy Touch, it began.

We are gathered here today for a beautiful consummation. For centuries we have been tormented, persecuted, murdered by Grimms. And since the time of Napoleon my family has sworn an oath to destroy a certain line of Grimms. We made it our personal vendetta—and today we have the youngest surviving Grimm of this line in our cold grip.

I shall kill this Grimm myself. And this night we shall have a night of celebration, a feast, a rite of triumph! Soon we will find his mate, and his mother, and they too will be exterminated—and there will be no more Grimms in his line.

That is only the beginning.

I swear to you that all Grimms will be exterminated before ten years have passed. I have invited you here today to fulfill the

It ended there, in mid-sentence.

It seemed likely that Denswoz had written it. From what Renard had told him, there was a good chance Denswoz had the Coins of Zakynthos, and the text typed here emanated the kind of megalomania they induced.

Nick opened a desk drawer, and after a quick rummage found a flash drive among the various pens and scraps of notepaper.

He smiled, and fitted the flash drive to the computer, then copied the document to it, and every other document he could access easily and quickly.

He checked—the computer was online. Denswoz must have been interrupted by something important, to leave an open line of external communication unguarded, given his strict control of cell-phone use. But then this was his stronghold—where he was overconfident.

Nick uploaded the contents of the flash drive as an attachment to Renard's email. Then he used the cell phone to send Renard a text:

Burkhardt here. Check your email. Attachment may be helpful. DO NOT CALL THIS NUMBER.

That was done.

Nick pocketed the flash drive and called Hank's number on the cell phone.

"Detective Griffin," came Hank's familiar voice.

"It's Nick." He kept his voice just loud enough to be heard on the phone.

"Where the hell have you—?"

"Hank, I don't have time. Listen. I went to check something out, walked into a trap. I'm at a place on the Columbia River." He gave Hank the address from the tax statement.

"I'm about two miles from there right now."

"What? Why?"

"Your car turned up out in these particular boonies. Looking over a roadhouse... seems like it's closed down. Listen, Nick, I can get a small army of Sheriff's deputies out there to raid the place and get you out."

"Hank? No. I've got something else in mind. If it doesn't work out... Anyway, I've got Lily Perkins here. She could end up being a hostage. Or caught in the... you know."

"Yeah. I'll drive out there, take a position where they're not going to see me from the place, you call me, tell me what to do."

"I like the way you think."

"Uh—I should tell you. I was with Monroe and Juliette and Rosalee and... Monroe insisted on coming with me.

And Juliette wanted him to and I couldn't turn down both of them…"

"Tell him the girl's okay. And Hank—be ready to shoot if you have to but be careful with your fire. Lily and I are going to be coming out to you…"

"You got it."

Nick ended the call and thought, *Now. Just one problem. There must be dozens of Icy Touch downstairs. And more coming.*

So how do we get out of here alive?

CHAPTER TWENTY-NINE

"Seriously, Hank, I'll actually feel better if I woge and scout the mansion out. I don't mean, you know, I'd go overboard and do anything crazy, just a little closer than this. Not *too* close but—"

"Monroe…?"

"What, Hank?"

"Stop talking. I need to think."

"Okay. Okay, fine. Just saying. I can be really *Blutbad quiet* out there, if I…"

"Monroe!"

"Okay, alright already. It's just—he's got Lily and—"

"I told you, she's with Nick and she's okay."

"But… I need to make sure she *stays* okay."

"Just let me think, dammit."

Hank tapped his fingers on the steering wheel of the unmarked car. Outside, the rain had thinned to little more than a mist, sweeping across the dark hood of the car in waves too soft to hear. The moon was tucked behind brooding gray clouds and the only light, now that he'd turned off the headlamps, was from the security lights on the black metal fence of the mansion house. He'd parked a hundred yards away, on the shoulder of the access road, where a thick growth of wild roses and big ferns blocked any view of the car from the large building. The access road ended at a closed gate. A gatehouse stood just inside the fence.

Monroe cleared his throat.

"So. If you have no strong objection, I'm gonna—"

"Monroe? I *do* have an objection," Hank said. "I do in fact object *strongly*. You're *not* going over there! Last time you went off half cocked, one of those damned vulture things stabbed you in the stomach."

"They're called Geier. Rather than vultures per se, they're—"

"Okay, fine, Geier. You want to hear what the plan is or not?"

Monroe sighed. "What's the plan?"

"The plan is to wait for Nick to call and tell us what the plan is."

Then he saw a light in his side-view mirror. And another.

"Oh crap. Get down!"

The two men ducked down as low as they could, Monroe half crammed under the dashboard.

Three cars drove by in quick succession. Hank waited, one hand in his coat, ready to jump up and yank out the Glock if he had to. He could hear the cars driving to the gate. He lifted up his head enough to see that they had passed.

"Can I get up now?" Monroe asked. "This is painful."

"Yeah." They sat up and Hank looked out the side mirror again. "Looks like they're expecting guests."

Monroe rubbed at a crick in his neck.

"Is hiding under the dashboard normal police procedure?"

Hank snorted. "No. Neither is sitting out in the rain with a Blutbad while Grimm's fairy tale monsters drive by. Nothing about this is police procedure. Was up to me I'd have the Sheriff's department here right now. And when we got Nick and the girl out we'd go to the FBI and tell them the whole damn thing and let the feds take over. This secrecy stuff bothers me. It's not legal and I don't think it's right."

"Do Nick and Renard know you feel that way?"

"Yep. They're not pleased about it. And I'm not pleased about skirting the law. But I'm sticking with Nick and doing it his way because... he's my partner. And he's always had my back. And because I guess maybe people aren't ready to know about Wesen yet."

"Maybe? There's no *maybe* about it, Hank. And by the way, 'monsters'... is kind of an offensive term, man. Some of them are probably Blutbaden. I don't appreciate the blanket prejudice. Terms like *monster...*"

"I'm going to back this car up and find another spot. Likely to be more guests before Nick calls again."

Hank turned on the engine without switching on the lights, and backed up slowly, the car bumping over ruts in the shoulder, till he was on the road again. He kept backing around the turn, hoping that no other cars appeared for at least a few seconds.

"There!" Monroe said. He pointed between a stand of madrone and ash trees. "Just enough room."

Hank nodded. He stopped the car, and then drove it slowly forward between the trees, hoping he wasn't going to get stuck on a fallen log. When he felt like he wouldn't be seen by drivers on the road, he stopped.

Less than five seconds later several more cars drove past.

"Not good," Monroe said. "They're going to the same place. That's a lot of bad Wesen. How is Nick going to—"

That's when Hank's cell phone rang. He answered instantly.

"Griffin."

"Hank. It's Nick... listen carefully."

* * *

Luckily, no one had found the dead Königschlange yet.

They were back in the room where Lily had been held, the dead man still lay on the floor. Nick picked up the small table beside the bed, got a good grip on two of its legs, and threw it, hard, through the window of the bedroom.

"Whoa," Lily said.

He hurriedly picked up the Königschlange corpse by its belt and collar and pitched it through the window. That was harder to do; it took all his strength to make sure the body cleared the edges of broken glass.

One of the corpse's feet caught on the glass but the weight of the body pulled it free, and the dead Wesen fell to the ground outside, landing in a litter of shards.

"Come on," Nick said. "Run!"

They hurried back into the corridor, ran to the stairs, up two floors—and straight into a woged Blutbad.

The Icy Touch thug snarled and leaped at Nick.

Nick ducked, warning, in an undertone, "Outta the way, Lily!" And then he used his Grimm reflexes to pitch the Blutbad over the stair railing. The Blutbad howled till he struck his head on the edge of a stairway and went silent, falling limply to the bottom.

Lily gaped at Nick. "How'd you learn to—"

"Never mind, just run!"

They pounded up the stairs, passed the top floor, until they reached the door that led to the roof.

The door was locked—but Nick was in too much of a hurry to try and find the key, and two slams of his shoulder popped it open. He stepped outside in time to confront a frowning middle-aged man with an assault rifle cradled in his arms: a roof sentry coming around the corner of the outbuilding housing the egress. Probably checking on the noise of Nick breaking down the door.

Nick hammered the sentry with the butt of his shotgun. The man went down, twitching but alive.

"Ouchy," Lily said, looking at the fallen man. Then she smiled. "Oh well. I *hate* these guys."

Nick closed the door from the stairs, whispering. "Okay, Lily. Here comes the tricky part. Be as quiet as you can."

He could hear shouting on the side of the house from where he'd tossed the Königschlange corpse. With any luck that little decoy would draw most of the sentries and keep them busy for a couple of minutes.

But when Denswoz got there, he'd know better.

"Where we going?" Lily whispered.

"Some, uh, Wesen like to have trees close around their dens so I figured… yeah, that one'll do."

They crossed the flat tarred roof to where several trees lined up next to the mansion. Two of them had grown past the three-story roof. The biggest looked like a redwood.

There was more than five feet between the tree's nearest branch and the roof. Nick could see it pretty well in the glare spilling over from the security lights out front. He set the shotgun down, flat on the roof and out of Lily's way.

"Wait here," he whispered.

Someone was shouting angrily from the other side of the building as Nick leapt from the roof onto the nearest branch, trusting his Grimm abilities. He teetered for half a second, then grabbed a higher branch to steady himself.

He held onto the upper branch and worked his way along the lower branch, as far as he dared, close to the edge of the roof. The big branch bent a trifle but held his weight.

Lily stood poised on the edge of the roof looking scared and uncertain, and hopelessly vulnerable in her thin shift and sandals.

"Come on," he whispered to her. "Stick out your hands

and jump for this branch, I'll catch you with my left hand."

She looked at him. Hesitated.

"Trust me, I'll catch you," he said.

She licked her lips—and jumped.

One of her feet hit the lower branch but the other missed and she started to fall past him, flailing for his hands as she slipped downwards. He clasped her left arm near the shoulder with his left hand, pulling her toward him. Balancing with difficulty, his right hand holding onto the higher branch, he lifted her until she found purchase on the lower branch with her feet. He grinned at her, and, though obviously scared, she grinned back. She held onto his arm, steadied her feet, and then took hold of the higher branch.

"Okay," he whispered. "We're gonna climb down. Follow me, as fast as you can without falling."

Nick climbed down through a strong smell of redwood pitch and foliage, showing the way, and Lily followed. He figured The Icy Touch were still searching through the house. But they'd reach the roof soon, and find their fallen sentry and figure out the rest.

Hurry.

He came to the lowest branch in the tree, looked around, saw no one nearby, and dropped down. He reached up and helped Lily, half catching her, and then setting her on the ground.

"Which way should we—?" she began.

He put his fingers over her mouth and signed for her to wait. They could barely see each other in the shadows, but she froze into silence.

Nick drew the pistol from his waistband, and crept to the nearest corner of the house. He could sense someone stalking toward it. He flattened against the wall, holding his breath. A dark silhouette holding a rifle stepped around the corner and Nick brought the butt of the pistol hard down on the sentry's head.

The man grunted and convulsively squeezed the trigger of his assault rifle. Two shots spurted into the ground, flame strobing against the shadows, and then the Wesen crumpled.

"Damn," Nick muttered. He ran back to Lily and, worried a round could have ricocheted off a rock, whispered, "You okay?"

"Yeah."

He stuck the pistol back in his waistband. There was shouting from behind the house. They were coming.

"Lily—we're gonna run to the front gate, round that corner. Run on ahead of me. Fast as you can! Use the cars for cover! Go!"

She sprinted away and he followed, slowing only fractionally to scoop up the sentry's AR15. He readied the semi-auto assault rifle and followed Lily around the corner.

The area in front of the house, inside the fence, was mostly concrete drive, a half circle of it extending from the front door, and it was crowded with parked cars. It looked like an unruly car dealership.

Dark figures emerged from the far side of the house. Probably Denswoz had spread his men around both sides, they were coming from the farther corner, to his left, on the side he'd dumped the Königschlange, and they'd be coming from behind. Nick fired the AR15 from the hip, keeping The Icy Touch locked on him so that Lily could get past.

One of them shouted in pain; another stepped back and returned fire. He crouched as he ran. Two bullets sang just over his head.

Time seemed to slow down as he rushed after Lily toward the gatehouse by the fence, hoping to cross the space without being shot down. The parked cars provided good cover, but running hunched over was slower.

Another gun cracked somewhere behind and he felt a slashing pain in his left shoulder. It didn't feel like it had hit him solidly—if it had it would have knocked him off his feet. There was a second shot from behind, and the round smashed through a car's windshield.

He kept running, zigzagging between cars, and then saw that Lily was pressed up against the wall of the gatehouse, beside the front door. The door opened...

A Hundjager—in full woge—charged out of the gatehouse door and Nick ran at him, afraid to fire for fear of hitting Lily. The Hundjager was snarling, bestial—and big.

Nick ducked to the right at the last moment, tripped the onrushing Wesen, turned, and fired the AR15, shooting the gatehouse sentry in the back of the head.

A bullet cracked off a car's fender just behind him. Then he realized that the gate was opening. Lily was inside the gatehouse and she'd thrown the switch.

Smart girl. Cool headed.

"Go!" Nick shouted as she reemerged, and he followed her through the gate before it was fully open.

A car came racing toward them, drove past, spun around and then pulled up to block their way. Monroe, in the back of the unmarked car, threw open a rear door.

"Come on, jump in!" he shouted.

A bullet smashed out a brake light on the car, and then Lily and Nick were inside. Hank floored it before Nick quite got the door closed.

They roared around the curve.

"Monroe—is Juliette safe?" Nick asked.

"Yeah, Nick—I don't think these creeps know where she and Rosalee are. We got her covered."

They went a short distance up the access road, and

then slowed next to the parked vehicle waiting for them. It was a white and silver Chevy SUV, facing away from the mansion. Behind the steering wheel was a scared-looking Eisbiber. Monroe had called around to find a local, friendly Wesen.

Hank pulled up and they all climbed out, leaving the car idling.

"Nick—how about if you just come with us," Monroe said. "Juliette'll never forgive me…"

"Hurry!" the Eisbiber called out the car window.

There was shouting from the mansion down the road. Not much time.

"Into the SUV, all of you," Nick said.

Hank looked troubled. "There's a police shotgun, and ammo in the trunk, and a vest. Wait—is that blood?" Hank stared at Nick's left arm. "You're wounded?"

"It's really and truly just a scratch. Now—trade you cell phones."

Hank looked surprised but took the cell phone Nick had been using, and handed his own over.

Monroe was staring at Lily.

"Um—you okay?" he asked her gently.

She looked at him. "Yeah. Who are you?"

"Who am I? I'm… my name's Monroe. I work with these guys. Come on. Let's get you back to Portland…"

He and Lily started to get into the SUV—then she ran back to Nick and hugged him.

"Thanks!" she whispered.

"My privilege. Well done for opening that gate—that was pretty quick thinking. Now go—you'll be safe with them."

She ran back to the car and Monroe helped her climb in.

"Nick," Hank said, "this is crazy. Don't stay here. Let me cover you, at least."

"You can't. That'll blow the whole plan. Anyway you

need to protect that girl. Go on, I know what I'm doing."

I hope.

They heard cars starting, back at the mansion.

"They're coming! Just go, Hank!"

Nick didn't wait for his partner's response. He jumped into Hank's car, slammed the door shut, put it in gear, did a quick three-point turn and hit the accelerator to speed back around the curve to the road in front of the mansion. He jerked the wheel to his left, braking when he was blocking the road. Then he put the car in park.

A cloud of exhaust fumes rose around him from the spinning maneuver, glowing in the shine from the security lights.

A car screeched to a stop between him and the gate of the Denswoz mansion. The two men inside looked like they were arguing.

Nick speed dialed Renard on Hank's phone.

"Come on, Renard, tell me you've done something," Nick muttered as he waited for the Captain to pick up.

Maybe this wasn't the best way to handle it. Maybe it wouldn't work. Maybe they should've had the Sheriff's department take over. But who knew what kind of creatures the Sheriff's team would find in there? And what they'd find out about *him*? They would probably get into a full on fire fight and The Icy Touch might well win that fight… Could he cope with being responsible for that kind of loss of life?

And maybe there was a back way out of the mansion anyway? Was there a boat, perhaps, on the river, that Denswoz would take if the place were raided?

"Circle around him!" shouted a gruff voice from the gate.

Come on, Captain. Answer! Nick willed Renard to answer his cell.

"Griffin!" came the captain's voice at last. He'd seen

Griffin's number on his cell phone. "Did you get him out of there?"

"Yes, sir, he did," Nick said, as a group of Wesen got out of the car in front of him.

Nick got out of his car as well, taking the AR15 along with him. He aimed the assault weapon across the top of the car with one hand, the other holding the phone to his left ear.

"Burkhardt? That you?" Renard asked.

"Last time I looked. You get the email, Captain?"

It was a little difficult to talk. Was it the exhaust making his mouth so dry or was it the fear?

"I got it. Useful stuff. And I *think* I have an arrangement made. But I'm not sure how long before..."

A shotgun boomed, blowing a side window out of Hank's car.

Nick ducked down, almost kneeling on his side of the car.

"Got to go, Captain. I'll be right here. I think I can get them to keep me alive till dawn."

"Maybe we can hand it over to the Sheriff's department..."

"Captain? They wouldn't finish the job. *We can*. It's got to be done this way. You know that."

Nick pocketed the phone and then shouted, "Tell Denswoz I'll surrender! But I want to talk to him first!"

Nick glimpsed a muzzle flash, heard the hum of a bullet from his left, and realized that someone was firing at him from the other side of the fence.

He turned, popped the rifle to his shoulder, aimed at the silhouette and fired.

Someone yelped and fell back.

He shouted again, louder, "I'm ready to surrender but only if I can talk to Denswoz!"

There were men murmuring in confusion, and then he

heard Denswoz's voice, shouting from somewhere near the gatehouse.

"That you, Burkhardt?"

"It is! No police—this is down to you and me. We've got two hundred years of history to settle, Denswoz! We'll make it the traditional rite of dawn—it all gets finished tomorrow morning! Give me your word it'll be a fair fight—and your leave to go if I survive! Swear it... and I'll surrender right now! But I want an oath from you just as serious as the one you swore to kill me!"

There was a pause.

Then the reply came: "I swear it! On the blood of my ancestors, I swear it! In the rite of the dawn you will have your chance!"

"I'm dropping my gun!" Nick shouted. He tossed the AR15 onto the roof of the car where they could all see it. "I'm coming over there!"

"Hold your fire!" Denswoz told The Icy Touch.

Then Nick put his hands up and walked into the Wesen's den.

CHAPTER THIRTY

"I, uh, guess you saw some weird stuff, Lily?" Monroe asked, as the car bumped over the country road.

She nodded dazedly. "Yeah. I did see some weird stuff. Some hella weird stuff."

"Right, but—they drugged you, so you only *thought* you saw…"

"No." She looked at him and shook her head firmly. "I wasn't on that stuff all the time. I saw Nick kill a cobra dude. And Nick told me about it—a little."

"Oh. He did. Well. We got to have a talk about that, and, uh, keeping things kind of under wraps—"

"This is just wrong," Hank interrupted as the Eisbiber turned onto the access road for the highway. "It's crazy to leave Nick there." He felt sick to his stomach thinking about what Nick was trying to pull off.

"Hank," Monroe told him. "Seriously, man, I know what Nick's planning sounds crazy, but I've been thinking about it and he's right—this has to be taken care of under the radar, kinda *sub rosa*. If the feds raid the place, or even the Sheriff—we can't know what The Icy Touch will do!"

"If we can't get backup then—we should go back," Hank said.

"Are you *nuts*?" the Eisbiber asked, laughing and moaning at once. "If we go back you'll put this girl at risk! Not to mention *me*! I'll let you out of the car, if you want, but…"

"I can't leave him back there," Hank said grimly, suddenly convinced of what he had to do. "Stop the goddamn car!"

The Eisbiber pulled up.

Lily looked at Hank, awestruck.

"You really going back there?" she asked.

"He's my partner."

"You mean you're, like, a couple?"

He looked at her. She wasn't joking. Monroe, though, laughed softly.

Hank showed her his badge.

"We're police detectives. He's my partner. Monroe, get her to Wu, he'll make sure she's protected. And he'll get her mom there, too."

Hank jumped out of the car, grimacing at the pain in his cracked ribs, and started back toward the Icy Touch mansion. As he went, he drew his Glock, checked to see if it was fully loaded. He didn't bother to holster it again.

Behind him, the SUV drove away. And then Hank was alone on the dark road.

Nick let a woged *Lowen*, one of the lion-like Wesen, force his hands behind him. He felt ropes tighten around his wrists—and he felt the Lowen's hot breath, smelling of raw meat, on his neck.

"I should be the one who fights you," the Lowen growled. "But I would make such short work of you…"

"I'll see if I can fit you in later," Nick said. But he didn't feel as jaunty as he sounded.

The Wesen pushed him through a crowd of onlookers; he saw a *Coyotl*, a *Steinadler*, three Blutbaden, a *Mauvais Dentes*, a *Wendigo*, a Hasslich and a Siegbarste. The Mauvais Dentes, like a man combined with a saber-tooth tiger, was as dangerous as Wesen came; the Hasslich, a troll, and the Siegbarste, an ogre, were powerful and murderous. And over there, a vulturous Geier standing beside three Hundjager. Most were woged; a few weren't but Nick could see their Wesen aspects anyway.

They all looked like they'd simply love to kill Nick Burkhardt.

There were likely other Icy Touch Wesen here. And all The Icy Touch in this place knew by now that he was a Grimm. And that Grimm, historically and typically, lived to kill Wesen.

It was not a good place for a Grimm to be alone.

One of the Hundjagers stepped up to Nick, and transformed to his human appearance.

It was Denswoz.

His tone was urbane, but anger simmered in his eyes as he spoke.

"Almost impressive, what you've done here tonight, Nicholas Burkhardt. But… really, it was just freakish chance. Someone allowed a young fool to take a guard post and… you suckered him. Not sure exactly how you managed it, but I can guess. I do congratulate you on getting the girl out of here intact—and eliminating a number of my men. I find I admire it."

"Admiration?" Nick said. "From you?" He laughed softly. "How flattering."

"Prattle away," said Denswoz, eyes glittering. "You'll soon discover there really is an afterlife. I plan to send you straight to Hell, first thing in the morning."

The other Wesen laughed at that.

"Easy enough for you to do," Nick said, looking him in the eyes. "Seeing as you've got my hands bound behind my back."

"I'll keep my word, Grimm, and you'll have your chance. Because I swore on the blood of my ancestors—I swore on all blood spilled by your kind! And not spilled just in fair fights—how many times have Grimms killed Wesen who had no recourse, no defense; creeping up on them and cutting off their heads as they slept? And how many times have Grimms killed Wesen children? Children, not even woged, shot and stabbed and burned by Grimms!"

"No Wesen child has ever been harmed by me," Nick said. "I count many good Wesen as friends, and I have been protecting them from your kind. And how many Wesen have *you* murdered? Doug Zelinski, the Blutbad who—"

"Shut up, butcher!" And with the word *butcher*, Denswoz slapped him hard across the face.

Nick was stunned for a moment, then he smiled.

"Again—that was easy enough for you to do. While my hands are tied."

"Take him to the ground-floor holding cell," Denswoz said to the Lowen. "As per the rite, he will die at dawn. Do *not* cut the ropes till I tell you! He's a Grimm! Do not turn your back on him! Don't trust him for an instant!"

"That's almost funny," Nick said, as they pushed him through the gate toward the house. "I'm surrounded by the kind of Wesen who kidnap innocent girls and drug them, who murder decent Wesen—but *I'm* the one who can't be trusted?"

With that, the Lowen roared, picked Nick up, and threw him bodily through the open front door.

Sitting behind the driver, Lily spoke to her mother on Monroe's cell phone, her eyes bright with tears.

The Eisbiber, Howie, was just now driving his SUV past the sign for East Portland city limits. But Monroe was feeling pensive. He was worried about Nick and Hank. What if Renard didn't come through? Nick was a tough Grimm—he knew what he was doing. Didn't he? Maybe he should've stayed with Hank. But that'd mean leaving Lily. He owed her father…

Smiling, Lily ended the cell call.

"She's going to meet us at police headquarters," she said. "By the time we get there she should be already be there!" Her lower lip buckled. She wiped her eyes. "I thought I was going to get raped and… probably end up killing myself. But it's really over now."

"You're going to be okay, Lily," Monroe said. "Um… we should talk about what to say to Wu. He doesn't really know about my part in all this. Or about Wesen. It's kind of complicated…"

"But what about *Nick*? It's really just him and his partner against all those… those *things*?"

Monroe winced at her use of "*things*," but decided to wait on that.

"Better them than me," the Eisbiber muttered. "Me, I'm a big coward—I can't believe I came along this far."

Monroe said, "You came along this far, Howie, because you're *not* a coward. But not many people can be like Nick. The guy's got a great big pair of…" He glanced at Lily. "Uh, he's really brave. Take the next exit, we'll head straight to police headquarters, hand Lily over to her mom there. Then you drive us about half an hour east, back toward your place, and you can drop me off. In fact, Howie, you can stop in, have a beer and some vegetarian chow at my cabin. Got some primo microbrew chilling there. Well, it's not exactly *my* cabin, really, but… Anyway you can meet Rosalee. She may adopt you. Here's the exit."

They took the exit onto a circular off-ramp, when Howie suddenly asked, "Wait, why's that guy right up on my tail?"

Monroe glanced in the side mirror on the passenger side—and saw a big semi-truck without a trailer, looming up.

"He's really taking tailgating to new levels! It's like—"

Then the semi-truck rammed the back of the SUV, jolting it hard.

Monroe grabbed at the dashboard, Lily screamed, and the Chevy fishtailed—then went out of control, bouncing off the ramp and into the soft wet grass by the road.

The SUV came to a stop—and stalled.

"Oh *crap*," Howie said.

"That truck do that on purpose?" Monroe asked.

His question was answered when he turned his head, his neck aching after the jolting, and saw the semi-truck angling toward them. It was clearly planning to run them down.

"Get this damn thing started," Monroe said urgently, unbuckling his seatbelt. "I'm gonna see what I can do."

He opened the car door, ran back toward the still-turning semi-truck, and woged as he went. He knew, somehow, there was another Wesen behind the wheel of that truck. The Icy Touch must have sent vehicles out to look for them, and somebody had seen the girl in the SUV.

Feeling his only partially healed wounds, Monroe raced directly toward the semi-truck as if he were planning to run it over and not the other way around. It was bumping along slowly in the wet, lumpy ground, just starting to pick up speed—and he took his chance to leap up onto its front end.

It was a Mac truck, complete with the little bulldog on the hood. He climbed up on the front of the truck, thinking the driver was going to shoot at him if he couldn't run him over—the windshield glass did shatter but not with bullets.

A fist came smashing through it. The fist drew back and was quickly replaced by a jet of red flame.

Monroe swung to the side, dodging the flame, somehow holding on to the frame of the windshield.

He heard the SUV's engine start, behind him.

Good for you, Howie, you kept your head.

The semi-truck was stuck in the mucky ground, its wheels spinning. The engine shut off as Monroe jumped to the ground—and the driver's side door opened.

Monroe looked up to see a fully-woged Daemonfeuer jumping down. The Wesen's head was scaly green, swept back from its forehead into hornlike extensions of the armored skin, something like a horned toad's. Monroe figured that maybe this was the one that killed that Drangzorn in the vacant lot.

The dragon-man narrowed his green, reptilian eyes and opened his scaly lips, exposing a red maw that suddenly exuded small licking flames and smoke—Monroe threw himself aside just in time to avoid the blast of flame.

He rolled, his Blutbad reflexes snapping into play, leaping up as the Daemonfeuer took a deep breath, the creature preparing for another burning exhalation.

Monroe ducked below the scorching plume, the flame searing just over his back, and he tackled the Daemonfeuer, slamming him hard against the edge of the open car door. The Daemonfeuer grunted, stunned, falling onto his side, and Monroe let his instincts have their way.

He ripped into the creature's throat… just as he'd killed the ranger, Lily's father, long ago.

The scales were hard to penetrate—but he bit deep and hard, and felt blood spurt into his mouth. The dragon man thrashed, and hissed—but soon it was done. The Daemonfeuer shuddered, and expired.

In death, it morphed back to human appearance. An ordinary man, pale and bloody in death.

Monroe spat blood, wiped his mouth, then shifted back to his own human form. But when he turned to the SUV, now driving onto the ramp, its wheels spinning with the slippery purchase—Monroe knew. Lily had seen him woge; she'd seen him turn Blutbad…

And she'd seen him kill as a Blutbad.

The SUV stopped on the roadside as another car drove by; the family inside stared at the stuck semi and the man with blood on his face as they went past.

Inside the Chevy, Monroe could see Lily turning to argue with Howie, waving her arms.

It began to rain, again, as he jogged over the wet ground as best he could. He reached the SUV and opened the back door.

Lily turned and, seeing him—she screamed and shrank away from him.

"Lily, it's okay. I'm not going to hurt you," he said.

"I saw what you did—what you are!" she whimpered.

"That was a bad guy…"

One I killed the same way I killed your father, he thought, feeling ill. *But that was different…*

"You have blood on your mouth!" she cried in horror.

"Sorry." He wiped his mouth again, using rainwater. "Some of us… we're called Wesen. We're mostly good people. There are bad ones—just as there are bad, uh, ordinary humans. Right? I mean, Nick wouldn't trust you with me and Howie if we weren't good people… Right? You trust Nick, don't you?"

"Howie?" She turned to look at the Eisbiber.

The Eisbiber sighed and said, "My people, we've got kind of a beaver thing going. We're not dangerous except to trees."

He woged—and she gasped.

Howie morphed back into his human aspect again.

"Monroe's right—most of us aren't bad sorts. These scumbags that took you... they're different. *They're* bad. Well, some are just... misled. You know?"

"That one I killed, that kind are always pretty rough characters," Monroe put in. "Source of the dragon legends, those guys. Daemonfeuer, we call them. Me, I'm kind of a wolfish sorta guy. There are trolls, ogres—like, from the fairy tales, you know? But we're another variety of people, really, is all we are. Most of us. Only, if you talk about this stuff, people will either think you're crazy and try to give you medication—or they'll believe you and come after us."

A Portland police cruiser was driving up, lights flashing. The people in the car that had driven past on the off ramp must have called them. They'd seen some kind of fight, the stranded semi-truck...

"The police are here," Monroe said. "You can tell them about me if you want, Lily. It's up to you. But... I hope you won't."

"What was the guy you killed going to do?"

"He was trying to kill us. Maybe take you back to that place Nick just risked his life to get you out of."

She wiped her eyes, and sniffled. Then she said, "Nick saved my life. You saved my life again. I won't say anything you don't want me to say."

"What about that guy's *throat*?" Howie whispered, as the cop got out of the cruiser to walk over to them. "How we explain that?"

"His head went through the windshield," Monroe muttered. "It's broken out. He cut his throat on it. Then I pulled him loose. Tried to give him CPR... Too late. Rain's washed the blood from the windshield."

"Works for me."

The cop walked up to them.

"Somebody want to tell me what happened out here?" he asked.

No, Monroe thought. *We don't.*

But he said, "Glad to, Officer! Well, it was like this... This trucker lost control of his semi, right behind us... and uh..."

CHAPTER THIRTY-ONE

Dawn. They'd be coming for him at dawn.

Nick sat on the floor, leaning against the wall, and looked around him. He had been thrown into an empty back room on the first floor, with bars across the windows. There was a Persian carpet on the floor, and nothing else. The only light came in through the windows from the security lamps behind the mansion.

He rubbed his wrists where the ropes had nearly cut into them, looked over the cuts on his arms, touched the bullet-scratch on his shoulder. He was bashed up, but his injuries weren't critical. He wondered if he had made the right decision in coming back to challenge Denswoz. It had felt right... and he'd learned to go with his gut, when it came to being a Grimm.

But this wasn't looking good.

Still, he had to get the coins away from the Icy Touch chieftain. He could feel their corrupting glow around Denswoz.

And he had to be *here*, to make sure it got done.

He'd managed to doze for a few hours after they'd taken off the ropes, his dreams fitful and dark. He'd awakened in this dark room, alone, thinking of Juliette. Was she really safe? Was she scared?

Soon it would be time to get up and stretch, and prepare for what was coming…

A few more minutes passed. Then he heard footsteps outside the door. Boots, several pairs. Low growling laughter.

He heard the turn of a key in the lock, and the door opening… Light from the hallway silhouetted several men.

They were early.

But then the familiar shape of Hank Griffin stumbled into the room, hands tied behind him, face tense with pain.

He fell to his knees, and then Denswoz, non-woged, came in behind him with two Wesen, a Blutbad and a Hundjager, both of them carrying AR15s.

Denswoz's eyes seemed to glow, just faintly. He had one hand in his coat pocket, moving restlessly in there. Nick assumed he was toying with the Coins of Zakynthos.

"Okay if I stand up?" Nick asked. "So I can help my friend here?"

"Go ahead," Denswoz said. "There's no help for either of you. Even if the police come looking for you. I have plans for your friend, here, as well as for you. We can kill you both and dispose of the bodies. We have a well-concealed place for that they'll never look in.

"Our bellies."

Nick ignored the revolting threat.

"Can I untie him?" he asked.

"Just as you like. I don't think he's going to be much good to you."

Nick could see that Hank looked dazed, was staring into the middle distance. There was blood on his shirt.

Seeing that, he had a strong impulse to lunge at Denswoz, and simply break his neck. But there were two AR15s pointed at him and Hank.

Nick took a deep breath and concentrated on untying his partner.

Hank moaned when the ropes came off, and tipped over—Nick caught him, easing him to the carpet.

"You cut into our *very* expensive supply of *Seele Dichtungsmittel*, with your *intrepid action* in the tunnels," Denswoz said, his voice heavy with mockery. "We're rather short on Seele, this month. We should've dosed the girl, when she got here, and we held off. But we haven't neglected Detective Griffin here. And we're fairly certain he didn't lie to us... was *unable* to lie to us. He told us that there is no police action on this facility that he knows of, no raid, nothing of the sort."

"Some of your people probably wanted to head for the hills, when I got away," Nick said calmly, as he massaged Hank's wrists.

"Yes. There was some dispute, as you may imagine. But... we have connections. Even if there was a police raid, our contacts would ease our way—and most of us would go free, fairly soon. And federal agents, or those clowns in the Sheriff's department—they wouldn't find much here. We've cleaned up the place quite well, since you got out. We'll be a convention of nature lovers, as far as they're concerned. Nor is there any talk on police frequencies about a raid on this property. But still—I wonder why you came back here. And why your partner is here."

Nick smiled. "You're not the only one who took an oath. And it wasn't only my kind who killed yours. You killed *mine*. I will kill you—and I just might get away with the coins. The ones you're toying with, right now..."

Denswoz quickly withdrew his hand from his coat pocket, scowling.

"Your kind never gives up till they're dead. So be it. You will be dead in a couple of hours. And I will demonstrate that we cannot be stopped. That we are invincible."

Nick smiled and shook his head.

"All you're demonstrating is that you are megalomaniacal. And sick from the coins."

Hearing that, Denswoz seemed to be the one who had to hold onto his temper, now. He turned, gestured to someone in the hall. They handed him a sweetened electrolyte drink in a sealed bottle.

"Here." He tossed the plastic bottle, and Nick caught it. "You can't say I didn't let you have a drink before you died, Detective Burkhardt. It's not poisoned or dosed, I promise you. I'll see you shortly."

The Icy Touch chieftain turned and left the room; the gunmen backed up into the hall, and the door was hastily locked.

Nick looked at the raspberry-colored drink.

"Just like you'd buy in a convenience store." He held it up to the light to check it was sealed, and to look for puncture marks. "Don't see anything. I'll test it for you, Hank."

He knew he was taking a chance but he was tremendously thirsty. He twisted the top off and drank deeply.

It was too sweet for his taste, but it strengthened him a little, and he felt no ill effect.

Nick waited, closing the bottle.

A few minutes later, Hank groaned again, turned on his back and, grimacing with pain, sat up.

"Something… drink…" he managed.

Nick decided he'd have felt the poison by now, if there were any. He unscrewed the top, and gave it to Hank.

"Knock yourself out, Hank. Just an expression."

Hank drank down half the remaining bottle, then put it aside, gasping.

"Oh God. Nick. I don't know what I might've told them. I'm not sure."

Nick shrugged. "You don't know anything that could hurt. Not today. I only told you part of it."

"My head is pounding…"

"They gave you *Seele Dichtungsmittel*. You told them the truth—that there's no police raid planned. Good that you told them that. It's true and they needed to hear it. But you shouldn't have come out here, Hank. Is the girl okay? And Monroe?"

"Yeah. On their way to town. I just… couldn't leave you here."

"They catch you trying to break in?"

"You guessed it." Hank moaned softly. "Hellfire, but that hurts." He rubbed his eyes. "Yeah, they… it turns out to be harder to climb over a fence when your ribs are cracked than I figured. And I didn't see the security cameras till too late. I fell off a fence on the inside, and one of the Monroe's evil cousins leaped out, couple more piled on and… I didn't even get off a shot. Feel like a jackass now."

"I know the feeling. They pretty rough when they interrogate you?" Nick could see that Hank's eye sockets were swollen from a beating.

"Gave me a good thumping. Then they dosed me with something. Like, blew it in my mouth with a tube. I don't remember much after that. Hope they didn't rape me."

Nick laughed softly. At least Hank still had his sense of humor.

"Naw. You're not that good looking."

"What happens now?"

"I challenged Denswoz to a fight. He's got an obsession about me—and my family. I knew he couldn't resist. And looking through my books in the trailer, I came across a couple of references to La Caresse Glacée. They have a penchant for rituals at sunset and dawn. I knew he'd probably set it up for dawn. I was counting on it."

"Ow, my head, my side, my face—lots of different kinds of pain. Like a smorgasbord. So, Nick? What's the plan? 'Cause I sure hope you have one."

Nick looked at the window. He couldn't see clearly, in the glare from the security lights. He got up, and peered outside, squinting up at the sky.

"Looks like… maybe an hour before dawn. So the plan is to…" He yawned. "To get some rest. Going to need it."

The sun was rising behind the line of fir trees, when Nick and Hank were brought under close guard out a back door of the mansion. The sky was almost blue, the overhanging clouds gray in the muted morning light.

They found themselves in a Mediterranean-style garden, with a circle of red crushed stone in the middle, surrounded by low green shrubs cut into topiary shapes— wolves, wild dogs, dragons. Enclosing the garden was a high black-painted iron fence topped with very sharp-looking spikes.

Nick noticed a dried brown puddle in the center of the circle: Blood. He'd probably never find out whose blood it was.

Around the circle stood a crowd of woged Wesen: the troll on his right, the ogre on his left, Blutbaden and Hundjager and Geier and Lowen and others. Most of them had guns in their clawed hands. The Lowen and the saber-toothed Mauvais Dentes and the pale-furred Wendigo, who looked at him with such fixed hunger—they were all there, and more, surrounding him on the edge of the red-gravel circle.

Hank was held back, the Lowen clasping the back of Hank's collar like an irritable father holding a small child. Hank swayed, blinking as he looked around as if suddenly confused. Nick knew Hank was pretending to be more fazed by injury and the Hexenbiest drug than he was in reality.

The Wesen growled and chuckled and muttered to one another. They bared their teeth and their clawed hands clenched and unclenched.

Wearing an old-fashioned costume of silk, breaches, a white shirt with French cuffs—like something from the early nineteenth century—Albert Denswoz pushed through the encircling rows of his followers. In each of his hands was a saber.

Denswoz was the only one not woged. Not yet. His eyes glowed faintly. The coins would be on his person, somewhere—Nick felt sure of that.

Denswoz approached Nick and thrust one of the antique sabers into the ground between them. It quivered there. A ribbon hung from a golden pommel shaped like the head of a falcon. The weapon was old, but it reflected the morning light with a kind of steely confidence.

"Napoleonic era sabers," Denswoz remarked, giving his blade a practice swing that cut singingly through the air. "Just a little curved, as you see. Springsteel blades! They're both nicely balanced dragoon sabers. Yours is a bit more... ornate. Do you recognize it, Burkhardt?"

"No."

"I suppose there's no reason you should. Your blade belonged to the murderer, your ancestor—Johann Kessler. One of my own ancestors took it from one of Kessler's descendants. Took it from the fellow's dead body, in fact. And the saber I hold belonged to Alberle Denswoz. It is only right that I should kill you with it. And I will use the same saber to kill your friend there. And I'll use it to slice open your woman, when I find her. And your mother—she is proving elusive, but have no doubt, I will find her. And then the long march to a reckoning will be completed! We will have triumphed over you, and soon—over all Grimms!

I promised you a chance, and you shall have it—though I doubt they taught you to use a sword in the police academy. Pick up your ancestor's weapon and die with a blade in your hand!"

Nick swallowed. Denswoz was right. He had no special skill with a saber, nor with a sword of any kind. He'd been hoping for hand-to-hand combat, or perhaps a duel with pistols—he was a pretty good shot.

He glanced at the sky. It wasn't fully light out yet. The day was only just beginning...

Denswoz reached into a pocket with his free hand, and his eyes seemed to glow a little more. He glanced around the circle of Wesen and waved his saber like a wand of benediction.

"Brothers and Sisters!" he called. "In the tradition of The Icy Touch, we consecrate the dawn with the blood of the rising sun! It is the Grimm who comes like darkness! The rite of dawn blooding is upon us! The Grimm will die under my hand! And this will be a sign of the triumph of all the world's warrior Wesen! Now at last comes the reign of The Icy Touch!"

Under the spell of the Coins of Zakynthos—the true source of the Icy Touch chieftain's power—the Wesen roared and hissed and screeched in a monstrous litany of affirmation.

"You're a lot of suckers, under the influence of the coins!" Nick shouted. And then he took up Johann Kessler's saber, swinging it as he'd seen Denswoz do so. It felt good in his hand.

"You'll find it has a good balance," Denswoz said, with a sharklike grin, taking up a swordsman's stance. "Let's see what you can do with it."

Nick turned sideways to Denswoz, and set his feet as he'd seen fencers do, raising the sword in an *en garde* stance.

The Wesen fell silent, entranced by the drama of the imminent fight. Nick could hear birds calling out in celebration of morning from the woods behind the mansion. Maybe his last morning ever…

"Denswoz," Nick said, "my ancestors killed some of yours. They didn't finish the job. I'm not a police officer now. I have no reason not to kill you. And it just feels… full circle."

"Quit stalling!" a Steinadler said, its voice creaking like the squawk of an eagle.

"Come to me, Grimm, and join your ancestors," Denswoz said, brandishing his saber between them.

Nick took a deep breath, and lunged, trying to stab his saber into Denswoz's right forearm, hoping to cripple it.

But Denswoz neatly avoided him, stepping to one side, deflecting Nick's saber with ease.

The encircling Wesen laughed and hooted and roared.

Nick slashed hard and fast down at his opponent's blade, trying to knock it from his hand, attempting to get a better sense of what Denswoz was capable of.

But the blade wasn't there to be struck—Denswoz adroitly swished it out of the way, doubled back and pierced Nick's forearm, lightly, with the tip of his saber.

Nick grunted in pain and jumped back.

The Wesen roared and squawked and snarled.

"Just lay down and die, Grimm!" the Lowen growled.

Nick was tempted to turn and slash through the Lowen's neck—striking an alternate target by surprise to take a few of the dark Wesen down with him.

But Denswoz chose that moment to attack.

The Icy Touch leader lunged, piercing Nick's left shoulder with the tip of his saber.

"My steel fang strikes, Grimm!" he cried.

Nick grated his teeth with pain and backpedalled, shrugging his shoulder off the steel—the same shoulder that had been scratched by a bullet the night before.

"And again, Grimm!" Denswoz snarled, ducking under Nick's swishing blade and piercing Nick's right hip with his sword tip.

Nick ducked back from the burning pain of the saber. He could see his blood running down his enemy's weapon. And he'd drawn no blood himself.

He's toying with me, playing to the crowd... The coins have made him overconfident...

And the coins were toxic. Like a drug they might energize him for a short time, then weaken him. Like hard drugs, the Coins of Zakynthos were vampiric.

Wear him down. Survive! Draw this out...

Nick chose to bide his time, deliberately going on the defensive.

He let Denswoz back him up, and he moved like a boxer trying to get his strength back, keeping his ancestor's falcon-crested saber between them, clumsily parrying his opponent's thrusts and cuts. Blood was running down Nick's arms, now, some of it making his saber grip slippery.

Denswoz tried a clanging combination of cuts, driving Nick back toward the Geier, so close he could smell the vulture Wesen's carrion breath. Soon, Denswoz would go for the killing blow...

But it seemed to him that Denswoz was weakening a little, the coins sapping him.

Nick glanced at Hank, saw a look of inquiry on his partner's face. Hank nodded toward a gun held by a Blutbad beside him. No doubt hinting he could get loose from the Lowen, grab that gun, maybe shoot Denswoz...

Nick gave a subtle shake of his head, and then felt Denswoz's blade raking across his ribs, on his right side.

Sucking his breath through his teeth with the agony, Nick reacted reflexively, his wrist and hand working neatly to flip round the Hundjager's blade, pushing it away.

Denswoz looked surprised at the speed of Nick's move.

And Nick was surprised by it too. *What if a Grimm has innate swordsmanship too—and I haven't been letting it come through?*

He made himself relax, and slide into the Grimm state of mind.

Let the Grimm control the sword.

His Grimm genes came from his ancestors—and it felt as though one of his ancestors was suddenly in control of the saber.

All at once Nick found himself slashing, cutting, using feinting, then contratempo. His blood was up; the pain receded behind fury, and his feet seem to know the right steps, as if he'd been taking sword-fighting lessons all his life.

Denswoz was startled, suddenly off his game, stumbling back.

Nick advanced with such skill that the Icy Touch chieftain's eyes widened, his mouth fell open, gasping as he strove to keep up.

Denswoz stumbled back under Nick's attack—and suddenly he woged, as if seeking an edge in Hundjager form. Denswoz snarled, Hundjager fangs bared in a furred muzzle.

But the woge took a moment of his concentration—and Nick saw his opening.

Nick stepped in, turning sideways to slip past his enemy's saber point—and thrust his arm out straight and true, in a *coup de main*. He drove the saber deep into Albert Denswoz's breast, the blade turned to slip between the Hundjager's ribs.

Denswoz howled in pain—and the Wesen thugs around them roared and shouted in rage as their chieftain went to his knees, dying.

"No!"

"Kill him!"

Nick drew the sword back for a *coup de grace*...

Then he heard Hank shout, "Nick!"

Nick turned, seeing the Lowen shove Hank aside and rush to try to save his leader.

Nick set himself for the Lowen's attack, but then the cracking rattle of an assault rifle went off and the Wesen spun toward the gun. Somehow Hank had knocked a Blutbad down, torn the gun loose from its grip, and turned it on the Lowen. The lion-like Wesen was thickly built and powerful and not immediately stopped by the bullets. But Nick slashed through the Lowen's throat with the saber, finishing him.

The Lowen whirled, clutching its neck, gurgling and stumbling in the way of a Siegbarste—which was probably all that stopped the ogre from coming at Nick.

Hank fired the rifle at the ogre's head at point-blank range and the creature staggered to one side.

Nick spun to face the other Wesen, three of them coming his way. One of them, a Hundjager, was aiming a pistol right at him—

Then the Hundjager's head seemed to explode—a moment later the crack of a sniper rifle was heard, echoing from the woods. And then a Blutbad went down, shot the same way.

The Wesen turned toward the woods beyond the fence—gunsmoke was visible but nothing else.

A squeal of tortured metal was heard from close to the mansion, and the roar of engines.

Hank fired the last of his clip as a troll rushed toward Nick.

Nick sidestepped the troll, and, giving his Grimm reflexes full sway, slashed at its hamstrings as it went by so that it collapsed, roaring.

He turned, ducked beneath the gnashing beak of a Steinadler, stepped back and hacked at the creature so hard its head flew from its shoulders.

Then Nick saw the black iron fence collapsing, to the right, and black-uniformed Wesen rushing through toward him.

They must be Icy Touch reinforcements. He and Hank had fought well, at least…

But then he saw Renard behind them, following the wave of incoming Wesen—and he realized that Gegengewicht had come at last. These weren't reinforcements for The Icy Touch after all—they were the better class of Wesen, here to destroy the cartel.

There were Steinadlers, Blutbaden, trolls, Lowen, among the onrushing Wesen troops, even two male Fuchsbau carrying elephant guns. And there were many others, and they far outnumbered the Icy Touch Wesen. The Gegengewicht were all dressed in black, neck to toe, a kind of uniform.

Hank had gotten a pistol—and he turned to fire it at an advancing Hundjager.

A few Icy Touch ran for the intact back fences, only to be shot off as they climbed by the Gegengewicht snipers in the woods.

Nick turned to Denswoz, who'd shifted back to human form. Nick knelt by him—and was surprised to see the Icy Touch leader open his eyes.

Denswoz looked at him accusingly.

"You… Burkhardt!" he croaked. "You knew they were coming… you set… all this up…"

"I hoped they would. Waiting for the Dawn Rite gave them time to arrive. You left your computer on. I copied the evidence we needed. Not very good 'information hygiene', Denswoz. Sloppy."

"I've failed." He spat blood. "They're all dead. But… she is safe… she is alive… and perhaps…" He coughed, and licked his lips. His eyes glazed over; death silenced him and he said no more.

But she is safe… and she is alive…

Who would that be? Nick wondered.

He found the Coins of Zakynthos in the dead chieftain's trouser pocket. He quickly stuck them in his own pocket, and turned to see…

A slaughter. The badly outnumbered Icy Touch were being torn to pieces.

It was horrible to watch, and Nick had an impulse to put a stop to it, if he could.

But then he remembered the poor girls The Icy Touch had drugged and abducted. And the hideous remains of Smitty's body.

Nick shook his head. Still carrying the saber, he walked away from the fight, letting the Gegengewicht mop up.

He saw Hank, leaning against the back wall of the mansion, clutching a wounded shoulder.

"Hurt bad, Hank?"

"It smarts, but nothing serious. You?"

"Same for me."

Renard walked over to them, a smoking pistol in his hand, shifting back to his human appearance as he came.

"Burkhardt. About those coins…"

"Sorry, Captain. Shoot me if you want. But I'm not turning them over to you. I'll arrange with my mother. She'll pick them up."

"She had them last time. And lost them."

"She won't make the same mistake. She'll find a way to keep them safe."

Renard looked angry, clearly about to challenge Nick.

Nick said, "Captain—look at what's going on, over

there. You think there's no connection? Denswoz used the coins to control The Icy Touch. Probably to turn decent Wesen, in some cases, into psychotics. It was a cult. And it killed him. You don't want the things. They're poison."

Renard's jaws clenched. Then a particularly piteous scream from the battlefield made all three men shiver.

"Maybe you're right." Renard took a deep breath, and walked away.

Hank grimaced at the bestial screams—as the Gegengewicht tore the Icy Touch gangsters to pieces.

"Let's get out of here. What do you say?"

"I'm with you, man."

Leaning on one another, they walked away, stumblingly, leaving the field of carnage behind.

Nick's left hand bore his ancestor's saber, slippery with blood.

CHAPTER THIRTY-TWO

Two weeks later... a windswept October morning...

Nick stepped back from the opened weapons cabinet in his aunt's trailer, where he'd mounted the saber. It looked fine there, hanging horizontally over the more traditional Grimm implements of destruction. It had more style, he thought, than the decapitation blade, the spiked mace, the special blunderbuss, the crossbow, the peculiar hooks. The saber, cleaned and shining now, had a certain elegance. He hoped his ancestors, wherever they were, felt that this vendetta was done; that it was at last truly over.

But the work of a Grimm might never be done. Not as long as there were Wesen like Denswoz in the world.

And Hank was right, Nick thought, as he closed the cabinet. There was a tension, a disharmony between being a police detective, and being a Grimm.

Maybe he couldn't do both.

He'd failed to maintain correct police procedure, when he'd interrogated the Geier. He had lost his badge as a result.

And keeping relevant information back from the authorities—the truth about Wesen involved in crimes—

was against the law. But as a Grimm—how could he do anything else?

He couldn't give up being a Grimm. Especially not after what had happened with The Icy Touch. It wasn't just about destroying bad Wesen—it was also about protecting good ones. The police department wasn't qualified to get that job done, not by itself. So he had to be a Grimm.

But could he continue being a cop?

Maybe not. Maybe he'd have to give up his job, even if he was reinstated.

He turned to the work table, thinking he'd make an entry—he'd started his own Grimm journal—on The Icy Touch, when someone knocked at the door.

Nick picked up the Smith and Wesson on the table, checked that it was ready to fire, and called out, "Who is it?"

"It's the damned fool who gets your back, who the hell you think it is?"

Nick put the gun down and went to let Hank in.

"Still raining out there?" he asked.

"If I say it isn't raining," Hank said, coming in, and unbuttoning his trench coat, "it'll be a lie the second it's out of my mouth. Liable to start any second. Weather around here likes to make fun of me. You remember when I took that vacation to Hawaii? I heard they were looking for police detectives in Honolulu. Was I tempted?" He sat down in one of the chairs at the work table. "Yes I was. Still am." He looked at the cot. "You sleeping here in the trailer?"

"Yeah, I'm kind of on the outs with Juliette again. And I get in Monroe's hair… or fur or whatever… when he's got Rosalee over. So I've been staying on the cot here." Nick sat across from Hank and leafed aimlessly through one of the old books. Extra casually, he asked, "They give you a new partner?"

Hank shook his head. "Nope. Matter of fact they haven't. I've been working with Wu and Renard but nothing much has come up. Not even good old-fashioned human murders. You get those coins out of town?"

"My mother sent a courier she trusts. They're gone. Somewhere safe. Anything new on The Icy Touch?"

"Renard cleaned up the scene out there pretty good."

"What about the feds?"

"Agent Bloom buys the story that The Icy Touch was more or less wiped out by a rival gang, out at the mansion. Kind of true. Fact is, The Icy Touch seems genuinely blown to hell. There must still be a few of the gang out there somewhere. But Renard says that after the info you picked up for Gegengewicht, they raided the rest of the Icy Touch gangsters in Mexico and Europe, so the punks are either dead or scattered—I reckon any leftover are just lying low, trying not to get their heads sliced off. Hey—Monroe give you a report on the girl?"

"Lily? Yeah. She's back with her mom. She might have a touch of PTSD. But she's doing well. He and Rosalee are kind of 'uncle and aunt' to the family now. The girl's got no problem keeping the secret. Far as Lily's mom knows, Monroe's just a police department informer who helped bring her in."

Hank chuckled. "And Monroe was almost arrested for her kidnapping. That cop who stopped them by the truck finds out that Lily is listed as missing, stranger abduction. She wasn't going to let Monroe go down for that, though. Hey—I do have a little news for you from the department. Jacobs wants you to come in tomorrow morning."

"Does he? He say why?"

"Not to me."

"Why didn't he just call me?"

"Says he did. You didn't pick up."

"I guess I've been kind of holing up in here." Nick reached over and switched on his cell phone, lying next to the gun. He immediately saw two missed calls from earlier that morning. "Missed a call from Juliette, too."

"How are things going with you and her?"

"Actually… We're kind of hanging fire. She went to visit some family. Just came back. I guess she had to decompress and think stuff over. Looks like maybe she made up her mind."

Hank stood up. "I got to go back to work. And you should go see Juliette."

Nick nodded. He thought about trying to talk Hank into getting some coffee with him. He wasn't in a hurry to see Juliette, not right now. In fact, the thought of seeing her scared him more than the dawn fight with Denswoz had. Because he was afraid she was going to break up with him.

You coward.

Hank waved goodbye and headed out.

Nick took a deep breath and called Juliette.

"Hi. Anybody there need an out-of-work cop?"

"Hi Nick. Um—could you come over this evening? We should talk."

He didn't like the sound of that.

"I could come over sooner?" *Let's get it over with*, he figured.

"Nope. Seven o'clock. Can you make it?"

"I'm pretty slammed with sitting around staring at the walls, but I guess I could fit it in."

"See you then. I've got to go. There's a scared Jack Russell terrier who needs my attention."

"Bye."

But she'd already hung up.

* * *

He got there at 6:45 and sat in his car outside the house. The wind blew fitful handfuls of rain on the car roof.

He listened to country music on the radio for a while. It seemed somehow appropriate.

About five till seven Juliette came out with an umbrella, and tapped on his car window.

"You going to sit out here for the last five minutes or do you want to come in?"

He cleared his throat. "I *could* come in."

She turned and went back to the house. He switched the engine off, and followed in her wake, hurrying up to the house. The rain was easing off but the sky was already dark.

Inside, he took off his coat, hung it up in the closet next to her wet umbrella. She went into the kitchen and he sat on the couch, and looked around the house they'd lived in together. They'd lived here for quite awhile, then she'd kicked him out, and he'd lived at Monroe's. Then she'd let him come back. And lately... he'd been sleeping on a cot at the trailer.

She came in carrying two glasses of red wine. Was it to ease the pain of breaking up?

She put the wine down on the coffee table and sat down next to him. She was wearing a dress, he saw now. Rather a pretty pale blue.

"Are your wounds healed up?" she asked.

"Sure. They weren't much—just a few scratches."

"No need to be macho."

He smelled food cooking. "That salmon I smell?"

"It is. With the sauce you like."

He looked closely at her. She smiled and looked back at him.

"Let's see," Nick said. "Pretty dress, wine, invitation just before dinner, my favorite salmon. These seem to me to be good signs. Am I wrong?"

"You're some brilliant detective, Detective. Right on the mark." She sipped her wine and then put the glass down. "Except for one thing."

"What?"

"You haven't kissed me yet. If you were so sure of your deduction, you would definitely have kissed me. Because I've been waiting for you to kiss me."

"You have?"

"What do you think, you big dope?"

"You're going to trust me again?"

"Can I trust you?"

"Yes."

"Will you tell me what's going on with you after this?"

"Yes."

"So kiss me. And you can move back in tomorrow morning. Providing."

"Providing what?"

"Providing you earn your keep tonight after dinner."

"How do I do that?"

"How do you think?"

So he kissed her.

"Lieutenant? You wanted to see me?"

Jacobs looked up from his computer monitor.

"Ah. Burkhardt. Want some coffee? Fresh from the machine down the hall."

"No thank you, sir."

"Detective, you going to think before you act, next time?"

"Well, I…" He stared at Jacobs. "'Detective?'"

The Internal Affairs investigator leaned back in his seat, and grinned. Then he opened a desk drawer, took out Nick's gold shield, and passed it over to him.

"You can get the gun from requisition."

"I'm okay with the department?"

"You're a problem, is what you are. There's stuff I don't understand about you. But a lot of people spoke up for you. Renard—he insisted he needed you. Even Hank Griffin grudgingly admitted you were some use to him, occasionally. There isn't anyone suing over the dirtbag... sorry, I mean the alleged dirtbag... that died out there, that day, when you were interrogating him. And I know any man can get carried away, especially when there are children in danger. Plus, all those girls signed a petition asking for you to be reinstated. Lily Perkins and her mom have written letters to the mayor, Chief of Police, and me, *insisting* you be reinstated. So I guess we better reinstate you."

Nick smiled—but he still felt uncertain. He picked up the gold shield, and hefted it in his hand, thinking, once more, *Maybe I really can't be a Grimm and a cop too. Having to keep things back from the department...*

Jacobs frowned. "You look like you're not sure you want to be reinstated."

"Lieutenant, maybe I should think about—"

The door to Jacobs' office banged open. Hank was there in the doorway.

"Sorry, Lieutenant. Kind of urgent. You give him his badge back yet? Because I need him. Well, anyway, the Captain claims I need him. He's sending us out together to check something out." Hank looked at Nick. "One of those cases that's... kind of your specialty."

Nick stood up, still hefting the gold badge.

"You and Renard could handle it. I was thinking maybe..."

Hank shook his head.

"Nick? *No.* Trust me. I need you on this one."

He gave Nick a significant look.

Nick nodded, feeling a little easier.

"You sure you need me on this, Detective Griffin?"

"I'm sure, Detective Burkhardt."

Jacobs snorted. "Will you too lovebirds get the hell out of my office and get to work?"

Nick nodded. "Yes, sir." He put the gold badge in his coat pocket and went into the hall with Hank, closing the door behind him. He looked around, and saw no one else in the hall. "What's this one about?"

"Oh it's *weird*. It's a *really* weird one..."

"Really? In Portland? Well, well. That's hard to believe. You can tell me on the way..."

ACKNOWLEDGMENTS

Much thanks to Micky Shirley for research and editorial input.

Thanks to Cath Trechman for skillful shepherding of outlines, and to Chris Lucero, Alex Solverson and Jessica Nubel at NBCUniversal.

And extra special thanks to Gary Labb, for police procedural clarity.

GRIMM
THE CHOPPING BLOCK

JOHN PASSARELLA

A set of human bones is found in woods near Portland.
When more remains are found, Nick and Hank discover
that missing persons cases in the city have increased
drastically in the past few weeks. As the detectives delve
deeper, they begin to uncover a gruesome Wesen truth.

A brand-new original novel based on the NBC TV series.

For more fantastic fiction, author events, exclusive excerpts,
competitions, limited editions and more

VISIT OUR WEBSITE
titanbooks.com

LIKE US ON FACEBOOK
facebook.com/titanbooks

FOLLOW US ON TWITTER
@titanbooks

EMAIL US
readerfeedback@titanemail.com